Blue Sky and *Green Grass*

Ron Walden

ISBN 978-1-95-726308-3
eBook 978-1-95-726309-0
Library of Congress Catalog Card Number: 2012932950

Manufactured in the United States of America.

ACKNOWLEDGEMENTS

I thank my loyal readers and friends who encourage me to continue writing these novels. It is satisfying to see my work in print. I could never accomplish this without daily help from my wonderful wife, Betty. She is my greatest inspiration and my toughest critic.

My friend Sheryl Oldham, once again, has done a magnificent job of editing. She makes me look professional.

Once again I thank my donut shop friends for their help. Many are retired troopers and offer valuable advice. I also thank my friend Amy for allowing me to use her persona as a model for the character Laura Toombes. She makes the story real. Thank you all.

These Books and More by Ron Walden available everywhere.
Cinch Knot
Pigs, politics, and Petroleum.
The Multinational Plot to Nuke the Trans Alaska Pipeline
Devil's Heart
Native American Lore and Modern Police Work
Ice Blue Eyes
An Alaska Story of Greed, Live, and Revenge

CHAPTER 1

Winter flying in Alaska is a treacherous undertaking. The temperature on this morning was minus fifteen degrees, close to the self-imposed limit of minus twenty when trapper Ken Whittle would stop flying. It was 9 AM, the daylight hour for this late January morning. He had been pre-heating the Piper Super Cub for nearly an hour while he loaded his trap basket and the gear he would take with him today. He had checked to be certain his fuel tanks were full (no need to check for water in the fuel; at this temperature it would be frozen). With the aircraft still tied down and the engine and wing covers removed, he started the engine, moving the throttle back to a slow idle. His Cub was on skis and sometimes it would begin to move when the engine was started. He carried his engine heater back to the shed and made a final walk around. He untied the little plane as the sky began to brighten. No clouds, the sun would soon be shining, it would be a good day to check his Susitna River traps.

By the time he returned from Viet Nam, the hippie lifestyle had become very popular, but Ken had no taste for it. He also had little taste for work. Young and strong, he bounced from job to job without finding a niche. He even took up with a group of hippies for a while. It was while with the three of them, two other guys and one girl, he traveled to Alaska. One of the men had heard there was easy money to be made in Fairbanks, so the group set off for the far north. Canadians didn't think much of hippies either. The four long-haired, shaggy, idealistic, young anti-war protesters set off for Alaska. They missed a lot of meals along the way to save money for gas. Several times it was necessary to camp on the side of the road while they repaired the Volkswagen bus with meager tools and little knowledge. After much arguing, the group reached Tok, and a fork in the road. The other three proceeded on to Fairbanks, but Ken Whittle took the left fork to Anchorage.

There were a lot of veterans and not much employment for young men without skills. He washed dishes, swept floors, and finally was hired as a bartender on 4th Avenue. The old Montana Club wasn't much, but it provided a decent paycheck, something he hadn't seen in a long time.

Early every afternoon the place filled with hookers, moochers, winos and other members of the street community. Among those patrons was a ratty-looking old man named Isaiah something-he couldn't remember his last name. Isaiah always sat at the far end of the bar away from the door. When Ken had the time, the old man told him stories about trapping in the north woods. He would tell the young bartender about the animals and how to set a trap for each one. His stories fascinated the young vet and he began to meet the old-timer outside the bar. Sometimes Ken would steal a bottle of liquor to give the old man and the two would talk for hours about trapping.

Ken subscribed to *Fur, Fish and Game,* a small magazine dedicated to trappers and trapping. He read each issue from cover to cover. What he didn't understand he would discuss with his friend Isaiah. That winter he quit his job and worked the trap-line with the old man. Soon his sets were catching more fur than his mentor. He stayed with Isaiah all winter and learned the art of fleshing hides without cutting the pelts. He learned about drying and stretching them. He found that life as a trapper wasn't easy, but he loved it. In the spring, after the sale of the furs, Ken took his earnings and invested in trapping gear.

He spent the summer on the Yentna River establishing his own trapping area. It was in that first summer, after setting up his trap-line, that he began to take flying lessons. He had finally found his calling. Two years later Ken received word that Isaiah had been found, frozen stiff, in his cabin. He had come to love that old man; he would miss him.

At age 62, hair turning gray and joints beginning to get stiff, Ken appreciated the ease of using the Super Cub to check his trap-line. It was, as the crow flies, only about 20 miles to Witsoe Lake where he would check his first string of traps. He would take a little extra time to look for any wolves in the area before landing near his first set. The sun was up now and Ken was relaxed, enjoying the flight when, near the lake, he caught sight of something in the trees about 150 yards from the shore. Changing course slightly, he circled around the site. It was an airplane in the trees standing on its propeller cone. The wind was calm and he landed straight ahead, then, taxied back to the shore-line. Hurriedly he took the engine cover from the rear seat and covered the engine cowling, not wanting to rapidly lose engine heat. Next he slipped into his snowshoes, zipped up his parka and made his way through the thick spruce thicket to the crash site.

Out of breath from the quick walk, he reached the airplane. Looking up through the windshield he could see the pilot in his seat. Using a piece of dead spruce as a ladder he climbed high enough to reach the door handle and open the door. It didn't look good, but he checked for pulse anyway. There was none. The pilot was dead and frozen in his seat. Ken had no way of knowing when the crash had taken place, but he had been on this lake four days prior and the plane wasn't there at that time. Trying to figure out what to do next, he spotted a shiny metal briefcase lying against the windshield. There was a bloody wound on the back of the pilots head. It looked as though the metal case had struck him from behind during the impact. For no particular reason he pulled the case from where it rested and tossed it to the ground. Sliding carefully down his make-shift perch Ken slipped into the harness of his snowshoes and tugged the rubber bands around his heels. He retrieved the briefcase and trudged back to the lake and his own airplane. Pulling the cell phone from his pocket he found he had no signal. "Figures," he thought.

Kicking off his snowshoes, he tossed them into the rear of the Cub. He placed the briefcase in the pilot's seat. Finally, he pulled the engine cover from the nose and stuffed it into the backseat of the little plane. He was about to climb into his seat when he saw the metal case. Out of curiosity he thumbed the latches. It opened. Ken was surprised when by what he found inside: CASH—lots of cash, thousands in cash, with a Colt Series 80, .45 caliber automatic pistol. Stunned, he closed the lid and put the case in the back with his snowshoes and engine cover. He started the engine, turned the little craft around and took off across the lake.

At 1,500 feet he keyed the microphone. "Anchorage Center, Piper 1362 Delta."

"Piper 62 Delta, Anchorage Center. Are you reporting inbound?"

"No, sir. I am reporting an aircraft accident."

"Piper 62 Delta, please change frequency to 121.5."

"Anchorage Center, Piper 1362 Delta on 121.5."

"62 Delta, what is the nature of your emergency?"

"Yes, sir. I have found a downed aircraft," he passed on the Global Positioning System coordinates. "It is a Cessna 206, yellow over white," he included the aircraft tail number. "This will be a fatality accident. The body of the pilot is still in the aircraft."

"62 Delta, please stand by while I notify Rescue Coordination Center and the troopers."

"Roger," Ken said, and then waited.

About one minute later, the voice was back. "62 Delta, are you still in the area of the crash?"

"Affirmative. I will land on Lake Witsoe and wait for the troopers. I will be out of radio contact until they are close to the site."

"Thank you, 62 Delta. The Troopers will contact you there. Please remain on 121.5 until you have been contacted. We would appreciate it if you would stop at the FAA office at Merrill Field and make a written report."

"I will do that." With that he circled back to the lake and landed.

Back on the lake and with the engine covered once again, his thoughts returned to the cash behind his seat and all the things he could do with that kind of cash.

Except for an occasional bottle of booze for Isaiah, he had never stolen anything before. But, if he took the money, who would know? He opened the case and counted the cash. It was banded in $5,000 bundles, totaling $104,000.

The temptation was just too great. He made the decision quickly and put $1,500 into the metal briefcase with the Colt. The rest he buried in his trap basket in the backseat. He put on his snowshoes and returned to the Cessna. Climbing up the make-shift ladder again, he placed the briefcase against the windshield where he originally found it. Since he had been wearing gloves all day, fingerprints would not be a problem.

Peering into the rear of the wreck he found a duffle bag tied into each of the four seats. Climbing down again, he hiked back to his own plane. Sitting inside waiting for others to arrive he couldn't help wonder about the cash and the cargo in the wreck. And who was this guy and why did he crash? The front of the Cessna had suffered surprisingly little damage. In Ken's unscientific appraisal the engine was stopped at the time of the crash. Maybe the pilot had lost an engine and stalled into the trees attempting to make it to the lake and a safe landing. He surmised the Troopers would figure it out when they arrived.

He had been inside his own airplane for nearly an hour when he heard the sound of an approaching helicopter. Ken climbed out of his Cub and waited for the Robertson R44 to land on the ice. He turned his back to the swirling snow the helicopter rotor blades had caused. As the rotors slowed he could see the pilot was a female trooper. She let the blades spin to a stop and energetically bounced to the ground, climbing up to place cold protection on the engine. Climbing down again she walked to where Ken was standing.

CHAPTER 2

The pilot, Alaska State Trooper Sergeant Karen Holmes, was a muscular woman with sandy-blond hair. There was an athletic spring to her step. She had attended Idaho State University with a major in criminal justice and was active in the Marine ROTC Program. Upon graduation she entered The Corps, went to Marine Corps boot camp and from there to Helicopter Flight Training. She had been assigned to a flight group in Florida. When she wasn't flying, she was working in the office of the Provost Marshal.

With enough experience under her belt she was deployed to Iraq in an Apache gunship. She loved flying the Apache because it fed her appetite for excitement. After her second tour she lost her craving for adrenalin and, upon completion of her enlistment, came home to southern Idaho. She chose University of Washington for her master's degree.

A year later with degree in hand, she was recruited by the Alaska State Troopers. With her helicopter portfolio completed and the trooper academy out of the way, she was ready to go to work.

She did her apprenticeship on road patrol and some investigations when an opening for a helicopter pilot was offered to her. She loved this life and the people with which she worked. Now, six years later, she was here investigating an airplane crash.

"Hello, I'm Sergeant Karen Holmes. Are you the one who called this into the FAA?"

"Yes, ma'am. Ken Whittle. I have a trap-line on this lake."

"You have been to the crash site?" she asked.

"Yes. I went to check on the pilot. I opened the door and checked to see if the pilot had a pulse. There was no need, really. He was frozen stiff. I came back here and tried to call on the cell phone with no luck. I got into my plane and climbed high enough to reach Anchorage Center. That's how I reported it."

"I'll take a formal statement later, but right now I need to see the pilot myself."

Ken nodded and tugged on his snowshoes. "I packed a trail into the plane, so if you stay behind me the trail should be solid enough for you to make it without snowshoes." He began his walk and she fell in behind.

"Were there any other tracks in the area when you arrived?" she asked.

"None," he replied. "It does look like a moose came through here." He pointed twenty feet to the right. "But nothing else, not even a wolf track."

As they approached the crash site she asked him to wait. She passed him on the trail taking a small digital camera from her pocket. After taking several photos, she investigated the spruce log propped up as a ladder. She looked at him inquisitively.

"Yeah, I put that there to climb up and check him."

She made her way up the make-shift ladder and touched the victim's neck. Ken had been right, there was no need. He had been dead for several days. Still perched on the spruce log, she took a small portable radio from her belt.

"Dispatch, Helo One. Do you read me?"

"I read you about three, but clear."

"Dispatch, have Captain Davis call me on channel eight."

In less than a minute, a male voice came on the radio.

"This is Captain Davis. What is the situation there, Sergeant?"

"The pilot is definitely 10-79. The plane is vertical in the trees. There isn't much daylight left today, can we get Era Helicopters to lift this whole unit out of here and transport it to our hangar at Lake Hood?"

"Stand by, Helo One. I will get right back to you."

Climbing down from her spot on the log, she turned to Ken.

"What do you suppose caused the wound on the back of his head?" she asked.

"It looked to me like that metal briefcase was in the back seat and came flying up to hit him in the back of the head during the crash." Ken paused. "Did you see the cargo strapped into the back seats?"

"Yes, I did. What do you suppose is in those bags?" she smiled as she asked the question.

"I don't know, but I can guess," he replied.

Her radio came to life again. "Helo One, Helo One."

"Go ahead, Captain."

"Stand by at the scene. Era Helicopters will be there with lifting equipment in about one hour. They have the coordinates and will meet you on the lake. Let them do the work, Karen. They are being paid to do it. Just keep the wreck and the pilot in sight at all times for evidentiary reasons.

"Roger that, Captain. I will stay on this frequency while I am on the ground. And if you have no objections I will get I.D. info from the witness and let him leave."

"OK, Sergeant. Your call. Stay in touch. Out."

She turned back to Ken. "Let me get some information from you and you can go check your traps. You won't have much time today, though."

When they finished Ken pulled off the engine cover and climbed into the little Piper. Warming the engine until the oil temperature began to rise, he taxied across the lake to where his first set of traps were set. He made a quick check of the traps on the south side of the lake. He was almost finished when the big red and white helicopter sat down on the ice near the trooper bird. While the Era pilot talked with the sergeant, the other man drug lifting straps and spreaders to the scene. It amazed Ken at how quickly the guy was able to ready the Cessna for the first lift to the lake.

The big helicopter took off and hovered over the wreck. Lowering a cable with a hook on the end to the man below, he began to gain altitude. The man on the ground motioned to the pilot which way to maneuver so as not to damage the cargo any further. They swung the yellow and white plane to the lake ice. The man on the ground closed the airplane door and adjusted the straps. Satisfied with the adjustments he climbed into the big helicopter and motioned for the pilot to take up the slack and lift the cargo into the air. It seemed to be balancing nicely, so he motioned for the pilot to head for Anchorage.

During the final lift, Sergeant Karen Holmes prepared her own craft for take-off. The two helicopters flew away in close formation.

Ken Whittle breathed a long sigh of relief, and climbed aboard his own craft and set a straight course for his home field near Big Lake. Thinking he was probably going to get away with his theft did not relieve his pangs of guilt.

Winter flying in Alaska requires as many hour of preparation as the length of the flight you will take. Putting the Super Cub to bed for the night, covering the engine and wings, putting a heater inside the cowling to keep it warm and unloading the airplane would take almost two hours.

He took the trapped animals into a fleshing room at the back of the house, carried the heavy trap basket inside and tended the fire. It had been a long day and he was tired, but all this needed to be done tonight. He removed the two mink carcasses and some traps from the basket and began to remove the cash. He carried the money into the kitchen area and placed it on the table. He spun the dial on his gun safe and opened the door. Re-arranging the items on the two shelves, mostly piled on top of the safe, he made room for the cash. With the money safely hidden, he locked the safe, went to the cupboard and poured a very large glass of Crown Royal.

Sipping his drink and thinking about what he had done left him with mixed emotions; guilt was the strongest one, but there was also elation and fear. He had never done anything like this before, always trying to stay within the law; another long sip of the whisky. It was time to begin caring for his catch.

The largest animal, a gray wolf, would require the most work and he started on it first. Several hours later he finished with the furs and sat back to take inventory. It was a good catch: one wolf, two mink, two lynx and a rare marten. In the morning he would have to return to check the traps on Ladyslipper Lake and Lockwood Lake.

The trapper washed himself, checked the fire and, feeling relaxed from the liquor, fell into bed.

Meanwhile, the two helicopters had finished at the state hangar in Anchorage. Mechanics had taken over caring for the blue and white trooper helicopter while Karen stayed with the broken Cessna. The crew of the Era helicopter had set the crashed plane near the hangar door. Crime lab troopers were on the scene with the Medical Examiner. It was their job to make official death determination and notifications. Once they began their tasks, Karen could safely leave the body and aircraft in their care.

Captain Davis had left the office for the day, but she had a mountain of paperwork to complete. Removing her parka and pouring a cup of hot coffee, she parked herself at the computer on her desk and began to enter the items from her notebook. She also downloaded the photos from her digital camera. It was nearly ten o'clock when she finished. Exhausted, she hand wrote a note for the captain and left it on his desk. A shower was going to feel good, she thought.

On her way out she met the night shift sergeant. Leon Otis, a six foot tall handsome young trooper with a penchant for practical jokes.

"Hi Karen. Heard you were doing the airplane crash up near the Yentna River. Who was the victim?"

"Don't know yet," she replied. "We can't get him out of the airplane yet. The NTSB investigators were supposed to meet with the Crime Lab guys at Lake Hood. They hadn't arrived when I left the hangar."

"Do you know what made him crash?"

"No, but it looked like the engine had stopped before he hit the trees. The guy did a good job of getting down in the trees and would have probably survived except he got hit in the back of the head with a metal briefcase during the crash. I think he stalled while trying to make it to the lake for an emergency landing. One strange thing, though. He had four duffle bags strapped into the back seats. Don't know what was in them, but my guess is marijuana."

"They always say drugs will kill you," he remarked, laughing. "See you tomorrow."

She waved and left the office building, zipping up her parka as she walked to her Chevy pick-up.

CHAPTER 3

Karen Holmes had been at her desk for nearly an hour when her telephone jingled. She had been so intent on the entries in her flight log that she was startled by the sound. She picked up the phone to hear the voice of a dispatcher who said she was forwarding a call of inquiry to line three.

Switching lines she answered, "Sergeant Holmes, how may I help you?"

"Sergeant, my name is Anthony Dunn. I am a realtor in Eagle River. I heard a report on the morning news about an airplane crash. Can you tell me about it?"

"Right now there isn't much to tell. Do you have some information about the crash?" she asked, reaching for a notepad.

"I'm not sure," he began. "When I heard about the crash I got to thinking that a business friend of mine flew to Fairbanks a few days ago and he has not contacted me since Sunday afternoon when he was leaving. I called the man he was to meet in Fairbanks who told me Jack Boardon never showed. I wondered if you could tell me if Jack was involved in this crash."

"What type of airplane did this man fly?" she asked.

"A Cessna 206, yellow over white with black trim," he replied.

"If you will give me your phone number, I will get back to you as soon as I learn anything." She listened and wrote down the number.

After hanging up she spun her Rolodex to NTSB. She dialed and asked for the person ever was in charge of the crash from yesterday. Her call was forwarded to Lou Mankawitz. Karen had worked with Lou on several other occasions. He was thorough and Karen trusted him.

"NTSB, Investigations, Lou Mankawitz. How may I help you?"

"Lou, Karen Holmes, AST. I understand you got the short straw on the wreck at Witsoe Lake. I'm working the case. Do you have anything for me?"

"Good morning, Karen. The Medical Examiner said he would call you when he was going to take the body out of the Cessna. He told me he would try late this morning. Three days at fifteen below makes a body pretty rigid. The plane is registered to a Jack T. Boardon of Wasilla. The description matches the pilot. I think it is him. I'm going to the hangar in a few minutes to look at the airplane and try to determine what caused the crash. Want to join me?"

"I can be there in about an hour. I have to give my captain a report before I can leave. Before you hang up, I need to tell you I just had a call from an Anthony Dunn of Eagle River. He claims his 'business friend' was flying to Fairbanks and hasn't been heard from since Sunday. It sounds like this may be the guy."

"We haven't touched the inside of the plane and I am really curious about those duffle bags in the back. I'll meet you at the hangar in an hour."

Just short of an hour later, they met at the Lake Hood hangar. Lou was outside talking with the ME when Karen arrived. He waved at the trooper as she stepped out of her white pick-up. Together they walked into the hangar. The Medical Examiner waited inside for the arrival of crime lab troopers.

"Until they finish we can look the plane over and try to determine what caused it to crash," Lou said. "They don't want us poking around inside until they have finished. The ME said they were done except for taking the body out of the seat. They shouldn't be more than a few minutes."

Karen peered through the side window. "I see the green duffle bags are still in there."

The two of them were walking around the Cessna, making a visual inspection when the back door of the hangar opened and two troopers in blue coveralls entered. They both waved at Karen as they walked over to talk with the Medical Examiner. In a moment the door opened again and one more coverall-clad trooper entered, pushing a metal folding gurney. It took the group only about three minutes to remove the body from the plane. Pictures were taken of the seat and cockpit area after the body had been removed.

"It's all yours, Lou," the ME said as he and his crew pushed the gurney out of the hangar.

"OK, Karen," Lou said. "Get out your notepad. Let's go to work." With a tape recorder in his left hand, he began to walk around the plane, commenting on the condition of individual parts as he went. "External damage is minimal considering the aircraft landed in a thick stand of spruce trees. The windscreen is cracked, but intact." The two continued to walk and take notes. After noting all external damage, he began to do the same thing on the inside. He noted that both the magneto and master electrical switches were in the off position, as was the fuel selector. He checked the fuel gauges; both tanks registered full. He turned off the master switch, and pulled his head from the cockpit.

"That's strange," he commented. He pointed to a yellow ladder standing a few feet behind the plane. "Bring me that ladder, will you, Karen?"

She followed and pulled the ladder to the front of the left wing.

"What is it that seems strange to you, Lou?"

"This guy knew what to do in an emergency situation. He had turned off the fuel valve and the electrical switches. He knew he was going to land hard and did all he could to prevent further damage. He did well. The strange thing is that both fuel tanks register full. He had been flying for more than half an hour and the airplane was vertical for two or three days, yet the fuel gauges read full. That doesn't seem likely."

He pulled the ladder closer to the leading edge of the wing and climbed up. Taking off the fuel filler cap, he peered inside. "Hmmm!" he commented as he pulled a small flashlight from his jacket pocket. Shining the beam inside the tank, he put his eye close to the opening. Lifting his head back, he studied the opening and once again looked closely at filler hole. "Hmmm!" he repeated.

"What is it, Lou?"

He was climbing down the ladder. "I don't think this was an accident. Wait here." He walked across the hangar and brought another ladder to put alongside the one Karen had found. "Climb up here and take a look with me."

Now, both of them were peering at the open fuel tank. Karen was puzzled.

"This tank is bone dry, but the gauge indicates full. It could have been broken in the wreck, but when I was shining my light into the tank I spotted something very unusual." He shined his light into the tank again. "Do you see a piece of black thread wrapped, just one turn, around the filler neck?"

She looked closer. "Now that you pointed it out, I see it. What do you think it's for?"

"I think it's possible someone sabotaged his fuel tanks. That thread could be holding the fuel indicator float at the full mark. Let's check the other tank." Climbing down he said, "If that is true, then this could be a murder."

After moving the two ladders to the other side of the aircraft, the two investigators climbed up to look at the filler cap atop the right wing. Removing the filler cap, Mankawitz shined his light at the opening.

"Look at this," he said. "Just like the other side."

Gently feeling with his index finger, he followed the thread into the tank as far as his finger could reach. "Hmmm!" he grunted once again.

"What is it?" Karen asked.

"The string is taut and leads off toward the center of the tank." Glancing toward the office door, he wondered if one of the mechanics had a fiber optic lens with which to peer into the tank. While Karen waited atop the ladder Lou climbed down and walked to the office. A few moments later he returned with one of the shop mechanics. They rummaged through a drawer in a toolbox to find a small box with an extension cord. The mechanic plugged the extension cord into an outlet. Bringing the end of the cord to the airplane from the small box, he produced a strange looking tool with a small LCD television screen and a coil of plastic tubing. A metal engine stand was pushed up to the wing where the mechanic set up the small T.V. Lou returned to his ladder as the mechanic handed him the end of the plastic tubing, giving him directions on its positioning and use. He was directed to place the tubing into the filler hole. As he did so, the mechanic directed him right, left, up or down. Pushing slowly, deeper into the tank, the mechanic told him to hold that position.

Turning the small screen around for Lou to see, he said, "I've never seen anything like this before." He pointed at the apparatus pictured on the screen. The thread was attached to the short arm of the fuel gauge float. Karen, too, could see the string attached to the mechanism.

"How the heck did someone get that in there?" the trooper sergeant asked.

"It takes a little doing, but we have a thing called mechanical fingers; you just make a loop, grip it with the fingers and maneuver it into place. I've done it to see if a tank float was working properly."

"Do you think this could have been inadvertently left in the tank by someone doing just that?" she asked.

"It could have on one tank perhaps, but not both. And usually we don't tie them off, just loop the string around the float and when the test is finished we pull one end and remove the cord," the mechanic explained.

"As a pilot, I always visually check my fuel on pre-flight. This man performed as a competent pilot during the emergency. I wonder why he didn't visually check his tanks before taking off." It was a question Karen would have to investigate.

Lou interrupted her thought. "This Jack Boardon leased a heated hangar at Merrill Field. I am only speculating now, but I think he may have filled his tanks the day before and put the plane in the hangar. When he powered up the next morning, the gauges still read full. He may have just been in a hurry to get his cargo in the air."

"That is a thought, Lou." Karen then made a suggestion. "I know you have more checking to do on the airplane. I have a drug testing kit in the truck. If it's OK with you, I will open one of the duffle bags and see what's inside. If it looks like drugs, I can test them right away."

"Good idea, Karen. Go ahead. Remember to mark where each bag was located. We have to weigh each one individually and match the weight to the seat it was in. We do this to verify correct weight and balance."

The mechanic pointed to a cabinet near his toolbox. "There is a small digital scale on the top shelf of that cabinet. You can use that if you need it."

Lou and the mechanic removed the equipment and pulled the ladders away from the wing. The two men had a short discussion after which the mechanic returned to his office. The NTSB man returned to the Cessna, opened the cowling and began to check the engine.

<h1 style="text-align:center">CHAPTER 4</h1>

While Lou Mankawitz set about checking the Cessna, Sergeant Karen Holmes opened the cargo door on the aft right side of the cabin seating area. She took several pictures before disturbing anything in the cabin. Satisfied there was nothing obviously amiss inside, she unfastened the seatbelt on the right rear seat. She carefully looked the bag over for marks, tags or anything to identify it. She found nothing on the bag or on the seat. Dragging the bag out of the aircraft, she took more pictures and weighed the bag.

She made a red evidence tag noting the total weight of 101.2 pounds. She attached the tag to the handle on the side of the bag and unsnapped the strap on the top. Unfolding the bag at the top and pulling the canvas flap from the inside, she could see what appeared to her like bundles of marijuana. She took out one of the brick-like packages and placed it on the scale. It measured 2.4 pounds. She took more pictures before cutting a small slit in the plastic-wrap packaging. With a test kit from her vehicle, she tested the contents of the packet and got an immediate positive reaction. Noting the results in her notebook, she reached for her cell phone.

When a voice answered, she said, "Captain Davis, Sergeant Holmes."

"Yes, Sergeant. How is it going at the hangar?"

"Busy, Captain. Number one, it looks like someone sabotaged the fuel tank gauges and emptied the tanks causing the plane to run out of fuel and crash. Lou is still looking at the engine to determine why it failed. I'll fill you in on the result when he's finished."

"So, this is beginning to look like a murder investigation?"

"It sure looks that way, Captain," Karen replied.

"You said that was number one. Is there something else?"

"Yes, there is. I just completed a field test on the contents of one of the duffle bags inside the plane. It tested positive for marijuana and, from the results of my test, I would judge it's high quality stuff."

"Sounds like a motive for murder to me. Stay on it, Karen. Let me know if you need help. I will send the crime lab boys down there to take charge of the evidence," he advised, and added, "It might be wise to take on a partner in this investigation. If someone killed once over this, they won't hesitate to kill again. We will talk about it when you get back to the office. Thanks for the update." With that he signed off.

"Lou," she called as she walked to the other side of the plane. "The crime lab guys are on the way to take charge of the evidence. I am going to weigh and tag the other three bags. I have already taken pictures, but I was thinking we should have them check the fuel caps and the wing area for fingerprints. Not knowing there was a crime, we didn't take precautions to protect what might be there; so, it might be futile, but I would hate to compound our mistake."

"Actually, we didn't disturb the scene much and I was the only one to handle the fuel caps," Lou responded. "They could just come up with something. I think this was done inside the warm hangar, so we might get lucky and find the guy didn't wear gloves."

"Dumber things have been done," she said as she went back to her task of weighing and tagging the other duffle bags.

Karen had finish with her chores by the time the crime lab crew returned to the hangar. She signed all the evidence over to them and asked them to check the wings, fuel tanks and caps for fingerprints. She was told they would do the job, but it could take some time to eliminate the excess prints. She was assured they would do their best. Satisfied she had done all she could at the scene, she returned to her own office where she drew up a Reader's Digest version of her report for Captain Davis. She walked down the hall to his office and tapped on his closed door.

"Come in," came a voice from the inside.

"It's me, Captain," she said upon entering. He motioned for her to take the chair across the desk from him.

Handing him the short version of her report, she sat.

"Do you really think I need a partner on this investigation?" she asked.

He was prepared for that question. "Yes, I do. It's too early in the case to know who we are dealing with and, until we do, I don't want anyone operating alone. The point isn't open for discussion. Now, who do you want to back you up?"

"Can I have someone from the drug unit? One of them might recognize someone I wouldn't suspect. I want someone with some moxie in case we do encounter a violent situation."

"I'll see what I can do. I'll have a talk with the drug unit captain." Captain Davis seemed worried. "You're a good cop, Karen. I don't want you or anyone else hurt. You are still in charge of the investigation. I just don't want you out there without backup."

"I appreciate that, Captain," she said in a quiet voice. "I want to follow up on that phone call from the victim's so called business friend. Perhaps he will give us some insight into who this Jack Boardon really is. I got the copy of his background check and nothing showed up there."

"OK, Karen. See me in the morning and we will map a strategy. By then I may have a suitable partner for you."

She stood and said, "See you tomorrow, Captain."

The following morning she had been in the office more than an hour, intent on completing the report from the previous day, when there was a throat clearing sound at her door. Looking up she saw a mountain of a man with dark, wavy hair, wearing black plastic-rimmed eyeglasses.

"Good morning, Sergeant. Craig Stanton. The captain said you needed a partner in a drug and murder case. Can we talk about it?"

"Come in, Craig," she greeted. "Call me Karen." With that she pointed to the chair in front of her desk. "Have you done investigations before, Craig?"

"Oh, yes." He grinned. "I have been a trooper for eight years and spent three years undercover with the drug unit in Fairbanks. The News Miner put my picture on the front page of the paper and identified me as an undercover cop. That sort of put an end to my usefulness in Fairbanks. I don't like to brag, but I can ride, rope and shoot with the best of 'em. Aw, shucks, ma'am, won't ya give me a chance?"

She chuckled aloud. "I guess I had that coming. I apologize. Sometimes I take things too seriously. Let's start again. Welcome aboard."

"The first thing I have to do this morning is meet with the captain and let him know what I will be doing today. First, we—you and me—need to learn what we can about the victim. NCIC didn't give us much." She took a sheet from the file and handed it to him. While he scanned the information, Karen continued. "I had a call from a man in Eagle River who claimed to be the victim's friend. He claims to have known the victim, Jack Boardon, for a long time. After we do that interview, we need to look at the victim's home address. Crime lab is scheduled to look at the hangar this morning, when they finish I think we should have a look at it, too."

"At this point there doesn't seem to be much to go on," Stanton said. "I have to agree with the captain, though. Four hundred pounds is a lot of weed. People have been killed for a lot less."

"OK, Craig, let's go see the captain and get on the road."

Twenty minutes later the two troopers, in Craig's patrol car, were on the way to the Eagle River realty office of Anthony Dunn.

The two troopers found the address of the realty office in Eagle River. It was a new office building, very nice, with a new sign over the portico announcing Dunn Realty, with a phone number. Inside, a pencil thin receptionist met them—a gorgeous young woman of about 25 dressed in a much-too-mini miniskirt and a hairdo with ringlets cascading down both sides of her pretty face.

"How may I help you?" she asked pleasantly.

Handing the blond a business card Karen said. "We came to talk with Mr. Anthony Dunn. He will know what it's about."

The woman walked like a model to her boss's door, tapped once and announced their request. Dunn immediately came to the front to escort them to his private, well-appointed office. Inside he indicated seats for them on a leather couch.

As he took a large leather chair opposite the couch, he said, "Pleased to meet you both. Please, call me Tony. Can I get you coffee or anything?"

"No, thank you, Tony. You and I spoke on the phone yesterday, Karen Holmes. This is Trooper Stanton. We wanted to talk with you about your friend Jack Boardon. We are investigating his tragic accident."

He nodded and got up to use the intercom to tell his secretary he wasn't to be disturbed.

Karen made the first inquiry. "Tony," she asked, "how long did you know Jack?"

He smiled. "We grew up together in San Jose, California. Our fathers both worked in the Silicon Valley. My father was an electronics engineer and Jack's father was a production supervisor, both at the same company. Jack and I went to high school together and played ball together. We chased around together a lot. We both went to San Jose State and graduated with MBA degrees. We were hell-raisers but never got into real trouble. A month or so before we graduated, we met an Air Force recruiter. The three of us did a lot of drinking together. He talked us into joining up and helped us get into flight school. We both became A-10 'Warthog' pilots. We both enjoyed flying, but Jack was much better at it than I."

Karen was doing her best to keep up with her notes while Craig, with a tape recorder on the table, listened.

"We were sent to Kuwait during Desert Storm," he continued. "It was unbelievably fun to cruise around the desert looking for tanks and to blow it up when we found one. One day we were cruising along on the Iraq/Kuwait border when we spotted four tanks hidden behind a sand hill that overlooked the main Kuwait highway. We saw the lead tank fire a shell that landed in front of a big, black Rolls Royce limo. As we circled around, the occupants of the limo got out, ran up the road and hid behind the embankment. There was another black car farther up the road, a Mercedes. It stopped in a small rock cut where it was hidden, but those folks in the Rolls were in trouble.

"Jack and I came back around and he put a rocket right in the turret of the lead tank. I was behind him and strafed the three tanks hiding behind the leader. I disabled two of those tanks with my cannon and damaged the third, but he was able to start up, smoking like crazy, and make a run for it. We circled around again and waved at the folks in the ditch. They waved back and the Mercedes came racing to pick them up."

"Wow!" said Karen.

"A few days later, the squadron commander called us to his office. Turns out, the family in the Rolls was that of some high-ranking Kuwaiti official. He was there to personally thank us and let us know how brave we were. I guess he didn't know how much fun Jack and I had doing it." He chuckled, reliving the experience. "This Royal somebody thanked us for saving him and his family, then thanked us again. It was embarrassing. What we didn't know was he had taken our names and information. Later, after rotating back to the states, we were both notified by registered letter that we owned Swiss Bank Accounts, a gift from the sultan, or whatever he was. It was quite a large amount, $500,000 each. When we got out of the Air Force, the money made it easy for Jack and me to start our business here in Alaska."

"That is an amazing story," Karen commented. "And the two of you have been in business together all these years?"

"Early on we were in the real estate business together, but after a while we split the business. I kept the real estate end and Jack went into property management. We had both acquired numerous properties and people were asking us to manage their business properties. Jack was very good at it and made a lot of money for the both of us."

"Would you give us the addresses of his business and his home?" she asked.

"Certainly, but maybe I can do a little better. I am the executor of Jack's estate and, if he is deceased, I have access to his home and office. I will get you keys to get inside both places. Please wait here and I will get them."

Upon his return they all said their good-byes. Back in the patrol car, Craig Stanton commented first.

"That is about the most fantastic story I have ever heard."

"I agree, but it should all be verifiable if it's true," Karen offered. "Let's go to Boardon's house first." Stanton nodded agreement as they drove out of Eagle River.

CHAPTER 5

A lengthy search of Jack Boardon's residence turned up nothing. He was an orderly housekeeper and tidy in his habits, but they didn't find anything that would tie him to the drug business. Satisfied there was nothing to be found in the home, the two troopers drove to Merrill Field and the hangar leased by Boardon. There was a key on the ring supplied by Dunn. In a back corner of the hangar was a small cubicle that had been an office.

In a file drawer was a thick file marked CESSNA 206 and a tail number. A check of the aircraft tail number confirmed it was maintenance records for the one Boardon had been flying. The same mechanic had signed all the records in the file. Karen noted the name of the mechanic, Carlton Leiber. Scanning the records, nothing obvious turned up. There was nothing unusual found inside the hangar. Feeling the frustration, they decided to have lunch before driving to Wasilla for a search of Boardon's office.

On the way to lunch Karen called for a background check on Carlton Leiber and received a quick response. He had a long sheet that included DWI, misconduct with controlled substances, theft and a list of lesser offenses. She read the list to Stanton.

"Sounds like our kind of guy," he said. "Do you think he could be the saboteur?"

"He appears to have the personality for it, but if he worked for Boardon, why would he want to sabotage his plane. Surely he would realize that he would be our first choice as a suspect?"

"You said it before, dumber things have happened." Stanton thought a moment and said, "Or, someone else put him up to it. After all, our friend Jack was living a double life. Maybe one of those lives caught up to him."

"In any case we need to find out more about his drug-dealing life. He could have made big enemies in that trade. I think we have a lot of work to do."

At lunch she began to make a list of questions begging for answers. She also made a note to contact Ken Whittle for a statement about finding the downed aircraft. Whittle should have called her before now, but perhaps he was busy with his trap-line.

Stanton paid for lunch. She would get lunch tomorrow she advised, not wanting to be indebted to the new partner for anything. Upon finishing lunch, they drove to Wasilla and, after considerable looking, found Wasilla Property Management in an old office building behind the Meta Rose Mall. Again they found they held a key to the front door, supplied by Dunn. The office was a mess. There seemed to be more files on the floors and coffee table than in the filing cabinet. What they found in the cabinet was very interesting. The files were full of deeds and rental agreements. It was astounding to see how much property was owned by the late Jack Boardon.

Also in the files were utility bills for his own property and for the properties he managed. Many of them had horrendous natural gas and electric bills.

"We are going to have to check all these places out," Karen said. "Let's take the file marked Matanuska-Susitna Electric Association. We can stop at the MEA office and get a physical location on, at least, some of these locations. Do you think it possible Boardon was growing his own product?"

"It doesn't seem likely, but anything is possible," her new partner replied.

Before leaving, they sealed the front door of the office with evidence tape and put up yellow tape stating, "POLICE LINE—DO NOT CROSS"

In the car, while on the way to the MEA office, she added more questions to the list she had started at lunch.

Karen explained to the office manager that they were investigating a crime and that they were in need of physical locations of the properties listed in the folder. It took nearly an hour, but the office manager came back with computer printouts for all the properties on the list. Karen thanked him and the two troopers searched the list for the nearest property.

The one they found was located about two miles up Palmer-Fishhook Road. It took a few minutes to get there, but when they arrived it was obvious it could be used for a growing operation. There was no house on the property, only a very large barn and two equipment sheds. Stepping out of the car, they were met with the familiar odor of marijuana.

Stanton and Karen began a walk around the big building, looking into windows and seeing nothing. The windows had been painted black to prevent prying eyes from seeing what was taking place inside. At one end of the barn was a new power pole with a very large and very new electrical transformer.

"What do you think, Craig, should we call the drug unit for back-up?"

"Sounds like a good idea to me," he replied.

She had her cell phone in her hand. "I am going to run this by the captain. If he agrees, he can call out the drug troops."

When the captain answered, she gave him a run-down on their activities so far today. She explained about the barn and requested the drug team. He said he would get them there as soon as possible and would call back with an ETA.

"In the meantime, don't go inside. Just wait for the drug unit and don't let anyone else inside either," Captain Davis advised.

From the console between the seats, Stanton pulled a tin of wintergreen Altoids. He offered some to Karen, she took one. He put one in his mouth and returned the tin back to the console.

"That little blond in Dunn's office was really cute," he commented.

"Why, Trooper Stanton! I'm shocked. You know it is against regulations to notice those things while on duty." She chuckled at his comment, adding, "Do you think the front she presented was real or medically enhanced?"

"First of all you should know, as my supervisor, that I was noting her description for my official report. And second, I think I should investigate and report the results of that investigation to my supervisor." Stanton was now chuckling.

"Neither I nor the report needs that particular detail, but if you feel a need to investigate, you go right ahead."

"Thank you, Sergeant. Glad to see you have a sense of humor."

"I try not to let it interfere with my thinking," she said dryly. "Speaking of Dunn, something about that man doesn't sit right for me. Four hundred pounds of marijuana is a lot of dope and, in the end, a lot of cash. Jack couldn't possibly have run all this operation on his own; he needed a lot of help. It didn't appear Jack had any office help. That means he was taking care of the property management business himself. Perhaps he didn't want the help to see what he was doing with these properties. In any case the growing operation would have required a lot of labor. He would have had a payroll. Someone would have been here to tend the plants. His help was likely paid cash with no records."

"Jack Boardon was a naughty boy. If he was here and alive, we could turn this investigation over to the IRS," Stanton quipped.

A large van came up the drive. Stanton recognized it as the drug unit crime scene vehicle. It had test equipment, Haz-Mat suits and all sorts of special equipment for dealing with suspected drug locations. First out of the truck was the commander of the drug unit, Lieutenant Bill Tolliver.

"How goes it, Craig?" he called as he approached the patrol car.

"Hi there, Lieutenant. Glad you could come to the party. Has Captain Davis filled you in on the details?" Craig Stanton and Bill Tolliver had worked together many times in the past and had, on occasion, shared a beer or two.

"Yes, he did. I have four guys with me. Where do we start?" Tolliver asked

"The windows are painted over, so we can't see in; however, there is that lingering aroma that should be probable cause for any judge. Sergeant Karen Holmes is in charge here, but I think we should just cut the lock off the front door."

"I think you're right, but you know as well as I do that these growers sometimes booby-trap the entry. I'll let my resident door buster handle it." With that he turned to meet Karen. "Hello, Sergeant Holmes. I'm Bill Tolliver, pleased to meet you."

"Good to see you again, Bill. I took one of your classes in the National Guard Hangar, two years ago."

"My crew is inside the van, suiting up. As soon as they are prepared, we will open the building and see what in inside." As he spoke, one of the crew, dressed in a white plastic protective suit, stepped out of the van carrying video equipment.

"Craig and I will stay out of the way while you do the initial ingress. Give me a call if we can help in any way."

The lock on the door was cut off with a bolt cutter. One man waved the others back while he inspected and opened the barn door. One by one the five men went inside. Through the door they could see Tolliver and his men had found the light switch. Twenty-five minutes later one of the men came back to tell them it was OK to come inside. The crew was efficiently going about the business of gathering evidence. There weren't any plants in the trays filled with dirt, yet the odor of hemp was almost overpowering.

Tolliver came over to greet them. "I just wanted you to see what was in here. It was a pretty sophisticated growing operation. It looks like they harvested a crop in recent weeks. I think whoever is working it will be back soon to start another. We are going to be a while, so if you want to do something else, go ahead."

"As a matter of fact, we have several other properties to check out. This may be the tip of the iceberg. We have to check out five other places that are probably just like this one," Karen advised him.

Tolliver gave her a card. "That has my cell phone number on it. Call me if we need to come to another location."

"Will do, Bill," she said to him as they turned to leave. "Good luck here."

Just two miles from the first property they found the second. Like the first it had no house but two equipment sheds and a half-buried building over 300 feet long. It looked like potato storage shed. Karen parked near the largest of the buildings. When they stepped out of the car they were met again by the familiar aroma of marijuana.

There were no windows in the building, but each end held a swinging door large enough to accommodate a large semi- truck. At the west end of the structure was another large power pole with another large transformer. The troopers found the large doors locked on both ends of the building. However, a metal man-size door had been left unlocked. Fresh vehicle tracks were visible and someone had apparently been using the east end to enter and exit.

With weapon drawn, but pointed at the ground, Sergeant Holmes poked her head inside the man-door. She didn't hear anything and couldn't see anything in the darkened building. Stepping outside, with the door ajar, she listened. After a few moments she pushed the door open and stepped inside. Taking a small flashlight from her duty belt, she shined it from side to side. The shed was so large the light didn't carry very far, but there wasn't anyone or any vehicle inside. She shined the light on the on the wall near the door and found a light switch. Turning the switch to the on position illuminated the entire storage shed with a row of overhead lights the full length of the vast room.

Holstering her weapon, she began to walk the left side of the roadway through the facility. There were storage rooms, more like bins, the entire length of the shed. Water pipes and a sprinkler system were plumbed down the entire compliment of small rooms. Each of the rooms was lined with trays of dirt. Each cubicle had a large mercury vapor light connected to a timer. It was the same all the way to the other end and along both sides of the long structure.

The last cubicle, closest to the entry door, was being used as living quarters. There wasn't much in the little cubicle, but on a small table, they found some mail addressed to Carlton Leiber, the aircraft mechanic. A coffee pot, a small refrigerator, a bunk and a wall locker were near the back wall. Under the coffee pot, in a drawer of a small cabinet was a baggie containing about an ounce of marijuana. Making notes and taking photos as they searched, they found maintenance books, small tools and other paperwork relating to the crashed 206 and other planes.

"Time to call Bill Tolliver," Karen said.

"They won't find much product, but this is definitely a grow operation. Craig replied. I find it interesting that our friend the mechanic is living here. All of that raises a question for me."

"What question is that, Craig?"

"I am wondering if Mr. Dunn owns an airplane and if Mr. Leiber does his maintenance work?"

"Good question." Karen pulled a phone from her pocked and dialed Tolliver. While it was ringing she told Stanton, "When I finish with Bill I'll call Lou Mankawitz and have him find the answer to that question."

CHAPTER 6

The two troopers were standing by their patrol car when the crime unit van came down the drive. Karen was on the telephone talking with Captain Davis. By the time the van came to a stop, she had put her phone back in her pocket. The door of the van opened and Tolliver and one other trooper emerged.

"You two may keep me busy for the rest of my career," he said, stepping down from the tall vehicle. "Is it like the other one?"

"Pretty much," Karen replied. "There are cubicles in here. Each has its own water and light control. It looks pretty scientific to me. There is one cubicle made into a living area. We believe it's occupied by the airplane mechanic. He isn't home right now, but he could come back at any time. Keep your eyes open."

"Are you going to stick around or leave?" Tolliver asked.

"We have three more properties to check out, so we will be leaving. I just talked to Captain Davis. He is sending some troopers to help you load and haul all this equipment. They should be here within an hour with a big truck. Craig and I need to check those other properties before it gets too late."

"OK, Sergeant. We can get you on the radio if the need arises. Let us know what you find." With that, Karen and Craig headed for the next site.

It was nine miles to the other side of the Glenn Highway to the next stop. It proved more difficult to locate than the previous two properties. Off the old Knik Road about a half mile at the edge of a large hay field was a bright red barn, a very large barn. The road in to the property didn't appear have been used recently. The description of the property claimed it sat on 82 acres with a well and a house. The road had been plowed recently, but there were no new tire tracks. The house looked abandoned.

As they got out of the car Craig said, pointing to the overhead wires, "There is no way this electrical system would support a grow operation like the others. I wonder why the power and gas bills are so high."

"I guess we should look inside and find out," Karen replied. "Let's check out the barn first."

Stanton nodded his agreement as the two walked the few paces to the man-door at the end of the barn. It was locked. They made their way around the outside of the huge old barn and failed to find a way to enter that wasn't secured.

"We will need a search warrant for this," Karen said. "Let's check out the house to see if it's open or locked. In any case we will include it in the search warrant request."

Stepping up onto the creaking boards of the back porch made Stanton, once again, think about booby traps. He had once had a partner injured in a situation similar to this one.

"Hold it, Sergeant," he said. "Let me have a look before we both get too close, just a safety check."

"OK, Craig, but you be very careful."

She stood quietly at the edge of the porch while Craig inspected the screen door and the windows, peering inside each one before returning to the door and trying the knob. It, too, was locked.

"Locked," he said as he motioned for her to follow. They walked around the house on the veranda style porch. At the front he once again checked the door and windows for signs of a trap. He didn't find any but was able to see through the windows that someone had recently been using this place.

"Do you want to call for a search warrant on this place or wait until we check out the last place on the list?" Stanton asked of his sergeant.

"It's going to be dark soon, let's go to the last place and take a look while we still have some daylight."

"Sounds good to me," he said as they walked back to the patrol car.

The last site on the list was farther up the Glenn Highway near the town of Sutton. The drive would take several minutes and Karen used the time to contact Lou Mankawitz. She made her request about Dunn and whether he owned an airplane. He said he would get back to her tomorrow morning. The roads were good, snow and ice free, but the berms on the sides of the road were piled high. There was snow in the trees and the Matanuska River was frozen over with the exception of the occasional open lead.

Their pace slowed to a crawl when they turned left on the old Jonesville Mine Road. Because of the snow-banks, the roadway was very narrow. Two cars could pass with caution, but the surface was icy, making the going hazardous. Several minutes later, near the end of the road, they located the property. Again they found the drive to be plowed but absent of fresh tire tracks. Driving slowly down the trail in the diminishing daylight, they watched for any sign of habitation. Breaking out of the trees, they found a small, well-kept home. A small one-car garage was to the left of the house.

Stanton stopped the patrol car at the garage door and both officers exited the car. "I'll check the house; you take the garage." Taking the small flashlight from her belt she headed toward the house. "Be careful," she added, calling back over her shoulder.

Stanton peered through the window in the man-size door. It was dark inside, and no sign of a vehicle. Without snowshoes it would be impossible to walk around the structure. Back at the side door he shined his light inside. It was empty except for a small workbench at the rear of the garage. Small tools and what appeared to be nuts and bolts were scattered among the tools on the bench. He did not attempt to enter the structure. After looking inside he joined his sergeant at the rear door of the small home.

Karen stared thoughtfully into space. "Do you suppose the last place we looked at was used to package the product and maybe he used this place to house his workers?"

"What makes you think that?" he asked.

"On the way out here, I was looking at the pattern of gas and power usage. The power usage at the first two places is fairly constant all year. The one on Knik Road and this one only have excessive use for short periods. I'm willing to bet this was used as a bunkhouse for workers."

"You make a good case, Sergeant," he agreed. "There doesn't seem to be much we can do here until we get the warrant. Shall we go back to Palmer and see what Tolliver has found?"

"Good idea. It's getting dark anyway." She shivered and added, "And cold."

They stopped in Palmer for a cup of coffee to go at Burger King. The coffee was gone by the time they arrived at the crime lab van. Bill Tolliver and his partner were inside the van when the troopers arrived back at the scene.

Climbing into the van, Craig and Karen found it warm and well lit. "Well, how did it go, Bill?" she asked.

"You had it right. It is a growing operation. It had been recently harvested and it looks like they are preparing for planting. The building is warm and the water is still working. We found a lot of lights, timers and other equipment. We are waiting now for that big van of yours to come and pick up this stuff. We inventoried it and have it piled near the door. There is a lot of equipment." Bill held up a notebook filled with entries. "We found a lot of aircraft records in that last cubical. The papers are all signed by the same hand by a Carlton Lieber. There are records for the Cessna you told me about as well as several other aircraft including a couple of Super Cubs and a Beechcraft King Air."

"Great job, Bill," Karen congratulated. "Craig and I are going back to the office to do the paperwork on all this and to try for a search warrant on two other properties. They didn't appear to be growing sites but are being used in the business. We will see you back in town."

Tolliver waved to them as they backed out of the drive. There was a lot of data-keeping to be done today and it was getting late. Within minutes headlights came up the drive. Bill instructed the driver to turn his truck around and back close to the door for loading. It took almost an hour to load the items and send the trooper van back to town. Weary and hungry, Tolliver and his partners sipped coffee and relaxed a few minutes before heading back to Anchorage.

CHAPTER 7

Ken Whittle rolled out of bed. It was chilly in the cabin. He slipped on a bathrobe before stoking the wood stove. He looked out the small kitchen window to read the temperature. It was 38 degrees below zero; no wonder the cabin was cool, he thought. He washed his face and brushed his teeth while planning his day. No need to hurry this morning, it was too cold to fly. He made coffee and sat at the table, thinking. He needed to go into Anchorage to make his official report about the crash he had found. He needed a few things from the grocery store and he was low on salt and borax for his hides.

Ordinarily, he would have to do some bookkeeping before going into town to see if he had money enough to do his shopping. That would not be the case today. He hadn't opened the safe since placing all that cash inside, not wanting to be tempted into spending enough of it to draw attention to his new wealth.

He was still having feelings of guilt about taking the money, but was relieved no one had asked him about it. He did wonder, however, why had this pilot been carrying such a large amount of cash with him? It seemed to Whittle that any legitimate business person would use a cashier's check for such a large transaction. He could not find a reason to justify that amount of cash. It must have to do with the drugs he had in the airplane, he concluded.

As the cabin warmed, he became more relaxed. Bacon, eggs, hash browns and coffee were on his menu this morning. He found himself humming "Rock of Ages" while fixing his breakfast. After eating he poured a third cup of coffee and tuned the television set to the weather channel. The high pressure area now over south central Alaska would remain stationary for at least two more days before temperatures would warm up. Ken didn't like the sound of that news. There were only a couple of weeks left in the trapping season. It had been a good season so far and he was not anxious to see it end. He would soon have to make plans to pull and store his traps for the season.

He started his old truck to warm it up while he went back inside to clean up his kitchen and make the bed. Checking the time, he found his cell phone to call the number on the business card the trooper sergeant had given him.

"Sergeant Holmes," she answered.

"Sergeant, Ken Whittle. I can't fly today, it's too cold. Would it be okay if I came in to your office to make that statement you wanted?"

"Good morning, Mr. Whittle," she greeted. "Yes, I plan to be in my office until around noon. I have a lot of paperwork to catch up on. What time do you expect to be here?"

"Early, it will take me a little over an hour to drive into town."

"I will tell the receptionist in the front to be expecting you," she advised. "See you then."

The old green '82 Dodge pick-up he drove looked bad, but it was clean on the inside and ran very well. The outside became coated in mud from the drive into and out of his property which was at the end of a mostly unimproved road. He had bought the cabin from an aging hippie who used the property to grow marijuana. The guy had put the place up for sale when he was arrested and needed money to pay a lawyer. That was when Ken had looked at it and decided it was perfect for his needs: a decent cabin, two outbuildings, some acreage, a small airstrip and privacy. The price had been right and Ken was able to scrape the cash together to buy it. Two years of hard work later and Ken had a comfortable home. Only one bedroom, but he seldom had visitors. He kept a snowplow blade on the old Dodge in the winter for keeping the road open. It was unhandy to drive in the city, but he wasn't going to take it off for this one trip.

It was just after 9 a.m. when he parked in front of Trooper Headquarters on Tudor Road. Inside, the receptionist called Karen to the front to meet her guest.

"Good morning, Ken. How was the drive into town?" she asked.

"Cold," he replied.

"Would you like some coffee to warm you up?"

"No, thanks. I have had my quota for this morning."

The Sergeant took him to an interview room where she had papers and files and forms on the table. She placed a small voice recorder on the table and asked if he would mind being recorded during the interview.

"Naw, it's OK," he responded. "Can I ask a question?"

"Sure. I will answer any question I can, but there are some things about our investigation I won't be allowed to tell you. What do you want to know?"

"I know it's none of my business," he began, "but can you tell me what was in the bags he had in the back of the airplane?"

"I'll tell you, but I would ask that you keep it to yourself," she said. "We tested the contents of the duffle bags and found it to be high quality, by that I mean high THC content, marijuana. I'm sorry I can't tell you any more than that, though."

"That's OK. I was just curious." With that he sat up straight in his chair and said, "Now, what is it you wanted to know?"

With that they began the interview which lasted a little less than one hour. After reading over the statement she had typed up for him, he asked where he should sign. She pointed to the proper place and asked the notary to come in and witness the signature.

She thanked him for his help and his cooperation and said they would be in touch if there was anything else they needed to know.

Satisfied he had done the right thing, he left the building and started his truck. It was cold inside. He spent the rest of the day in town shopping. It was humorous to him that he had all that money in his safe and was unable to think of anything to spend it on.

With the groceries loaded into the cab of the truck to keep everything from freezing, he drove home. Once there he carried everything into the house, stoked the wood stove and lay down for a short nap.

CHAPTER 8

Late that afternoon from his desk, Anthony Dunn dialed his intercom. "Miss Toombes, see if you can locate Carlton Lieber and have him call me right away."

"Right away, sir." Ten minutes later Lieber called back. The secretary forwarded his call to her boss's desk.

"Carl, I know it's cold outside, but I want you to load all the product we have and take it to the hangar at International. Load the King Air, check the fuel, and make a walk-around. Get it ready to go by 3:30. I'm going to Fairbanks and I want you to go with me. We will be back some time tonight. We will leave both our vehicles inside the hangar while we're gone."

"Sure thing, Mr. Dunn. Do you want full fuel on board?"

"Yes, that will get us both ways. We won't be on the ground long in Fairbanks. Dress warm for working up there," he cautioned.

He left the office after giving last minute instructions to Ms. Toombes. His real estate office was a busy one with many transactions requiring registry with the recorder in the courthouse. Laura Toombes had proved to be efficient as well as easy to look at.

"I may be late in the morning, but keep my schedule the way it is. If things go as planned, I will have to go into Anchorage in the afternoon. I have to go to the bank. Call my lawyer and set up an appointment for right after lunch. Tell him we have to discuss what to do about my partnership deals with Jack Boardon. His death is going to complicate my life a great deal." He stared into space a moment, and then asked, "Do you have any questions for me?"

"No," she said. "I can take care of everything. Just call me if there are any changes. By the way, will you be at your cell phone number?"

"Most of the time, yes, but I may be out of range occasionally. See you tomorrow."

In Alaska, the majority of people traveling during the winter carry cold weather clothing in their vehicle. Dunn was one of those people. At the airport he parked his SUV inside the hangar, took a heavy parka and insulated boots from the rear of the truck. He carried the load to the waiting Beechcraft and tossed them inside before making a last minute inspection of the plane. Lieber turned off the lights and closed the hangar door.

Lieber met Dunn as he came around the tail, looking at the control surfaces. "Is everything OK, boss?"

"Yes, everything looks good. Are the wing de-icers working properly?" he asked the mechanic.

"Yes, sir. I cycled them just to make sure."

"How much product is there?" Dunn asked.

"Twelve bags, one hundred pounds each," Lieber confirmed.

"Weather said it is clear and cold all the way to Fairbanks. It should be a nice trip. I filed a flight plan when I called for weather and I will open it on the way." Climbing the air stair into the cabin with Lieber following, Dunn said, "Close it up, and we will get going."

With calm air, they took off to the north, directly toward Fairbanks, climbing to 12,000 feet. With the autopilot dialed in, Dunn sat back to enjoy the night. The aurora was brilliant in the sky. Mt. McKinley stood in majestic splendor, shimmering in the light of a full moon. A couple of minutes after crossing the Tanana River, Dunn began his descent for a landing at Fairbanks International Airport. Staying on the runway to the last taxiway, he turned off and made his way to a large commercial hangar—the last in a row of such hangars. As he shut down the engines, a cargo van came around the hangar and backed to the air stair.

Before exiting the craft, Dunn spoke quietly to Lieber. "Don't unload anything until I give you the word."

"Got it, Boss," was the reply.

"Let's go into the office," said a huge black man. His name was Mosely Cain, but everyone called him "Moose." "It's too damn cold out here."

It was only about fifty yards to the hangar entry door, but at 45 below zero, it seemed to Dunn like a mile. Inside he unzipped his parka while Moose poured two cups of hot coffee. Moose and a partner Dunn didn't know owned or leased four Boeing 747 freight hauling airplanes. They maintained a, mostly regular, schedule carrying freight to destinations around the world. The venture generated a large cash flow, but the aging aircraft and rising fuel prices ate up almost all the profits. With contacts from his military career during the Gulf War, Moose had set up a lucrative drug smuggling business. He had known Anthony Dunn from those military days and, by accident, learned he was involved in the marijuana growing business with another old friend, Jack Boardon. Moose had devised the plan to trade heroin and cocaine for the marijuana that he sold for cash in New York City.

"My pilot said Jack was a no-show on the last flight. What happened?" Moose asked.

"He ran out of fuel and crashed shortly after takeoff. Jack didn't survive. The troopers are looking into the accident now. He had 400 pounds of weed with him when he went down. The cops are a little more than curious about that." Dunn sipped his hot coffee. "There is no way to tie him to me, except through the property management business and all of that is legitimate. I'm going to miss old Jack."

"Yeah, me too," said Moose. "Will this have an impact on our arrangement?"

"No, we had just finished cleaning up after the last crop harvest, so there is nothing for the troopers to find except lights and growing trays. It will be costly to replace all that, but we have other property and can be growing again within a couple of weeks. It was time to renovate anyway. The THC content was down in the last crop. The soil needed changing. Gotta look out for quality," he quipped, laughing at his own joke.

"Do you have the whole 1200 pounds with you today?" Moose asked.

"Yes, do you have my product?"

"Of course, and the $100,000 cash you wanted. This shipment of heroin came from Thailand. Good stuff."

"Get it for me and I will have my mechanic unload the weed." Dunn wanted to get back to Anchorage. "Call me about mid-March. I should have a delivery date for you by then."

"Will do," said Moose. "See you in a couple of months."

Dunn took two leather cases from the old desk and the two men walked back to the King Air where he told Lieber to go ahead with the unloading. Five minutes later the van pulled away, Lieber closed the air stair and Dunn started the engines. In seconds heat began to warm the entire cabin. While the mechanic strapped into the right hand seat, Dunn called for clearance for take-off. Once in the air and headed home, he decided all had gone well and was satisfied with his profit.

Dunn helped the mechanic get the big twin into the hangar and close the door. He told Liber to meet him at O'Sullivans Restaurant and he would buy dinner.

According to the thermometer on the instrument panel, it was beginning to warm up. It was now only minus eight degrees.

CHAPTER 9

Karen Holmes had been in her office for more than an hour when Craig Stanton arrived carrying a fistful of papers. It was a stack of search warrants for the properties in Palmer.

"We got 'em!" he said. "How do you want to handle this? Are you and I going to serve them ourselves?"

"Good going, Craig," she replied and then added, "Captain Davis has made arrangements for the drug unit to do the searches. You and I will join them later and coordinate cataloguing and listing the evidence. In the meantime, how about you drive up to Eagle River and speak with the secretary at Dunn's Realty. See if you can find out anything about Dunn personal habits and if he does a lot of flying." She held up a finger for him to wait while she dialed the telephone.

"Good morning, Lou," she said into the mouthpiece. Sorry I haven't been able to get back to you before now. What did you find out about Anthony Dunn's airplanes?"

"That's OK Karen. I have been out of the office most of the time anyway." Lou had an office in the federal building on 5th Avenue. "You won't need to take notes. I have a written summary for you if I can find time to bring it to you. First, our friend Mr. Dunn has a Beechcraft King Air. An older model, but it's well-kept and pretty. I remember seeing it and I admired it at the time. The King Air is a turboprop twin. They are fast and comfortable, capable of flying to the Lower 48. His last flight was yesterday afternoon. He filed a flight plan for Fairbanks and returned just after nine last night."

"Business trip, no doubt," Karen commented.

"Right, if you want to believe that. Just for your information, he had one passenger listed going both ways."

"I don't suppose there is any way to find out who the passenger was, or where he went in Fairbanks?"

"I can't do everything for you, Karen. You are the investigator." He chuckled and added, "Also, for your file, Dunn owns a Super Cub he keeps in a small rented hangar at Birchwood Airport in Eagle River."

"This guy has a lot of expensive toys. He must sell a lot of real estate."

"That is the kind of stuff investigators investigate." Lou chuckled again. "Anyway, I will bring this file to you sometime today, probably late this afternoon.

"Craig and I will be out of the office most of the day, but the receptionist will put it on my desk. Thanks for the help, Lou."

Turning back to her partner, she gave him the information she had just learned. "See if you can find out what kind of business he had in Fairbanks yesterday. Any skinny little secretary worth her salt should know that kind of stuff," she teased.

"I'll try to get her full cooperation," he replied, as he lifted his long frame from the chair. "Will the lunch tab be a per diem expense?"

"Only if you get all those questions answered," she replied. "How about I meet you at property number five on old Knik Road? I'll have been to all the other properties and hope to have all the evidence lists by then."

Knowing she would be out in the cold most of the day, Karen took a pair of insulated boots from behind the driver's seat and laced them up. They would be clumsy for driving, but she would save time at the scene. It took a little less than an hour to drive to the property on Palmer-Fishhook Road. Upon her arrival, she found troopers busy listing items, large and small, as evidence. The trooper in charge was a short, stocky man wearing a Beaver fur hat. He had noticed her driving into the property and met her outside.

"They told me you would be here, Sergeant. I'm Joe Rhines," he said, holding out his gloveless hand. "We are nearly finished here. Good thing, too, my people are getting cold. We need to find a coffee shop and warm up."

"Are you familiar with Joe's Cafe?" She gave him the address and directions. "I am going to check out the other properties and meet everyone at the farm house on old Knik Road. The house is warm inside, and it is close enough to be able to check back at the other places if the need arises. I should be there around noon. Have you heard anything from the other teams?"

"Not much, I think they are like us, trying to finish and get warm," Rhines said.

She waved and walked back to her truck. A few minutes later, the scene was repeated at property number two. Checking with all the other teams and giving them the same instructions, she drove to the last location, with a stop at the Noisy Goose restaurant in Palmer for a cup of coffee to go. The last team had the door unlocked and was finishing with the evidence gathering when she arrived, still sipping her coffee.

The team leader met her at the door and explained what they had been doing. He said they were finished in the kitchen area and she could set up her temporary office there.

"Have you found anything incriminating during the search?" she asked.

"Not much. Your assumption was correct, I think. They used this as housing for the agricultural crew. There is evidence that several people were living here. I was amazed at how clean the place was. Usually, when a bunch of men inhabits a place it gets trashed. Not this time—no garbage, no dirty clothing, no liquor bottles, no dirty dishes. It's as if housekeeping just left. There is food in the cupboards, but the refrigerator is clean. It appears they were planning on using it again, but they left it clean."

"Any evidence they were growing marijuana on the property?" Karen inquired.

"None. Like I said, they lived here, but that was all."

"Thanks," she said. "The other teams will be here later and we can all get together to compare notes. I will take notes on things to be followed up on, but the main report can wait until we get back to the office. Thanks for all your help," Karen said politely.

It was 1:45 when Stanton came in, smiling. "I have news, boss," he said, grinning.

"Does this mean I will be getting a bill for per diem?" was her reply.

"Not this time." He paused, taking his notebook from his jacket pocket. "According to the secretary, Dunn has more money than God," the trooper began. "She says she is puzzled by that because his real estate business is good, but not enough to justify his trips and his toys. She told me that Jack Boardon and Anthony Dunn were partners, years ago, but had split the business about four years ago. From that point on Dunn operated the real estate end and Boardon ran the property management business. Most of the properties we are looking into right now are jointly owned by Dunn and Boardon." He paused, turning the pages of his notebook.

"You had a busy lunch," Karen commented. "I will pay per diem for this one."

"She told me Boardon, with two long O's, was half crazy. She said Dunn didn't want him coming into the office. She also thought he was using hard drugs. She never saw him do it, but his personality kept changing and he began to have mood swings. She said she was afraid of him." Again, he paused to turn the page.

"She also told me," he continued, "that Dunn did a lot of banking away from the office. He would go to different banks, not the real estate office bank. She never asked about that but was curious. She thought it was just personal business."

"I asked about the mechanic, Lieber," he said. "She thought he was a drug user, too. She said he was never dirty, but he never looked clean. He was always scruffy looking, to use her words."

"The two of you had quite a conversation. Do I need to think about a wedding gift?" she teased.

"Not yet, but I did like her," he said as he poured a cup of coffee from the thermos on the table.

"Good job, Craig. I never expected that kind of cooperation from her. Drink your coffee while I finish this report." She smiled at him and continued with her writing.

The two of them worked most of the afternoon compiling lists of evidence and observations. Both were getting tired and stiff from the process. Karen stood and stretched her tired muscles when her radio came to life. The roving patrol watching the properties on the other side of the Glenn Highway was reporting a trespasser at property number two.

Karen and Craig responded immediately, as did the two troopers who had been working at the property all morning. With lights and sirens, the three-car convoy made it to the potato storage shed in less than five minutes. The on-scene trooper reported the person inside the building would not come outside. Upon their arrival they found the trooper, beside his car, trying to communicate with whoever was inside.

Karen and Craig joined the trooper who gave them a brief summary of the situation. Karen spoke into her radio asking for the name of the owner of a 1982 Ford F150, giving the license plate number. The response was almost immediate, Carlton Lieber.

"Lieber, is that you inside?" Karen called.

"Yeah, who wants to know?" was the reply.

"Sergeant Holmes, Alaska State Troopers. You are trespassing on a crime scene, sir. Come on out here and we will talk about it."

"I don't think so. You might shoot at me," he responded.

"Are you armed, Mr. Lieber?" Karen asked.

Karen motioned for the other two troopers to take a position on either side of the vehicle entrance and near the man-door. They quickly and quietly moved in, both with weapons drawn.

"Mr. Lieber, we can't allow you to stay in there. Come on out where we can talk," she asked once again.

"I don't want to get shot."

"Open the door and hold your hands outside so we can see you are not armed, and you can come out without anyone getting hurt. Come on out, Mr. Lieber."

There was long silence from inside the building. In a few moments, the man-door opened a crack and two empty hands appeared. One of the troopers at the door grabbed the hands and pulled them outside. He spun Lieber around and the nervous man lost his balance and stumbled to the ground. The trooper put his knee in the middle of his back and locked a set of handcuffs on his wrists. While he was still on the snowy ground, the trooper searched the mechanic for weapons. Finding none, he helped the man to his feet.

Shaken, Lieber said, "You said you wouldn't hurt me."

"Oh, you aren't hurt, Mr. Lieber. We just had to see if you were telling the truth about being armed. Now calm down and tell me what you are doing here."

"My office is in here," he said, half-shouting and angry.

"What office is that Mr. Lieber?" Karen asked.

"I'm an A and P mechanic. All my maintenance records are here, or were here. I see they are gone now."

"Who is it you work for?" she asked.

"I was working for Mr. Boardon and Mr. Dunn, but Mr. Boardon got killed the other day. He was in an airplane crash and I know everyone will be asking a lot of questions about his airplane and I was the one who worked on it."

"Did you have anything to do with the accident?" she asked again.

"See! I knew everybody would blame me," he whined. "Ain't it possible he just screwed up and crashed?"

"Yes, I guess that is possible." She paused a moment before asking, "Mr. Lieber, would you be agreeable to coming with us into the Palmer office to get your picture and fingerprints taken? If you do this voluntarily, we might not have to arrest you, just get some information and you can go. In fact, I will follow you back into Palmer in my vehicle if you want to drive your own truck. Is that all right with you?"

"Yeah, I guess I can do that. But you won't arrest me, right?"

"If you cooperate, that's right," she explained.

He agreed and the small caravan drove back into Palmer.

CHAPTER 10

The weather was warming, and Ken Whittle wanted to check his trap line. Two sections of his string had been unattended for nearly a week. For small furbearers that could be disastrous. Eagles, owls, ravens coyotes, wolves, shrews and a hundred other carrion feeders would raid his traps if they got to them first. He had pre-heated the plane, and loaded his trap basket and supplies. He started the engine, throttled back to a slow idle and made a final walk around the plane. He untied the wings and climbed inside. There were only a couple of weeks left in the trapping season, but with the weather warming, he might not be able to keep his traps out until the end.

He began at the farthest end of the trap line and worked his way toward home. It went quickly because there were few animals in his traps. The cold weather probably accounted for some of that, he thought.

His final sets were on Witsoe Lake, the scene of the crash he had discovered. As he flew over to check out the landing area, he noticed a set of fresh ski tracks. The craft had landed, circled back, taxiing to where the crash had occurred. "That's strange," he said aloud to himself. He landed and came to a stop near where the other airplane had stopped.

Getting out of his own plane, he looked carefully at the tracks. Someone had stepped out of the airplane and walked to the shore where the Cessna had crashed. The ski tracks were those of a small tail dragger. Probably a Super Cub like his own. The boot prints led him to the crash site where someone had milled around for several minutes. "Looking for what?" he wondered. "Should I pass this information on to the troopers?" He decided he would have to think about that.

Daylight was fading when he finished on Witsoe Lake. He noticed the wind had picked up as he flew toward home. By the time he had covered the airplane and unloaded his furs and gear it was late and dark. When he finally made it to his cabin and opened the door, he knew immediately someone had been in his home.

Cautiously, he began to check out the cabin. Only minor things had been disturbed. In the bedroom he found the gun he kept under the mattress was still there; however, its position had been changed from the way he always kept it. He checked the woodstove for booby-traps. He looked under the sink and behind the toilet. He looked behind the curtains for microphones or recorders. He found nothing. The last place he needed to check was the safe. Opening it, he found the stacks of cash exactly as he had left them. He gave a sigh of relief and made a pot of coffee. Removing his parka and hanging it on a peg behind the door, he stoked the fire and waited for the coffee pot to finish.

Sitting in his chair, sipping the hot brew, he tried to figure out who had been in his cabin. He didn't think it was troopers. They would have come with a search warrant and asked him to open the safe. No, it had to be someone looking for something in particular, like the cash in the safe. There were myriad possibilities. All that marijuana in the wreck meant the pilot was in the drug business. Could it be someone looking for drugs? It didn't seem likely, since the troopers took all of it with them. It always came back to the cash.

Why did he have both cash and marijuana in the airplane? Had he already made a sale before the crash? Possible. One hundred four thousand dollars is a lot of cash and would have been a big marijuana sale. Maybe he had a partner who was looking for the money. That seemed likely. He took another sip of his coffee; it was getting cold.

He got up to pour a fresh cup when it struck him. "How did he know who I was and where to find me? I could be in real danger," he thought. "I guess some precautions would be in order."

Putting on his parka again, he walked out to his fleshing shack. It was divided into two rooms—one for fleshing hides and one for salting and storing the furs. Upon entering, the first room was the fleshing area; it was closer to the door for ventilation. The room at the rear was stacked with piles of salted hides. One stack was all beaver pelts; the hides had been stretched, salted, and rubbed with borax to absorb the fat. He pulled the hides aside and shined a light on the floor to locate the nails. It took more than an hour to make a lift-out door in the floor.

In the kitchen he found a large plastic tub with a moisture tight lid. Taking the cash from the safe, putting it into gallon-size freezer bags, and placing it all in the plastic container, he carried the package to the fur shed. He hid the container under the floor and replaced the makeshift door. With gloved hands he raked up debris from the floor, rubbing it into the newly sawn cracks in an attempt to disguise its location. Satisfied with his efforts, he pulled the stack of beaver pelts back into place atop the hideaway.

Back inside the cabin, he removed the heavy parka and poured himself a whisky. Sitting in his chair near the stove, he thought about booby trapping the doors and windows. One more sip of the liquor and he discarded the idea. "If they want in, they will get in," he thought. Tired and hungry, he fixed himself a sandwich, had another whisky, and climbed into bed. Before going to sleep, he thought about the gun under his mattress and decided to put it under his pillow—a handier place. Relaxed now, thinking about all the hides to be fleshed tomorrow, he fell asleep.

Early that same day, Carlton Lieber had made a frantic call to Anthony Dunn. He told of being caught by the troopers and fingerprinted. They had asked him many questions, to which he had given vague answers. Lieber had overheard a conversation between two of the troopers in which one of them mentioned Ken Whittle as the trapper who had found Boardon's crashed plane. He was frightened.

"What should I do Mr. Dunn?" he asked.

"It sounds like they were just checking you out. You should have stayed out of the warehouse. That was dumb on your part," chastised Dunn. "I want you to stay away from Jack's properties. They will be watching all of them. Just go about your business as if you never knew him. Go over to my hangar at Birchwood and when I get back this afternoon I want you to change the oil in the Super Cub." Thinking for a moment, he continued. "Do you have enough money to keep you out of trouble for a while?"

"I'm broke, Mr. Dunn. Mr. Boardon was supposed to pay me last week, but he had that wreck."

"Alright, you go to Birchwood and work on my Cub. I will come by the hangar and give you some money. I want you to keep a low profile. I don't want anyone suspecting a connection between you and me other than that you are my mechanic, understand?"

Dunn told Laura Toombes he would be out of the office for about three hours but would be back later in the day. With that, he drove to Birchwood Airport and flew away in a northwest direction. He had found the crash site easily. Troopers had told him Jack had crashed on Witsoe Lake. Flying over the lake, he saw the ski tracks of the trapper's airplane and the place where troopers had lifted the big Cessna out of the trees. He landed and walked to the site. There was absolutely nothing to see there.

Before leaving the office, he had consulted the computer and found a property listed to Ken Whittle. A computer image of a real-time satellite picture showed a small airstrip on the property with no airplane present. That property would be his next stop.

The place was fundamental and primitive, but tidy and, for a trapper, an ideal location. Dunn walked along the snow-packed trails to each of the two outbuildings. One had a lock on the door, but through a small side window, he could see it was where the trapper prepared his furs. The other building was a shed containing an aircraft engine heater, tools, gas cans and the usual things found in a shed used to support the use of an airplane. Things were neat and tidy in the shed, saying something about the personality of the individual using it.

At the house, he found the door unlocked. Inside was warm and clean. There was a coffee cup in the sink, but, as with the shed, things were in their place and neat. Dunn searched the bookshelves, cupboards, and drawers before moving to the bedroom. There was a revolver under the mattress, loaded, but no cash. Back in the living room/kitchen, he pondered the safe. It was a Browning, a very strong safe with lots of locking lugs. He attempted to move it, but found it had been bolted to the floor. "This would require a different tactic," he thought.

Checking the time, and noticing the fading daylight, he started his engine and flew back to Birchwood Airport. He gave Lieber some cash and left the Super Cub for the mechanic to pull into the hangar.

Back in his office, he greeted his secretary and entered the office, closing the door behind him. From a small red address book, he took a number. It was the foreman of the crew he and Boardon had hired to manage their growing operation.

"Don Bettis," answered the voice on the other end.

Bettis looked like any other vegetable farmer in Palmer, and in fact owned fifteen acres he cultivated for that purpose. Bettis was one of the few people Dunn trusted. More than six feet tall and usually found wearing bibbed overalls, he was well known around Palmer. The trio, Jack, Tony and Don, had met while on duty, during Operation Desert Storm. It was not until they met again, in Alaska, they had become close friends.

"Don, Tony," he replied. "I suppose you heard about Jack?"

"I read it in the paper. What happened? Do you know?"

"How about dinner tonight and we can talk about it?"

"I'll get a booth in that little Italian joint in Wasilla. Seven o'clock?" Bettis asked.

"I'll see you then,'" Dunn replied.

Turning off his cell phone, he picked up the desk phone and dialed Laura Toombes. "Come in here, please."

The two spent the next hour reviewing the recent transactions and confirming their registration with the borough offices. She was always astounded to see how much paperwork was required to transfer ownership from one party to another.

When they finished, Laura went back to her desk and turned her thoughts to the young, handsome trooper who had taken her to lunch. She thought it best to keep that fact secret from her boss, since much of the conversation was about him. "I wonder if he will call me again," she pondered.

CHAPTER 11

The past couple of days had been tiring. The sergeant and her partner had spent long days inventorying evidence and trying to make sense of the evidence the teams had collected. They had not found any papers, receipts or other evidence of product being sold. The volume of marijuana that must have been grown here was phenomenal. There was ample evidence of what was grown and the scope of the crop; however, it appeared that the crop had been harvested, hung to dry, and then moved to another location for packaging. It was certainly a professional operation.

Karen Holmes checked the time, and stood up and stretched her aching muscles. They were nearly finished now. Evidence had been removed and stored and only paperwork remained. The two troopers had worked all morning finalizing their reports.

"How about some lunch?" Karen asked. "I'll buy today."

"I like that idea," Craig agreed. "Where do you want to go?"

"How about the Sea Galley?" she suggested.

"Sounds good to me. We can take my patrol car."

With hands stuffed inside pockets of their parkas, they hurried to the car. As they pulled away from the parking area, Stanton gave his location and intention to go to lunch. He reported Karen was with him in the car.

"Stand by," was the acknowledgement. "There is a request for Sergeant Holmes to report to the hangar ASAP. Lieutenant Nelson will brief you when you arrive."

"10-4," Stanton replied.

The helicopter had been pulled out of the hangar by the time they arrived. Lieutenant Nelson, the boss at the hangar, was directing the fete. He waved to them as they got closer.

Zipping her parka as she exited the patrol car, she spoke. "Hi, Dan. What have we got?"

"Two paramedics are inside getting their equipment for a rescue on Flattop Mountain. We had a call that a cross-country skier is injured, but we don't have an accurate account of how badly. You need to take the Medics up there and bring out the injured party." He handed her a map with a red circle drawn on it. "The report gave this as the location; the southeast side, close to the summit. You can take Stanton with you to handle the witnesses."

"Sounds easy enough," she said, looking at the map. The medics were coming out of the hangar with a stretcher and several plastic boxes of medical supplies.

She swung into the pilot's seat and began her pre-flight check while the medics loaded their gear. Flattop Mountain is a popular spot for hikers, skiers and other outdoor enthusiasts. Only a short distance from the city and accessible by automobile, the trails are sometimes treacherous. Although not terribly steep, they are narrow and lie on steep hillsides. Many people are injured each year and occasionally someone is killed there.

Karen started the engines and called the tower for permission to take off from the ramp at the state hangar. Permission was given and the helicopter lifted off. In only minutes, they were near the parking area. As the big helicopter approached, a group of people in the parking lot motioned for them to continue and pointed in the general direction of the injured skier. She continued on her course and found another small group of Samaritans seemingly giving aid to a person on the ground. Two of the citizens giving aid to the person on the ground began to wave their arms when the helicopter came into sight. They were near the top of the mountain and the sergeant found a landing spot about fifty yards above the trail.

Loading their medical gear on the stretcher, the two medics carried everything down the hill to where the injured skier was lying. Stanton asked the bystanders to step aside while the medics tended the patient. Hooking him up to monitoring machines and calling on the radio, they advised the hospital the patient had an apparent severe neck injury. They asked that an ambulance meet them at the state hangar on Lake Hood. The people who found him had done an excellent job of keeping the patient still and warm until help arrived. Several minutes elapsed while the paramedics stabilized the skier and placed him on the stretcher. They enlisted several of the bystanders to help carry the heavy load to the helicopter.

Stanton had a notebook full of names and addresses as well as abbreviated statements from them. He asked each one to come into the office and make an official statement. Once loaded, Karen motioned the people on the ground away and started the engine. Clouds were beginning to close in on the mountaintop. The pilot was relieved to be off the mountain heading back to the hangar.

The ambulance was waiting when they arrived. There were now four medical personnel on the scene, making it easy to transfer the load to the ambulance.

Karen and Stanton watched the red lights swing toward downtown Anchorage.

"I'll still buy you lunch, Craig," she said, grinning at him.

They were eating their salad course when Stanton asked, "How did you ever get into flying helicopters?"

She gave him the short version between bites. She was proud of her skills and accomplishments, but wasn't comfortable talking about it. The halibut was served by the time she finished her tale. "Besides," she said. "Since I'm not built like a supermodel I needed an edge when competing with skinny blond secretaries."

"In my opinion, there is more to a package than the wrapping. I'm not trying to sound gratuitous, but I would rather have you for a partner than any blond I know. And, I would rather have you for a back-up than almost any man I know. I don't want to hurt your feelings, but I think you are a terrific lady."

"Thanks for the compliment, Craig," she said, finishing her deep-fried halibut and fries. "I just couldn't help kidding you about the secretary." She grinned and sipped on her coffee. "By the way, what happened to the skier? It looked like he was hurt pretty bad."

"He was. They said a concussion and possible skull fracture. He is a seasoned cross-country skier. Witnesses said he was moving up the trail when some young person being towed by a huge dog was coming down. The skier couldn't control the dog and was having a runaway coming down the trail. He called out to the guy coming up and he stepped off the trail on the downhill side. When the dog towed the young skier by the other one they bumped and the uphill skier tumbled backward into the rocks below the trail. The other one couldn't stop and was drug all the way to the parking lot at the trailhead."

"I hope he recovers," she said sympathetically.

"I have dealt with the injured skier before. His name is Bob Erwin. I was called to direct traffic near Beluga Point a couple of weeks ago when an ice climber fell. She got caught in her ropes and was hanging upside down with a broken back about fifty feet above the highway. When I got there, Erwin had been climbing another ice face only a mile up the road. He came to me and offered to get her down. Anchorage Police Department was handling things, so I asked if they wanted the assistance. They agreed and Erwin grabbed his gear. He went up that ice face like a spider, untangled the ropes, and brought her down. The whole thing took him less than five minutes. He really knew what he was doing. I admired him for that."

"He sounds like a good guy. I'm glad we could help." The coffee had tasted good and she ordered another cup.

Stanton was drinking iced tea. Swallowing a big gulp he asked, "Do you have any thoughts on who killed Jack Boardon? I can't see where we have any evidence to directly connect anyone, though his business partner could have had a hand in it."

"We have to find out where he was going with 400 pounds of marijuana. We can assume it was for sale. Lou said he never filed a flight plan, but I asked him where he thought Boardon was headed. He said it was just a guess, but Fairbanks seemed a likely possibility. Coincidentally, his business associate, Mr. Dunn, filed a flight plan and flew to Fairbanks a couple of days ago. Do you think they were seeing the same people there?"

Stanton thought a moment. "Laura Toombes said he never told her where he was going, but he sometimes did that. She said those flights were always a mystery to her."

"Another thing, do you think our friend Carlton Lieber had anything to do with sabotaging the fuel gauges in in the Cessna? He certainly had the opportunity and the knowledge to accomplish it," she speculated.

"Lieber has a connection to both Dunn and Boardon. How would it work to put some pressure on him? He seems like the nervous type. Perhaps we can shake him up enough to say something we can use," Stanton suggested.

"Sounds to me like as good an idea as any. Think about it tonight and in the morning we will meet in my office to make a plan." She picked up the ticket, read it, and laid a credit card atop it. "I said I would get lunch. It was worth it, Craig. I'm beginning to like the way you think."

CHAPTER 12

Don Bettis was waiting for Dunn when he arrived, and waved to him as he parked his SUV. Anthony Dunn was dressed in black slacks, blue shirt, gray sport coat, and black loafer-style shoes. Bettis was clad in his usual bibbed overalls, denim shirt, and a lined denim jacket. They said hello and walked into the restaurant together. The waitress brought them menus.

When she had gone, Bettis looked around, and then asked quietly, "What happened to Jack?"

"He ran out of fuel and crashed north of here. He had 400 pounds of product with him and was on his way to Fairbanks," Dunn replied in a near whisper. "He also had $100,000 of our money with him. He was supposed to trade with Moose for heroin, but he didn't make it. The troopers said he had around $1,500 in a metal briefcase. I think I found out what happened to the rest of the cash."

"Where did it go?" Bettis asked.

"A trapper from Big Lake found the wreck. The troopers told me he had been at the scene for quite a while before they arrived." Dunn again checked to see if anyone was listening. "I think he found the cash before the troopers got there. I checked out his cabin. He has a big Browning gun safe. I am guessing he put the money in the safe. I checked and found the safe bolted to the floor. Judging by the rest of his property, I would say he is a thorough and careful man." He sipped his water, looking Bettis directly in the eyes. "I need to know how deep you are willing to go in this business."

The waitress came back to take their orders. Each ordered the spaghetti dinner with meat sauce and meatballs, and a glass of Chianti.

When she left Bettis answered, "I don't mind getting my hands dirty, but it won't be free."

"I'm glad to hear you say that, because I have a business proposition for you." The waitress was back with the wine. When she left he continued. "With Jack gone I am going to need a new business associate. Someone I can trust."

"What do you have in mind?" Don Bettis inquired.

"Jack and I were partners in several properties. Some of them we used for growing product. Some are rentals, and some we just keep for investment. I need someone to take over the property management business. Jack made a lot of money at it and he was a lousy businessman. You already know the growing end of the trade. You can manage that as well. You can hire someone to replace you and run the agricultural crews."

"This all sounds very good, but I don't think I like what happened to your last partner."

Dunn chuckled. "Can't say I blame you there, but Jack got ambitious. I heard he was going to 'borrow' four bags of our product and keep the heroin he got in trade. This business is built on trust, since there are no notarized contracts with anyone. Jack violated that trust and it cost him." At that point, the waitress brought their meal. She poured the last of the bottle of Chianti into their glasses and asked if they wished to order another bottle. Dunn said no and the waitress walked away.

When she had gone, Bettis asked, "It sounds like you have something in mind. What do you want me to do?"

"The troopers picked up my aircraft mechanic and printed him, got his picture and asked him a lot of questions," Dunn said. "He is a good mechanic, but I am worried about his loyalty. I think if the cops press him, he will make a deal to save his own hide. He is a danger to this whole operation."

Bettis thought a few seconds. "So, the mechanic rigged Jack's plane?"

"You can think that if you want, but the mechanic has to go. Disappear, permanently." Dunn whispered.

"And," Bettis asked, "what about the trapper with the cash?"

"That, too, will have to be dealt with." He took another forkful of sauce-laden spaghetti and chewed it up. He sipped his wine again. "Do you think you can handle this?" he asked, wiping his mouth.

"I don't see anything I can't handle. I will need a little operating capital and information about both these people." He wiped his mouth and tossed his napkin on the table.

Dunn took the dinner ticket and put a $100 bill in the leather folder. As the waitress went by, he handed it back to her. "Thank you. It was a very good dinner." With a nod of his head, he motioned for Bettis to follow him outside.

Both men climbed into the SUV and Dunn started the engine. After turning up the heater, he reached into the back seat for a large manila envelope. He handed it to Bettis.

"Everything you will need should be in there. If you need more cash, ask me for it. I want to caution you about one thing. I have a secretary who knows nothing about our business. Do not call me at the office. You have my cell phone number. Always use that, and speak only to me. Is that clear?"

"Yes, it's clear, and unnecessary. I may look like a hick farmer, but don't play me short. You said this business is based on trust. Trust is a two way street. I appreciate your caution; but, remember, my involvement is as deep as yours from this point on."

"I'm happy to hear you say that." Dunn held out his hand. "Here's to a new partnership."

Bettis shook his hand. "Let's make it a profitable one," he said as he stepped out of the car.

As he drove back to Eagle River and his townhouse, Dunn reviewed the evening. It had gone well and his fears about Bettis had been allayed. It was going to be up to him to deal with Lieber. Dunn hoped that could take place within the next couple of days, but he was not going to press his new partner.

His townhouse had a carport, not a garage. The weather was warming, so tonight there would be no need to plug in the electric engine block heater.

<h1 style="text-align:center">CHAPTER 13</h1>

By the time Stanton arrived the following morning, Karen had been in the office more than an hour. He stepped into her office with a cup of Kaladi Brothers Coffee and an apple fritter. He handed her the cup and the bag with a smile.

"Good morning, Sarge," he remarked cheerfully.

"You seem awfully cheerful this morning," she said. "I feel I should worry when my partner starts to enjoy his work. I must not be giving you enough to do."

"Investigating is my life," he said. "I live and breathe investigating. I can't get enough investigating," he joked. "It's why I became a trooper."

"Well, come sit down, Mr. Investigator. I am about to make your life complete." She pointed to the chair in front of her desk, pulled a file over in front of her, and opened it. "I have here the answer to your prayers." She sipped the coffee and opened the bag. The fritter looked delicious. Karen ate it while Stanton talked.

"I've been thinking about Lieber. I don't think he is capable of planning this crime on his own. Someone had to have put him up to it. Someone he trusted. Someone who could give him something he wanted or needed. Someone who also needed him," Stanton was building his argument. "Who, on our list of acquaintances, fits the profile?"

"It would seem only one name fits, but remember we don't have much to go on. We don't know who Boardon's other business associates were, if he had any. We know he didn't do all the work himself, so, he may have had a disgruntled employee. In the dope business there is always the danger of a rival dealer. We may have many possibilities. However, you are right about one thing, we have to start somewhere and his known business associate is a good place to start. How do you want to confront Lieber? Do you want to find him and have an off-hand conversation or should we pick him up and bring him in to the interrogation room?"

"I would rather call him on the cell phone and take him to lunch. He seems like the nervous type and if we can get him comfortable with talking to us, we might get him to make a mistake. I think we should try to convince him that we are after his boss, Anthony Dunn."

Karen thought about that a moment. "You could be right. He might spill his complicity if he thought we weren't after him. I can go with that, but let me start the ball rolling by checking bank accounts for Dunn and Boardon. The marijuana they were growing generated a lot of cash. They had to put it somewhere. I will get us some help with that aspect. Meanwhile, call our good friend Carlton Lieber and make a luncheon appointment."

"Can you think of anything I've missed?" Stanton asked.

"No, I think this is a good place to start. We have a lot of open territory to cover, but we have to start somewhere. Let me know how you do with your phone call." Karen finished her coffee and took the last bite of apple fritter as he walked out of the office.

Her next task was to update the captain. She would also ask him to have someone check out those bank accounts. Captain Davis was pleased with the direction Karen and her new partner were taking. He informed her that checking bank records sometimes took weeks, but he would see if he could expedite this one. A murder would raise the priority level.

Her desk phone rang as she reentered her office. "Sergeant Holmes," she answered.

"Karen, Craig. Lieber wants breakfast. Are you up for that?"

"Where?"

"Lilly's Restaurant on Tudor Road. He said he was heading there now."

"I'll ride with you if you will bring me back to the office when we finish."

"I'll meet you at the car," Craig told her.

The two troopers discussed strategy while driving to the restaurant that was only a short drive from the office on Tudor Road.

"Do you want to take the lead or would you rather I do it?" she asked.

"I don't want to sound like a brash upstart, but, if you don't mind, I would like to try getting him to talk. I think I can draw him into a conversation with a little more ease. You have those stripes and may intimidate him. I know you sure intimidate me."

"Yeah, right," she said, trying to look stern. "That's probably a good idea, if he needs any prodding, I can handle that part. You have him pegged, though. He is nervous and wants a way out. Just keep a little pressure on him and try to make him feel like we are his only friends."

Stanton turned into the restaurant parking lot. The old Ford was parked near the door in a handicap zone. Karen followed Craig into the café and spotted Carlton Lieber sitting in a booth at the rear of the dining room. Stanton slid into the booth next to Lieber while Karen sat across from the two.

"Good morning, Carlton," Karen greeted. "How are you this morning?"

"I'm good," he answered sheepishly.

"I'm buying breakfast this morning, Carlton." Stanton informed the mechanic.

"Order whatever you want. I think I'm going to have steak and eggs. What about you, Sergeant Holmes?"

"The steak and eggs sounds good to me," replied Karen.

When the waitress came for the order, she brought a coffee pot and poured three cups.

"How is it going for you, Carlton?" Stanton asked.

"OK, I guess." He seemed reluctant to talk. "I got enough work to get by."

"You must have lost a good customer when Jack Boardon died. That must have cut into your business pretty good," Stanton offered.

"Yeah, but Mr. Dunn has two airplanes, and I take care of them both. He treats me really good."

"Mr. Dunn seems like a nice guy." Craig tried to keep the conversation going.

"Yeah, he likes me. He took me to Fairbanks with him the other day, in that big twin turboprop King Air. It was a nice trip. He even bought me dinner at O'Sullivan's when we got back. He has me do stuff for him sometimes," the mechanic bragged.

"He must trust you, then. Did he ask you to help Mr. Boardon the night before his last flight in the Cessna 206?"

"He didn't have to. Mr. Boardon already asked me to help him load and get the airplane ready for morning."

"Did he fuel the airplane the night before?"

"Yeah, he always did that."

The waitress brought their breakfast and poured more coffee.

"That seems a little strange to me, Carlton. You see, he crashed because he ran out of gas. The FAA told me that he was only about twenty-five minutes from Merrill Field when he crashed, out of fuel. What do you supposed happened to the full tanks he had the night before?" Stanton asked. "Do you think it could have all leaked out during the night?"

"I don't know what happened," Lieber muttered.

"I checked with the fuel service he used and they said he did gas the airplane the night before. They told me he never took off without full tanks, even on short flights." Stanton was cutting his steak into small pieces and salting his eggs and potatoes. "So if his tanks were full when he took it to the hangar, what happened to the gas?"

Lieber was toying with his food. "Don't ask me," he said. "Why are you asking me those questions?"

"Sorry, Carlton. It's just that you told us you helped him load the airplane the night before and you are, or were, his mechanic. Was he having trouble with his gas tanks?"

"I kept that airplane in first class shape. There wasn't anything wrong with it, and don't try to make sound like I did something wrong, 'cause I didn't."

"That's not it at all, Carlton. I am just having trouble figuring out what happened to all that gas. The FAA team said the floor of the hangar was clean, so it didn't leak out on the hangar floor. Help me out here, Carlton. I'm trying to figure out why he ran out of gas."

"I already told you I don't know what happened to the gas." He still hadn't eaten his breakfast.

Stanton finished his last piece of toast and was wiping his fingers on a napkin when he turned to the mechanic again. "I have to ask, Carlton, did you take the gas out of Mr. Boardon's Cessna?"

Lieber was nearly frantic now. "Why would you think that? I fix airplanes; I don't wreck 'em."

"Well, Carlton, the FAA investigators said they found evidence that the fuel gauges had been rigged to read full. It would take an aircraft mechanic to do that, and a good one at that." Stanton watched Lieber's eyes. "I just want to know if someone paid you to make Mr. Boardon think his tanks were full when they were almost empty."

"I'm not saying another thing until I see a lawyer. Are you going to arrest me?"

"Heck no, Carlton, I don't want to arrest you. But if someone paid you to do something to the Cessna, then I might arrest him for murder. If you did it on your own, then I guess I will have to arrest you." Stanton took a huge gulp of his coffee. "I won't ask you anything else, Carlton. You can call a lawyer. I'm sorry, but I didn't think you were the one with the plan to kill Jack Boardon. I guess I was wrong."

At that point, Karen interrupted. "Come on, Craig. Just cuff him up and he can call his lawyer from jail. I told you he wouldn't talk to us, even to save his own hide. I think we have enough of a case to get an indictment, pin this on him, and close the case."

Carlton sat wide-eyed. "What is she saying? Are you going to arrest me for murder?"

"It sounds like the Sergeant wants me to arrest you, and she's my boss." Stanton picked up the breakfast ticket and read it carefully, killing time.

"Now, wait a minute!" Lieber exclaimed. "I just did what I was told. Forget the lawyer. I ain't takin' the fall for something I didn't do. It wasn't my idea."

"Then, whose idea was it?" Stanton asked.

"I can't say. He might decide to shut me up, too." Carlton sounded truly frightened. "I ain't saying any more. Take me to jail. I'll be safer there."

Stanton turned to Karen. "Sergeant, can't we cut Carlton a break? He has been cooperative and I believe him. We can pick him up any time, if the need arises. I think he just needs some time to think about it."

"I don't know, Craig. We would be taking a very big chance of him skipping out. That wouldn't make us look very good," Karen said.

"I ain't going anywhere. I ain't got a place to go." Lieber was becoming frantic.

"Look at it from the Sergeant's point of view, Carlton. We have all this evidence that implicates you in the death of Boardon. You say you didn't do it, but the evidence says you did. There is no way we can turn you loose on just your word. We have to have something to go on. Something we can investigate; something that would make you a witness, and not the killer."

"Oh, man," Carlton whined. "I knew this would happen." He stared at his plate in silence for a long while. Finally, he looked up and spoke to the Sergeant. "I can't give you any names. He would kill me like he did Mr. Boardon. All I can tell you is that he is the head of the drug business in this area. He has lots of money and he has lots of friends. I don't want him to know I said anything. I ain't telling you his name, 'cause he would know it was me. I promise. I won't leave, but please don't put me in jail."

Karen looked at Craig. "Do you still believe him?" she asked. "Are you going to take responsibility for him?"

Stanton turned to Lieber. "You see how it is, Carlton. I will be in it with you if I let you go."

"I promise I won't go anywhere. I'll do whatever you say, but please don't put me in jail."

"Sergeant Holmes, I think I believe him. He might just be able to find out more about the drug business for us. If he did it would make him look a lot less guilty when arrests begin."

"Alright then, but he is your responsibility." Karen really was dubious about letting Lieber go free. She turned to Carlton and said, "I want you to keep in touch with Trooper Stanton. From now on, he is your best friend. Don't let him down."

"I want you to find out the name of the drug contact Dunn made in Fairbanks. I want to know where and when the growing operation will resume. I want you to check in with me every day." He took a card from his shirt pocket and handed it to Lieber. My phone numbers are on this card. Don't lose it, and be careful who sees it."

"You can count on me." Lieber's whole mood had changed and he was now smiling with relief.

"Get out of here now, and remember what you are supposed to do."

He slid out of the booth and walked quickly out the door and to his pick-up.

Karen hadn't eaten much of her breakfast. She drank the last of her coffee and turned to her partner. "I hope this doesn't come back and bite us."

CHAPTER 14

Late January is a very slow time for farming in Alaska. Don Bettis had a great deal of free time to devote to his new endeavor. Dunn had furnished him with a personal history of the mechanic. The man was considered a good mechanic by anyone who had used him in the past. His personal life did not reflect the same knowledge, however. He had no money in the bank and lived in a small cabin on land owned by Jack Boardon. In return for rent, the mechanic did errands for Jack. His only telephone contact was his cell phone; Jack paid for it, too. The FAA constantly contacted Lieber to correct unfiled, late or missing logbook entries. As he read the file, Bettis only shook his head in disbelief.

The farmer decided the first place he should check out was the cabin Lieber lived in; it was located on a one-acre parcel between Wasilla and Palmer. The property was one mile off Trunk Road. The side road was gravel but well maintained. The cabin itself sat on the back of the lot. Lieber's truck was nowhere to be seen. Bettis parked in front of the cabin, stepped up on the small porch and knocked on the door. There was no answer. He tried the door and found it unlocked. Inside the place was a mess. The floors had not been swept for a very long time. There was a pile of garbage—paper plates, soup cans, pizza boxes and a lot of other trash in the kitchen area. The entire place reeked of accumulated foul odors. The kitchen table was littered with tools and FAA forms. Bettis didn't understand them, but there were several forms designated 337. They seemed to be aircraft modification forms. Again, Bettis was shaking his head.

The small bedroom was in the same disarray as the rest of the house. The bed was unmade and there was soiled clothing scattered everywhere. The bathroom, too, was a mess. It was small with a stained toilet, a filthy lavatory sink, and a leaking shower stall. Filthy towels hung on the rack.

Back in the living area, Bettis saw that a wood stove provided heat, while the kitchen range was propane. It appeared the resident did not spend a lot of time in the place. Too bad, the faulty chimney on the wood stove would make a great cause for a fire. The problem, it seemed, was finding the man sleeping at home.

Back in his truck, Bettis sat a few minutes, thinking. A cabin fire here would be an ideal solution, but finding Lieber here was going to be difficult. He turned around in the yard and drove away toward another property Jack owned. It was an old potato warehouse where Lieber kept an office of sorts. Bettis had a key to let himself in if the troopers were not there. Dunn had told him they raided the property and were watching it by patrols. This assignment was proving to be more difficult than he had anticipated.

When he reached the warehouse, no one was there. He let himself in and found the cubicle used by Carlton Lieber. The troopers had taken everything from the area, but he found where the mechanic sometimes spent the night. Not wanting to be found by the patrol, he kept his inspection short, locked the door behind him, and left without being seen. While driving to his own farm, Bettis began to realize how hard it was to get away with murder.

After returning to the office, Karen had given Stanton the task of searching the banking records provided by Captain Davis. Stanton was buried in the columns of numbers when someone disturbed him. It was Karen, wearing her parka.

"I just got a call and have to fly the helicopter north on the Parks Highway. Life Med Helicopters are busy and they need me to medevac a patient. There has been a truck/auto collision north of Talkeetna. Keep at what you are doing. I don't know how long I will be, but I'll be back this afternoon. I will see you then." She gave him a short wave and left the office.

Craig was not an accountant and, for that matter, could barely balance his own checkbook. The figures in Dunn's accounts, however, were easy to interpret. They had been broken down for him by category. Payments on property were in escrow and trust accounts. Profits were paid into business accounts and expenses withdrawn from those accounts. His personal accounts were as easy to understand. He paid his monthly expenses and bills by check. Stanton could not find anything wrong in any of the accounts.

What was missing was the cash from any drug sales. "Where did all that money go?" he wondered. He needed professional help. He called his friend and personal accountant, Miles Lawton.

"Miles, Craig Stanton," he said when the accountant answered.

"Hi, Craig. It's early in the tax season for you to be calling. How have you been?"

"You know me, Miles; I wait until the last minute every year. This is trooper business. Do you have a little time to work me in to take a look at some bank accounts?"

"Sure, Craig, the pace hasn't become hectic yet. When do you want to come in?""Right away, if I can. I have some questions about some banking ledgers and need professional advice."

Lawton's office was only a mile north on Tudor Road from his own.

"It will cost you lunch," Lawton joked. "Come on over. I will take a look at your stuff as soon as you get here."

"I'm on the way," Craig said. "Thanks."

Ten minutes later, he was in the accounting office. He swore the accountant to secrecy and the two men began looking at the sheets. After an hour the accountant said the accounts were all accurate and in order. "I do see something unusual, though, Craig."

"Oh, and what is that?"

"The cash flow in his business is tremendous. The part that puzzles me is that his escrow payments and other income fall about fifteen percent short of his deposits. There doesn't seem to be a record of where that cash came from."

"OK, but before we turn him over to the IRS, take a look at this other set of books. This is another person, a business partner of sorts. They owned property together as friends. This second person is now dead. I need to know if the extra cash in the first accounts could have come from that association," Craig informed the accountant.

The two men scanned the second account and made comparisons as they had done in the first. It took only three quarters of an hour to do the second account. When they had finished, the accountant said, "This is just like the first set of books. His deposits and payments exceed his income by more than twenty-five percent with no accurate record of where that cash came from. All the business recorded, however, appears to be legitimate."

"What you are saying is both these accounts have more cash coming in than their business shows, is that correct?" Stanton asked.

"I can't say this is a detailed audit, but from what I saw, yes, that is correct," Miles concluded.

"When do you want that lunch? Are you hungry now?"

"Of course, I'm a small business owner. We are always hungry."

"You always like Outback Steakhouse. How about lunch there?" Stanton offered.

"Sounds good to me, I'll follow you over there," replied Lawton.

An hour later, Stanton was back in his office. Karen had called and was back in Anchorage. By the time he finished the note from dispatch telling him she was back in town, she was at his door, unzipping her parka.

"Did you miss me?" she asked.

"I just came back to the office myself. I may have some news about those bank accounts," he reported. "Do you want some coffee before I give you the news?" he asked.

"Yes," she said. "Hold the apple fritter this time."

When he returned with her coffee, he found she had removed her parka and changed her shoes from the insulated boots she had been wearing to oxfords, which were more comfortable. He handed her the coffee that she took with both hands.

"How did your rescue turn out?" he asked while she sipped her hot brew.

"I really don't know. The roads were icy. Two women in a new Subaru Forester lost control and slid broadside into the front of a Carlisle Freight truck. The truck T-boned the car on the driver side, killing the driver of the Subaru. The passenger is in bad shape. The trucker has a broken shoulder or arm. I brought both of them back to town. The trucker should be OK, but it doesn't look good for the lady. The last report I had was that she is critical. The Parks Highway is still closed while they do the investigation."

"Sorry to hear that." Stanton replied. "Do you want some time before we start to work?"

"No, I'll be OK by the time I finish my coffee. Thanks for getting it for me, by the way."

He responded with a wave of his hand.

"While you are finishing your coffee, let me lay out a scenario for you. Tell me what you think." He paused to collect his thoughts. "What if we underestimated our friend, Carlton Lieber? What if he was more than just an aircraft mechanic? Suppose he was also the liaison between the marijuana business and the real estate business. Remember that both Dunn and Boardon used Lieber as a mechanic. You and I figured we could manipulate him. Suppose Dunn and Boardon figured out the same thing. Suppose they both used Lieber to insulate themselves from the illegal end of their enterprise. That would mean our friend Carlton knows a whole lot more than he is telling us about the drug end of the business."

Karen took one last sip of coffee before tossing the empty cup in the wastebasket. "If all that were true, it could simplify our life; but what makes you 'suppose' all of this?"

"The short version is that both Dunn and Boardon show considerably more cash in payments and deposits than either of their businesses generate, roughly 15% more for Dunn and 25% for Boardon. Surely, the drug business is netting more cash than they are showing in their businesses. They are probably putting it in hidden bank accounts. The point is that it appears to me like the proverbial iceberg and we are only seeing a small part, while the rest remains hidden." He smiled at her. "Does this sound a little far-fetched for you?"

"Not at all, Craig. In fact, I have had questions along those lines myself. Your finding the discrepancy in the bank accounts confirms my suspicions. Great job. Now, how do we go about making use of this information?"

The two troopers immediately set about designing a strategy for obtaining hard evidence, which at this point was almost non-existent.

CHAPTER 15

By 4:30 in the afternoon, daylight was fading fast. Snow on the ground reflected light and made it seem light a while longer. Ken Whittle had not been out of his cabin all day. He had spent the day working on furs and reading. The cabin was warm and a day of relaxation seemed like the right thing today.

He didn't see any headlights but heard the engine in the quiet afternoon. The drive came onto his property from the east; his cabin faced south. Stepping to the window over the sink in the kitchen, he could look out to the road entering his yard. The light was poor, but the dark shape of a pick-up was parked on the road. It was stopped with the lights out. No one had exited the truck as far as Ken could see.

Whittle had been on alert since the day someone had come into his cabin. He had a Remington pump shotgun behind his chair, but now he wanted something else, too. He went to the bedroom, retrieved his .357 Magnum Smith and Wesson revolver, and returned to his chair. He tucked the revolver beside his left leg and picked up his *Fur, Fish and Game Magazine*. He waited. Several minutes went by before he heard footsteps crunching in the snowpack. They stopped in front of his steps. Several more minutes passed before the visitor climbed the steps and tapped on the door.

"Come in," Whittle said, dropping his hand to the butt of the gun.

The door opened slowly, only a few inches and a voice called, "OK if I come in?"

"I said come in, now come in and close the door before you let out all the heat." Ken held the pistol grip in his hand.

As the door opened wider, a bearded face poked around the door. "I just came to talk with you. Are you Ken Whittle?" the beard asked.

"That's me," Whittle replied, trying not to sound friendly.

"Good, I've got the right place." Closing the door behind him, he turned back to Whittle and asked, "Mind if I sit down? I want to talk to you."

"What about?" Ken asked, again trying to sound gruff.

"Nothing serious, mostly out of curiosity," he began. "I was told you found an airplane wreck a few days ago. I just wanted to ask a few questions about it, if I may."

"I found a wreck, but I can't talk about it. I'll answer any questions I am allowed, but keep it short."

"Aw, hey, I understand. I was just curious because I think the guy in the wreck was a friend of mine. I did some work for him and he owed me some money. He was going to pay me when he got back from a trip to Fairbanks, but I haven't heard from him. I went by his office and he hasn't been there either. Do you know the name of the guy you found?"

"Troopers said his name was Jack Boardon. I didn't know him. I just found his plane, wrecked, while I was checking my trap line." Ken held a tight grip on the revolver, not exposing it. He thought the conversation was a distraction and remained suspicious.

"Oh, gosh! That was the name of the guy who owed me the money," the beard exclaimed. "What happened, do you know?"

"Troopers said he ran out of gas." Whittle was getting nervous. "Now if that's all you need to know, I like my privacy. Don't bother coming back."

The beard stood up. "I understand, sorry to have bothered you." He turned to leave, opened the door, and turned back again. "By the way, did you happen to find anything at the airplane?"

"The troopers took everything at the wreck when they left. You didn't tell me your name."

"Don, Don's the name," the beard said as he opened the door and stepped into the night.

When he heard the crunching footsteps walking away, the trapper went to the kitchen window and watched as the beard climbed into his truck, turned around and drove away.

Ken poured a tall whisky in a water glass and returned to his chair. "This is beginning to get very strange," Whittle thought. "There are only a couple of weeks left in the season, anyway. I had better start pulling my traps tomorrow, and I had better start packing up and get out of here as soon as possible. I think break-up and spring will be nice in Arizona." Break-up is the time of year when the frost leaves the ground and everything turns to watery mud.

As he sipped his whisky, he could only worry and wonder if this was meant as a warning or if Don was looking for something. It was likely he noticed the safe while he was there. It was also likely he would believe the cash was stashed inside.

When he had finished his drink, he tucked the .357 into his belt and went outside to make a thorough search of his property, especially his fur shed. All was locked and undisturbed as far as Ken could tell.

In the office the following morning, Stanton met with Karen to discuss Carlton Lieber. Karen read the summary Craig had written, trying to digest the contents.

This new report certainly opened a myriad questions, the answers to which Lieber had cautiously avoided.

"It looks like we need to have another talk with our favorite mechanic," Karen remarked. "Do you think you can talk him into coming into the office and answering some of those questions?"

"I believe he is scared. I think he will come in, but as to answering those questions, I just don't know. He may be more afraid of Dunn than he is of us."

"We may have to put pressure on him. We still have him on the hook for murder. As long as he thinks he is our witness, we might get him to open up. We have new questions and more information now. He won't know how much information we have. You did a great job of working his paranoia the last time we talked with him. Let's try that tactic again. If he clams up, we can always threaten him with arrest again; in fact, we can arrest him. We have enough on him to put him away."

"I would sure like to keep him talking," Stanton said. "At this point he is the closest thing we have to inside information." He thought a few seconds. "I'll call him and see if I can get him to come down here and chat."

"Good, I'll be in my office," said Karen.

An hour later Carlton was in Karen's office. The three of them passed the time of day. It was obvious to Karen and Craig that the mechanic was very nervous and tense.

"You seem up tight this morning, Carlton," Stanton began.

"This whole thing is getting to me. I can't even sleep at night. I'm scared," he said, wringing his hands and looking at the floor.

"Relax, Carlton. We have tried to be your friends, but you are sure making it tough on us," Stanton began. "You were a little less than truthful when we talked before."

"Why do you say that?" Lieber wanted to know. "I told the truth. You know I did."

"Yes, I think you did, Carlton, but it wasn't the whole truth. I've learned that you left a lot of detail out of your story." Stanton opened the file folder on his lap.

"You gotta believe me, Trooper Stanton. I didn't lie."

"I don't think you lied, Carlton. I just think you left out some important facts. For instance, you forgot to tell us that you were more than a mechanic for both Dunn and Boardon. You were their runner. You did favors for both of them. You carried money for them both for paying work crews. You helped Boardon load the marijuana in his airplane the night before he crashed. I think you were involved in the growing and distributing of the marijuana Dunn and Boardon were selling. It looks to us like you were one of the big bosses."

Leiber looked at the trooper with eyes wide. "No, sir. That ain't right. I didn't do any of that stuff. Sometimes I ran errands for both of them, but I wasn't no boss. No, that ain't right."

Karen worked hard to suppress a grin.

"If I'm wrong, I apologize, Carlton. But that's the way it looks to me. Straighten me out if I have my facts wrong," Stanton said.

"Look, I just delivered messages. I took orders to the growing crews. I delivered supplies and sometimes meals when they worked long hours. Mr. Dunn and Mr. Boardon took good care of the workers." Lieber was trying to explain. "I wasn't no boss. I just delivered messages and supplies. That's all." He was frightened. "Mr. Dunn wanted Jack to crash. He had me rig his gas gauges and empty his tanks." Again, Carlton Lieber's eyes widened. "Oh, God! If Mr. Dunn knew that I told you that, he would kill me. I mean really kill me."

"We aren't going to tell him, if that is what you are worried about," Stanton said, attempting to console his witness. "But, you have to realize we can't protect you unless we have the whole truth. We need to know everything you know about Dunn's drug business. We need names, places, and dates. We need to know all his contacts and what he is dealing in besides marijuana. Are you willing to tell us all that?" Stanton had him now.

CHAPTER 16

Ken Whittle took off in his Super Cub as soon as it was light enough to see the runway. Much of the equipment and bait he ordinarily brought with him was missing today. He was going to pull all his traps. He had experienced a good season so far and his fur was top quality. Any fur he brought in today would have to be fleshed and salted, but he would be able to finish that chore in a single day. He flew to the far end of the trap line and worked his way to Witsoe Lake. It was late in the afternoon and light was fading when he took off from the lake. Loaded with carcasses, traps and cold weather gear, his airplane approached gross weight when he took off. He would need to land with a little extra care when he reached his own airstrip.

It was Whittle's habit to overfly any landing spot, even his own. He found it paid to look for moose and caribou or other obstacles before landing. As he flew over his little airstrip, he noticed a pick-up parked in the trees a short distance from the house. Thinking it was possible the beard had returned, he decided to land as short as possible and quietly walk to the house. Perhaps he could surprise whoever was snooping around. He made a low approach and landed as slow as he dared with the load he was carrying.

Ken climbed out of the Cub and reached back inside to find his pistol. He found it behind the front seat and tucked it into his belt. Next, he found his rifle and checked to make sure there was a shell in the chamber. He found five extra rifle cartridges and dropped them into the pocket of his parka. Stealthily he moved toward the cabin. As he moved closer, he saw the door to the tool shed was open. The lock was in place on the fur shed. That meant whoever was here was in the house. Circling near the brush line and being as quiet as possible, he moved to the house. The front door was open. Staying near the brush line, he moved to where he could look through the door. He spotted the intruder near his Browning safe. Then he saw his welding torch inside. It appeared the burglar was about to attempt to use the welding torch to cut open his safe.

Whittle sneaked to the end of the porch and slid under the railing. The intruder was busy with the torch and did not see him step to the center of the door, rifle in hand.

"Turn off the torch," Whittle ordered.

Startled, the man spun around, still holding the cutting torch in his hand. Slowly he closed the gas valves and laid the torch on the floor of the cabin. It was the man with the beard, Don.

"Did you come here last night just to case the place for a robbery today?" he asked.

"Not really," Don replied. "But you were so unfriendly last night, I didn't think you would open the safe for me, so I came back to do it myself."

"Is there anything in particular you are looking for?"

"As a matter of fact, there is. It seems there was a great deal of money missing from that airplane you found. Last night you said you didn't want to talk about it so I came back today to look for myself."

"Who sent you?" Whittle asked.

"Nobody. Curiosity just got the best of me." The intruder began to shift his weight and turn slightly to his left. Suddenly he pulled his jacket open and reached inside with his right hand taking a small automatic pistol from a shoulder holster. Clicking off the safety, he swung the gun up to fire.

Before he could complete his motion, Ken pulled the trigger on his rifle. Shooting from a chest high position, Whittle's bullet caught the man in the chest under his right arm. Don's gun fired, but his shot was wild as he jerked backward from the shock of the striking bullet.

Ken could see the man was dead, but checked for a pulse anyway. No pulse. Out of habit, he reached out and turned off the oxygen and acetylene tanks. Not sure what to do next, he reached for his cell phone and dialed 911. Troopers began to arrive within minutes.

The first trooper on the scene was Tom Jameson. A twelve-year veteran, not yet forty years old, he looked like a cop: wavy black hair, square shoulders, straight posture and a stern, no-nonsense look about him.

"Who called 911?" he asked.

"I did," Whittle began. "This is my place. When I came back from trapping, I saw a strange pick-up parked up the road. I landed and stopped up the runway. I was suspicious because a guy came here late last night. He came into the house and was looking around. When he was leaving, I asked his name and he just said 'Don.' I thought it seemed odd. When I flew over my airstrip this afternoon, I saw a pick-up parked up the road. I had a hunch the guy had come back, so I sneaked to the house and found him inside getting ready to cut open my safe. I told him to shut off the torch and he did. I asked what he thought he was doing and he pulled a gun. I shot first. That's when I called you."

The trooper took a notebook from his pocket and began to write. "What is your name, sir?" He asked for his driver license, if he was the owner of the property and a dozen other questions. An ambulance and three more troopers had arrived. A large van with four other trooper/investigators arrived. While they were all busy doing their respective jobs, Whittle taxied his airplane to the house and covered the engine. He unlocked the fur shed and carried the new animals inside. The traps were unloaded and hung on nails on the side of the tool shed. The trap basket he put inside the fur shed. Ken locked the door before returning to the house.

Ken found Trooper Jameson inside with the others. When the trooper saw him standing outside, he stepped out to speak to the trapper.

"Mr. Whittle, is there somewhere you can spend the night? I'm afraid we will be most of the night with our investigation and you won't be allowed back inside until we have finished. I want you to know we checked the physical evidence against your story and everything checks out. I see no reason to have you stay here until we are finished. Just let us know where you will be."

Whittle gave the trooper his cell phone number and said he would be at "that new motel" in Wasilla. Jameson thanked him and told him he could go.

Relieved to be vindicated, Ken stopped at a liquor store in Wasilla and bought a new bottle of Crown Royal. He checked into a room and showered. The local pizza joint would deliver. With all that done, he sat at the small table in the room and poured a very large glass of whisky. His nerves were shot and he needed the drink badly.

An hour later, the pizza was delivered, and he gave the driver a fifty and told him to keep the change. The pizza smelled good and he was feeling a little tipsy. He poured another whisky to go with his Pizza. By the time he ate his fill of the pizza and finished his glass, he could no longer hold his eyes open. With his last conscious thought of the day he wondered, "Who sent that guy?"

CHAPTER 17

Karen's copy of the daily police report had a brief paragraph about the shooting in Big Lake. She probably would not have given it a second glance except she caught the name. Ken Whittle was the shooter. The paragraph said it was justified and Whittle left the scene. The investigation was incomplete.

She buzzed Stanton and asked him to come to her office. When he came in, she handed him the daily report. He read it quickly.

"Holy smoke! Isn't he the one who found Boardon's wrecked airplane?"

"I can't imagine there is more than one Ken Whittle in Big Lake, or the state for that matter. I think we need to set up a meeting with Mr. Whittle." She began to search her file for his cell phone number.

"This report doesn't give the victim's name. While you try to set up a meeting with Whittle, I'll try to find out who the victim was and what happened last night," Stanton said before returning to his own office space.

Karen located the telephone number and dialed. She was about to hang up when a sleepy voice answered.

"Hello?" the voice answered.

"Hello, Mr. Whittle. This is Sergeant Karen Holmes with the Alaska State Troopers. Do you remember me? We met at Witsoe Lake; I was flying the helicopter."

"Yes, I remember. Can you hang on for a minute?" Without her response, he quit talking. Half a minute later she heard the toilet flush. "I'm back. What can I do for you, Sergeant? Does this have to do with the wreck or is it about last night?"

"A little of both, Ken. My partner and I would like to come up to meet with you. It will take us about an hour to get there. Where can we meet you?"

"I stayed in a hotel in Wasilla last night. It will take me that long to get a shower and get going. How about I meet you for breakfast in an hour?" Whittle said, giving her the name of a restaurant.

"We will be there, sir. Thank you."

Stanton returned. "I called the crime lab boys. They say the victim's name is Don Bettis. Whittle came home from trapping and found Bettis in his house with a cutting torch. It looked as if he was going to cut open the big gun safe in the living room. Whittle surprised him, Bettis pulled a gun, an automatic, but Whittle had his rifle on him and shot first. Bettis' gun discharged, but went wild. He was dead before he hit the floor."

"Did you get a history on Bettis?" Karen asked.

"They are printing it out for me, but the headlines say he is suspected to be involved in a marijuana growing operation in Palmer." Stanton was grinning. "Does this have a familiar ring to it?"

Karen was deep in thought for a few seconds. "Do you think it's possible he worked for Dunn? Otherwise it would be a great coincidence." She paused again, looked up and said, "I think when we get back to town we need to have another talk with our good friend, Carlton Lieber. Maybe he knows this Mr. Don Bettis."

At the restaurant in Wasilla, Whittle ordered a huge breakfast of pancakes, sausage, three eggs, juice and coffee. Stanton and the Sergeant ordered only coffee. The waitress brought three coffees and went back to the kitchen.

"I was surprised to see your name in our daily report, Ken," Karen began, sipping her hot coffee. "Can you tell us what happened?"

Whittle told his story the way he had told it the night before. He hadn't lied; the story was true, as far as it went. He went on to tell about pulling his traps for the season and coming back late, landing with failing daylight, seeing the truck parked up the road from the house. He told about his visit the night before by Don. It was all pretty straightforward and truthful.

"That is very interesting, Mr. Whittle. What do you suppose this fellow was looking for?" Then it struck her, "Did you keep something from the crash, Ken?" she asked. "Something he came looking for?"

Whittle's eyes widened. "You were there, Sergeant. You know I didn't take anything out of the airplane. What could I have taken?"

"I know, Ken. It's just that Bettis must have been looking for something specific. It must have been important or valuable to him if he was willing to pull a gun on you, especially if you already had your rifle pointed at him. I can't help wondering what could have been so important, can you?"

"I sure don't have any idea, Sergeant."

"We have learned that Mr. Bettis may have been employed by Jack Boardon. When he crashed Boardon must have been carrying something Bettis wanted, and he thought you had it. If he thought it was in your safe, it must be small. The only personal items, not on his person when he died, were a metal briefcase and four bags of marijuana. Those bags were 100 pounds each, so he wasn't looking for missing dope. When we took charge of the Cessna, it had to be inventoried. In the metal briefcase was a Colt .45 and $1,500 in cash. I can't imagine what else was in the airplane Bettis could have wanted."

"Sergeant, I don't think I like what you are implying. You were there. You know I didn't take anything from the plane," Whittle said, halfway through his breakfast.

"I have told you everything I know, but if you are going to accuse me of something, I want a lawyer."

"I haven't accused you of anything, Mr. Whittle. I was just wondering, aloud, why an employee of Jack Boardon came looking for the man who found his boss dead in a plane crash. It just doesn't make any sense to me. I was hoping you would be able to help me figure it out, but if you want a lawyer, that's fine, too. Just be aware, Ken, that we will find out what this is all about, and when we do I hope you have been telling us the whole truth." She and Stanton stood to leave. "We'll get the check, Ken. See you later."

Stanton was driving and as he turned onto the Parks Highway he looked at Karen. "I think you struck a nerve," he said grinning. "What made you think to ask him that question?"

"Just a shot in the dark," she said, grinning back at him. "It started out as an innocent enough question, but his reaction got my attention and I just had to pursue it. Now I am more curious than ever. He must have taken something from the crash. Common sense says it was money, but we found $1,500 in his briefcase. If Whittle took money from the plane and left that much in it, two things strike me. One, if he left $1,500 in the case to throw us off the track, there must have been a lot of cash in there; and two, if he did that, Mr. Whittle is a clever man who has already killed one man. We need to be very careful when dealing with Mr. Ken Whittle."

"Well, Madam Sergeant, I applaud your deductive skills. I never would have followed that track. Where do we go from here?"

"It's time we had another conversation with your friend Carlton Lieber. We don't know enough about Don Bettis. It may be that Lieber knew the man and can tell us how he was connected to Boardon and perhaps to Dunn. Anthony Dunn's name comes up too many times. Lieber said if Dunn knew he was talking he would 'kill him.' What if Dunn sent Bettis to visit Whittle? I know that's a big jump in logic, but in my mind, he is the only one on the list we have who could manipulate a scheme like this. For what reason, I have yet to figure out. He seems to have more money than is involved here, or at least more than we know about."

"You are thinking far ahead of me on this one," Stanton said, speaking about her logic thus far. "You could be right. Everyone in this case has dirty hands, and we still have no idea about a motive for any of the participants, except for Lieber. I think he is just working for a paycheck."

"We have to find a way to get Lieber to give up more details, facts, and figures. I think he is going to be our key to solving this case.

CHAPTER 18

Mosely "Moose" Cain was relaxing in his rented New Jersey townhouse when the phone rang. It was only 1 in the afternoon, but Moose had only been out of bed a short time. Not many people knew his cell phone number, so it must be important. He stood up and walked to the bedroom door, looked in at the sleeping woman and closed the door.

"Hello," he growled into the phone.

"Moose, Tony. There are problems here, not for you or me, but problems, nonetheless. You remember I told you Jack was dead in a plane crash?'

"Yeah, I remember."

"Well, last night his crew boss, Don Bettis, was shot and killed by the trapper who found Jack's plane. I sent him there to find the $100,000 that came up missing from his airplane. I think he took it out of the plane before the troopers arrived," Dunn explained.

There was a short silence. "Can any of this come back to us?" Cain asked.

"No, I don't think so. He worked for Jack and I never had anything to do with the growing operation. Jack ran all that. I had met Bettis and contacted him to find the cash. Our only contact was by phone, except for one evening meeting a few days ago. As far as I know, no one saw us together—at least no one who knew us," Dunn informed his business associate.

"What about the last load, do you still have it?" Moose asked.

"Gone as of yesterday. You remember Marshal Dillon? He flies for FedEx now. He takes our product on his flight to Seattle. It went out yesterday. It was delivered last night. The cash should be in our Cayman Island account by this afternoon."

"It sounds like you have everything under control," Moose commented.

"I believe so," Dunn said. "The troopers came to my office once, but they wanted to know about Jack. I told them about our business dealings and they seemed satisfied."

"Too bad Jack got greedy," said Moose. "I liked him, but he was about to screw up our system. I think we did the right thing in eliminating him. But don't get careless. Tie up all the loose ends and keep a low profile. We have two weeks before I go back to Thailand and pick up another shipment. We need to have all this under control before then."

"Bettis getting killed puts a kink in the growing operation. I have to find another crew foreman. There is one man on the crew who might fill the bill. I'm going to have to talk to him and feel him out. I should have an answer on that by tomorrow. Everything is ready to go for a new crop, but I will have to get a few new grow lights. I have a source for that and we should be growing in a few days."

"I have to go now. I have company. Keep me posted. Stay under the radar, good buddy," Moose advised his old friend.

———————

Dunn told Laura Toombes he would be back in a couple of hours and left the office, driving to a house he owned jointly with Boardon and rented to Melvin James. Melvin was an ex-cop from a town on the Kuskokwim River. A Village Public Safety Officer, or VPSO, he had been accused of assaulting a seventeen-year-old high school girl. He had never been prosecuted, but was fired from his state job. James had applied for positions on several police departments, but his past had always ruined his chances.

Living in Fairbanks, broke and drunk most of the time, he had met Jack Boardon by chance. Jack and his foreman, Don Bettis, had been in Fairbanks hiring farm hands for a growing operation in Palmer. With nothing else on his horizon, James had hired on. The work was hard, but not much of it. It paid well and kept him out of the tavern. Bettis relied on Melvin to do the daily supervising of the crew while he ran the overall operation: keeping supplies on hand, paying the electric bills and making sure the crew stayed out of sight of the law.

When Dunn stopped in front of the rented house, he saw Melvin's old Plymouth K-car in the driveway. If anyone recognized his own car at the address, they would undoubtedly think he was there to collect the rent. Dunn parked his SUV in the drive and stepped up on the small porch. He knocked on the door. In a few seconds, he heard movement inside the house. It was a few more seconds before the door began to open. The figure on the other side was barefoot, dressed in tee shirt and jeans. His was uncombed and his breath was horrible.

"Yeah?" he said through the narrow opening.

"Are you Melvin James?" Dunn asked.

"Yeah, that's me," he said, rubbing his sleepy eyes.

"I am Anthony Dunn and I need to come in and talk to you."

The door began to open wider. "Come on in," the man said, walking to the kitchen sink for a glass of water. "What do you want?"

"Are you working these days?" Dunn inquired.

"I'm a farm hand. No farming this time of the year." He sipped the water.

"You were working for Don Bettis, is that correct?"

"Yeah, that's right."

"Bettis is dead. He was shot last night. Now are you interested in what I have to say?"

"What happened to Don?" Melvin asked in surprise.

"He was doing a burglary up at Big Lake and the owner came home."

"I worked for Don, and he didn't strike me as a burglar. He did a lot of stuff, but I can't believe he was a burglar."

"I don't know many details, but he's dead. I need someone to take his place and I was told you could handle the job. Are you interested?"

"Sure, I'm interested, but I'm not doing any burglaries that will get me killed."

"Don't worry about that. What I need is someone who can run the growing operation and the work crew. Do you think you can handle that?" Dunn wanted a commitment from Melvin before he could continue.

"Yeah, I can do that. Most of the crew are hard-working guys and don't take much supervising."

The house was as unkempt as its occupant was, Dunn noticed unhappily. "I plan to start a new crop right away. What I need is someone who can run the entire operation. You will have to run the crew schedules, handle payroll, keep the crew supplied with fertilizer and anything else they need to keep the crop growing. I want to maintain the same system we had before. Keep the crew living on one of the places, away from the grow sites. I want it run about the same as Bettis did it. Do you have any problem with that?" Dunn inquired. Melvin shook his head. "Above all, you need to have as little contact with me as possible. I will give you a cell phone number to use if you need something. You will make more than the rest of the men, but you will earn it. This position carries a lot of responsibility. Can you handle it?"

"Of course, I did most of all that for Don anyway. How soon do you want to start?"

Dunn handed James a small notebook. "This is a list of items you will need and where to get them. There are phone numbers of suppliers in there. Don't let anyone else see this notebook." Dunn took an envelope from his inside pocket. "There is a large sum of cash in here. You will need it to purchase what you need and to take care of the men. Keep good records. The records are for me, no one else. I need it to keep track of the expenditures. This is a business, and as such, we must make a profit. That is your job."

"I hate to start out this way, but I am going to need a little money for myself. Expense money, you might say."

"Take $500 from the envelope. Put it on your ledger." Dunn looked around the house. "And clean this place up. It's a health hazard. Keep me updated on your progress every three days. If you need something not on the list, call me."

"Thank you, Mr. Dunn. I won't let you down. Bettis ran a good operation and I will try to do the same. By the way, call me Mel. I hate Melvin."

"Do you have any questions before I leave, Mel?"

"Not right now, Mr. Dunn. I'll be in touch."

As he drove away, Anthony Dunn wondered if he had done the right thing by hiring Mel. He had always done a good job for Bettis and had never had contact with the law while working for him. Melvin James would have to hire at least two more men to bring the crew up to full strength. That would be his test for efficiency.

While driving back to the office, Dunn called Laura Toombes to ask if there was anything new he needed to take care of today. Everything was going fine, she informed him. Good, he thought. I am getting behind at the office and need the afternoon to catch up.

CHAPTER 19

It was late in the day by the time Stanton and Sergeant Holmes left the office to meet with Carlton Lieber. The two troopers were in the same booth at Lilly's Restaurant when Carlton arrived. His eyes darted around at the customers in the café before reaching the booth.

Karen pointed at the seat across from the two officers. "Have a seat, Carlton. Would you like coffee or something to eat?"

"Just coffee," Carlton said, his eyes searching the customers once again. "I don't like sitting here with the two of you, especially in the middle of the day like this."

"You're the one who suggested this meeting place. You said you didn't want to come to our office. Come on, Carlton. Make up your mind. Let's get to it, Carlton. I think you are leaving out a lot of the facts of your story. I want the straight facts. You had better quit jerking us around like you've been doing." Karen wanted to put him on edge.

"Hey, Sergeant, lighten up. Old Carlton here is just protecting himself. I can understand how he feels. He'll be square with us if we give him a chance." Stanton was on Carlton's side; he liked that.

"Yeah, Sergeant, I saw how Bettis got smoked. He was a careful guy," Lieber commented. "I have a right to be careful."

Now Stanton took the lead. "What about Bettis. Did he work for Dunn, too?"

"Not really. He worked for Jack, but he knew Mr. Dunn. I saw the two of them talking a couple of times. I don't know what they talked about, but they seemed friendly. I think he did errands for Mr. Dunn sometimes."

Once again, Stanton asked the questions. "Were Jack Boardon and Anthony Dunn in business together? I mean in the marijuana business. We know the two of them had business dealings in the real estate business. Bettis worked for Jack in the marijuana growing business. If he knew Dunn, maybe Dunn had a connection with the marijuana business, too."

Lieber glanced around the room again, and leaned forward in the booth. "If he finds out I told you this, he will have me buried," he whispered. "Jack and Mr. Dunn were in it together. Jack ran the grow operation and Mr. Dunn was in charge of the selling. They never sold stuff on the street. Everything was packaged and shipped out to wholesalers. Jack was taking a load to Fairbanks to be shipped out on a cargo plane. I heard, but I never saw it first-hand that Jack would trade their marijuana for cocaine and heroin. I heard a rumor that he was carrying a lot of cash with him the day he crashed. The night I went to Fairbanks with Mr. Dunn, he met a cargo pilot there and gave him the marijuana. In return, he got two big packages. We brought them back here. I never saw them again. I don't know what Mr. Dunn did with them."

"You, somehow, forgot to mention this the last time we talked. Why was that, Carlton?" Stanton prodded.

Karen was listening intently. This confirmed what she had supposed. Boardon and Dunn were in this together. She, however, never suspected the two men were wholesaling their product. The crime lab had told her the THC content of the marijuana in the plane was very high. That would make it a high price item when being traded. She had many questions but let Stanton continue.

Lieber hung his head, looking into his coffee cup before answering. "I was afraid if I told you what I knew that you would think I was involved in the drug business, and I ain't. I have smoked a joint or two and I drink beer when I can afford it, but I never sold any drugs. Honest, I never."

"I believe you, Carlton. I think you are a just guy trying to make a buck, but you have to look at it from our position. We have bent over backwards to give you a break and to take care of you, and yet you keep half the story from us. We have to wonder if our trust was misplaced," Stanton told Lieber.

"Hey, man," Carlton said, again looking around the room. "I know I held out on you, but I have to be careful. Mr. Dunn hired me to rig Jack's airplane so it would crash. I know exactly how dangerous Anthony Dunn can be. I don't want to be another accident." Carlton Lieber was truly frightened.

"If you want our help, you will have to quit these games and tell us everything you know. What's more, you have to let us know if you find out anything else is going on over there." Karen spoke quietly, but her intent came through.

"We're not hard to get along with, Carlton." Stanton tried to console Lieber's fears. "But, if you expect us to protect you, you will have to be 100% honest with us. You know we have to check out whatever you tell us, so just tell the truth and we will stay friends."

"OK, OK, I got it," Carlton conceded. "There ain't much else I can tell you anyway."

"What about that cargo pilot you met in Fairbanks," Karen asked, politely.

"What about him," Carlton responded.

"Who was he and who did he fly for?" she asked.

"Mr. Dunn called him 'Moose.' I don't know his real name. Mr. Dunn said he owned a Boeing 747 and flew all over the world. I think he just got in from the Far East on the night we met him. He sure was a big person. That must be how he got the name of Moose.

"You say Dunn picked up two large packages there. Did he get them from Moose?" Stanton asked.

"They did the deal in the hangar, but after Mr. Dunn got the packages he signaled me to turn over the 1,200 pounds of marijuana to Moose's men. That's what I did. I helped them load those bags into a van and they left." Carlton seemed less nervous now.

Stanton pressed him again. "And that's when you loaded the two packages on Dunn's plane and came home. Is that right?"

"Yeah, that's right. Mr. Dunn was in a good mood all the way back to Anchorage, too," Lieber chuckled. "He ain't in a good mood all that often."

"What happened to the two packages when you got back to Anchorage?" Karen asked.

"Mr. Dunn put them in his car and I never saw them again. Mr. Dunn was in such a good mood that he bought my dinner that night. First time I ever ate at O'Sullivan's. It was really good—and expensive."

Stanton asked the next question. "You said you heard that Jack and Dunn didn't sell stuff on the street. What do you think happened to those two packages?"

"Mr. Dunn was in the Iraq war, some kind of hot-shot pilot, I heard. He made a lot of friends there. A lot of them are flying for airlines and cargo haulers now. Some of the growing crew told me once that he thought one of his old buddies was taking the stuff out of state. I don't know if that is true, but it's what I heard."

"Did you ever hear who his buddy was or which airline he flew for?" Stanton asked.

"Nah, all that was just talk after work while we were all drinking beer at the farm in Palmer. I got invited because I was there delivering groceries and more beer."

Stanton thought a moment and turned to Karen. "Can you think of anything else we need to ask Carlton right now?"

"No, Craig. I think he has been forthcoming with us and I admire him for it." She turned to Carlton. "You did well today, Carlton. From now on let's both try to stay on the other's good side. Agreed?" Carlton lowered his head but nodded in agreement.

"Take off, Carlton," Stanton said. "But stay in touch."

Lieber walked as though a weight had lifted from his shoulders. The two troopers watched him as he left the restaurant and walked across the parking lot. He sat in his pick-up a long time before starting the engine.

It was beginning to snow as they left the meeting place. They were both thinking about what they had learned.

"We have to go back to the office and try to sort all this out. We still don't have any real evidence with which to confront Dunn, but we got a lot closer. Before we're done, you may have to visit the skinny blond again. You are so good at getting her to give you information." Karen laughed at her partner. "I don't know about you, but I have had enough coffee for one day."

"I'm with you on the coffee, and if someone has to grill the secretary, I guess I could do it. It's tough duty, but that's why I thrive on investigating. You know investigating is my life." They both laughed.

CHAPTER 20

Karen walked into her captain's office. It was time for her to report progress on the Jack Boardon case. He greeted her and told her to take a seat while he finished signing several letters and forms. This had become his daily late afternoon ritual. When he finished he turned to his sergeant.

"Sorry about that, Karen. The secretary needs these forms and letters to copy and distribute by the end of the day. Now, what's on your mind? Have you found out anything in the plane crash case?"

"Only in general terms, Captain. Nothing specific, only rumors and guesses." She wanted him to know that she and Craig were making progress, but as of that moment, there was no credible evidence to report.

"You know about the shooting at Ken Whittle's house in Big Lake. We have learned that the victim, Don Bettis, worked for Jack Boardon and was acquainted with Anthony Dunn. Our informant claims to have seen Bettis talking with Dunn on a couple of occasions. He also says Bettis was the crew boss at the growing operation on Boardon's property. What makes this so interesting is that our informant says Boardon used his farm properties to grow high THC content marijuana. Bettis was the one who supervised the farm crew. The product was packaged and traded for cocaine and heroin. Our informant was present on at least one of these trades. He says Boardon dealt with a man, usually in Fairbanks, who owns a large cargo plane and flies all over the world. He claims the pilot, a man called Moose, brings cocaine and heroin into the U.S., trades it for local marijuana, and takes the marijuana to the East Coast where it is sold to wholesalers." Karen continued, "Our informant tells us that Dunn sends the cocaine and heroin via another cargo pilot to the West Coast, again to be sold to wholesalers. Nothing is sold on the street in Alaska." She paused.

"It sounds, from what you tell me, like you have hit on the mother lode of the Alaska drug business," the captain commented. "Do we have hard evidence to substantiate any of this?"

"Not yet," Karen reported. "That is one of the reasons I came in to see you. I think I need some direction, simply because we don't have any evidence." She looked him in the eye and asked, "Do you think we need to inform the Feds about what we've learned? It seems to me as though we're caught in the middle. The plane wreck was definitely a murder. The marijuana farming is a violation of Alaska law. Those things we can pursue and I'm sure we will eventually indict the guilty parties. My question is, what about the federal violations for importing heroin and cocaine? What about interstate transportation of drugs for distribution? Who is transporting the cocaine and heroin down the West Coast? Do we arrest them or do we follow the drugs and find the outlet on the other end? We have a lot more questions than answers at this point."

"You make some good points, Karen," said the captain. "What is your opinion, and what would you like to see happen?"

"I'm in unfamiliar territory, Captain. If left up to me, I would call the Feds and get their advice. In the end, the interstate stuff will go to them anyway and the murder and growing violations will still be our jurisdiction."

"I agree." He wrote a note on his pad. "It is too late today to call the federal building, but first thing in the morning I will contact them and ask how they want to handle it. As soon as I get an answer from them, I'll contact you. I hope I can have that for you tomorrow.

"Thanks, Captain. Craig and I will be waiting to hear from you."

"Speaking of Craig, how is it working out between the two of you? Are you getting along?"

"We got off to a rocky start, my fault, but I have since learned to appreciate him. He's a good investigator and he's great with the informant. He has great instincts and a good sense of humor. He needs it all, working with me." Karen was laughing at herself.

"I'm glad it's working out for you both. See you tomorrow."

Craig was waiting at her door when she returned to her office. He followed her inside. "I had a conversation with the lieutenant of the drug unit," he commented from behind her back. "He and I worked together in Fairbanks a couple of years ago. I asked him if he had heard any rumors about our growing operation or anything about large-scale importing of cocaine and heroin. They haven't heard anything about the imports, and I never volunteered anything. He did say there was a rumor about a big growing operation in the valley, but he didn't know where it was or who was involved. One of the reasons is that the dope never showed up inside the state and they never looked for it."

"I just talked to the captain about that. He's going to contact the Feds in the morning and get back to us on what they want to do about those interstate violations. We still have to deal with Boardon's murder and with the marijuana growing operation."

"The little talk we just had with Carlton certainly confirmed your suspicion about Anthony Dunn. My hat goes off to you on that one." With that compliment, Craig moved on to his next question. "I think I should have another lunch with Laura Toombes." He held up his hand. "I know the SOPs about fraternizing with someone involved in an active investigation. I promise to keep it professional, at least until the case is closed." He was giving her the "I promise, Sarge" grin.

"Do you really think she knows anything, or is this personal?"

"It's professional, at this time," he said. "Seriously, though, I think Dunn keeps his drug business out of the office. However, she surely hears things she would deem suspicious. There must be phone calls or strangers coming to the office that are not involved with the real estate business. Perhaps I can find out something about those strange flights by Mr. Dunn."

"I would like to know who her hairdresser is," Karen teased.

They agreed to call it a day and start again in the morning. Karen stayed in her office to finish her daily paperwork and bring her logbook up to date. She checked the time; she had another hour's work to do before she could leave.

Craig Stanton returned to his desk, looked at his watch, and decided to try to contact the secretary. She answered on the second ring.

"Dunn Realty," she answered.

"Miss Toombes, this is Trooper Craig Stanton. I'm about finished for the day and called to ask if you were free for dinner."

"Oh. Hi there, Craig. I'm so pleased to hear from you. I was thinking about you earlier today and wondering if you would call."

"I have been very busy on a case I'm working. Otherwise I would have called sooner." He liked this blond, but he knew he could not get personally involved with her until this case was resolved.

"Do you really mean it about dinner tonight?"

"Of course, I mean it. I'm still in uniform. I have to mean everything I say. It's my duty."

"Oh, Craig, you are such a tease," she giggled.

"How about it?" he asked. "What time can I pick you up for dinner?"

"I have to keep the office open another hour. I'm waiting for a client to come in and sign some papers. Will that be too late?"

"No, I have to go home and change into civilian clothing. That way I don't have to mean everything I say." They both laughed. "Where would you like to go for dinner?"

"To tell the truth, I would settle for pizza and a six-pack at my place. Is that all right with you?"

"It sounds just perfect," he said.

She gave him directions to her place. She was a little giddy. It was not her habit to invite gentlemen to her home, but, after all, she thought, he is a trooper.

By the time Stanton got home, showered and changed clothes, it was late. He called her on the road to Eagle River where she lived. He liked the idea of spending a quiet evening with a beautiful lady.

CHAPTER 21

Without conscious thought, Craig Stanton was whistling while walking down the hall toward his sergeant's office. He felt especially good this morning for some reason.

"Good morning, Sergeant," he greeted in a musical tone.

Karen looked up at him and grinned. "My, aren't we in a good mood this morning?"

"Yes, even though I worked late last night—investigating," he replied.

"I admire your diligence, Craig," she teased. "Did she put up a good front?"

"Sergeant! I'm shocked you would ask such a question. You can't think I am the type of guy who would kiss and tell, do you?"

"And surely, Craig, you don't think I'm the type who would ask her partner about his love life?" Karen laughed.

"I did learn a couple of things, though. For instance, she confirmed that Dunn knew Bettis. She overheard Dunn talking on his cell phone to someone he called Bettis. Another time, she overheard him talking with a man called Moose. She didn't know who he was but thought it was a funny name."

"I can tell by the happy look on your face that you consider this good news."

"The results of any investigation are like the links in a chain," Craig explained. "One piece is connected to the next by the evidence. We had heard there was a man by the name of Moose whom Dunn met in Fairbanks. I don't believe this is a coincidence. Investigating is my life, Sergeant. You know that. Anytime an investigation leads to something useful, I'm happy," he said.

"Well, Mr. Investigator, where do we go from here with this information? If we confront him with it, he will suspect his skinny blond secretary of blabbing to us."

"That is true, but it puts one more bullet in our gum." He grinned again and asked, "Have you heard from the captain this morning?"

"Not yet, but I will as soon as he contacts someone at the federal building." She stood, picking up her coffee cup. "Want some coffee while we wait?"

Half an hour later her intercom line rang. It was the captain. He asked Karen and her partner to come to his office.

"Good morning," the captain greeted.

"Good morning," Karen and Craig said in unison.

Captain Davis slid a notepad to the center of his desk, perusing the scratches on it. He looked up and said, "The two of you are turning out to be heroes. I just got off the telephone with a DEA agent by the name of Sam Goodyear. He has been investigating the drug import business for a couple of years. In all that time, he learned that someone was bringing cocaine and heroin into the U.S. from the Far East. That's it. The two of you have learned more by accident than they have in two years' of intense investigation." He gave them a short smile. "Goodyear wants to meet with the two of you here in the office today. Will you have time for a meeting?"

"Just let us know what time and we'll be here. We need to talk with Dunn again, but we were holding off until we heard from the Feds," Karen advised her captain. "We want to prod him a little, but we don't want to tip him off that we have him tied to the drug growing business. We have a witness to tie Dunn to Jack Boardon's murder, and we suspect he is the boss in the drug growing and trading business, but we don't have a solid motive for killing Jack. So far all we have is one person's word against his. We need proof."

"I will let you know what time to meet Goodyear," the captain advised.

Karen asked, "Do you want to attend the meeting with Goodyear?"

"No, I don't think I need to be there, but keep me informed," he said. "I'm going to call Goodyear and try to set up a meeting in your office for 1 p.m. Is that a good time for you?"

"That will be good, Captain. We will have all our notes ready for the meeting." She paused, thinking, and then added, "I have two questions, Captain. Do we trust this guy? And can we expect to get anything in return for the information we are passing on to him?"

"Give him anything he wants in regard to the drug import information, but be cautious about damaging our cases. Try to maintain jurisdictional credibility. We want him to go after Dunn's contacts for interstate transport for sale, but we don't want to jeopardize our murder case or our marijuana growing case. Keep those close to the vest, but be cooperative with him. Perhaps he will give us something we aren't aware of at this time."

"I understand, Captain." She glanced at her partner. "My chief investigator and I will be careful and cooperative."

"Chief investigator?" the captain asked.

"It's an inside joke, Captain."

"Try to keep the jokes to yourself. Most Feds don't have a sense of humor."

"Will do, Captain." With that, Stanton and Holmes went back to her office.

After talking it over they decided to make a trip to Eagle River to visit with Anthony Dunn. Laura Toombes showed every one of her brilliantly white teeth in a friendly grin when she saw Craig Stanton. They asked if Dunn was in. Laura checked with him and showed them to his office, smiling at Craig as they went.

Karen shook hands with Dunn and Stanton said good morning. He offered them each a seat and asked what he could do for them. He was a very friendly man.

Karen opened the conversation. "Mr. Dunn, we just stopped by to tell you of a development in the case of Jack Boardon. You may have heard about a shooting up at Big Lake. It seems someone was about to use a cutting torch to open a gun safe in a trapper's home. The trapper saw him and when the robber pulled a gun the trapper shot him. The trapper is the same one who found Jack's airplane wreck. The safe cracker was a man by the name of Don Bettis. We have learned that Bettis had worked for Mr. Boardon. We wanted to ask you if you knew this Don Bettis."

Without hesitation, Dunn shook his head and said, "No, I can't recall ever meeting anyone by that name. Jack hired lots of laborers, but I seldom ever met any of them."

"That's what we thought, Mr. Dunn, but we needed to ask anyway." She paused, trying to read Dunn's face, without success. "By the way," she asked, "you told us that the two of you had business dealings together. Are all the legalities of his death causing any problems for you?"

"No, we took precautions since we are, or were, both pilots. We had life insurance policies on each other. Enough to buy the other one's share of the business in the event either one of us died. I certainly never expected to have to use it to settle with Jack's estate. This has been very stressful for me. Jack and I go back a long way."

"I understand your grief, Mr. Dunn. We didn't come here to cause you any more hurt, but we had to know if you knew Don Bettis." She stood. "We have taken enough of your time, sir. Thank you. Please call me if there is anything I can do to help you."

"It's always a pleasure to talk with you, Sergeant."

Laura Toombes was waiting in the outer office to say goodbye to Craig.

"Who does your hair, Laura?" Karen asked in parting. Craig gave his sergeant a look of utter disgust. Karen knew she would pay for that one later.

In the car and at lunch, the two carried on a good-natured banter about Laura Toombes and Craig Stanton. Karen teased him unmercifully and he defended himself with skill and finesse. The two officers were beginning a solid friendship, each trusting the judgment of the other. The topic of discussion changed, however, on the way to the office from lunch. The mood became serious as they discussed the tack to be used when the DEA agent came to the office. They decided to volunteer as little as possible, but to answer all his questions as completely as they could. Beyond that, they would improvise.

Promptly at one o'clock Goodyear checked in at the front desk. Karen went to meet him and show him the way to her office. Stanton was already there. Introductions were made, and they got down to business.

Goodyear, a short stocky man with no neck and an Oklahoma accent, opened the conversation. "I want to congratulate the two of you on obtaining information my colleagues and I have tried to learn for more than two years. We are excited about what you have learned. Your captain has given me a copy of your murder case. We do not intend to interfere in that. The captain also had concerns about your jurisdiction in the marijuana growing case. I just want to assure you that the DEA has no interest in either of those cases. However, we will give you any help and assistance you require in either of them. With that said, I want to give you this file." He handed Karen a manila folder. Metal clips held all the papers in place inside and a neat nametag on the cover was inscribed with a case number, nothing else. "This is the file containing two year's work. It had come to a standstill until you helped us get it going again. For that we are grateful."

Karen opened the file and scanned the pages.

Goodyear continued, "You can keep that copy. You will find we have been chasing an unknown person all over the world. We knew what he was doing, but could never find out who he was. With the name you gave us, Moose, and the fact he owned a large cargo plane, we traced it to an old military pilot from the first Gulf War. His name is Mosely Cain. He has an old Boeing 747; he owns it outright. He flies more or less regular routes around the world, contracting with civilian and military shipping companies, and he is regarded as a reliable transporter. The name of his company is Amarada Cargo. He is incorporated in the U.S., Nevada to be specific. He seems to have two regular routes: a northern route and a southern route. The northern one runs New York to London to Amsterdam with side trips either north through Russia or south through the Middle East countries, and varying sometimes to Laos, Cambodia, Sri Lanka and Viet Nam. The Southern route hits the same major cities, except takes side trips through the southern hemisphere and returns to the United States from either Hong Kong or Manila."

Stanton voiced the next question. "If he flies to all those destinations, why is he stopping in Alaska to pick up marijuana?"

"Good question," Goodyear replied. "We think, and this is only speculation, your grower is turning out some high quality weed. Our best guess is that he is bringing cocaine and heroin from Southeast Asia and trading some of it for high quality marijuana on a stop in Alaska. We also believe their only motivation is money. Cain is able to find high quality marijuana here that he can sell for high prices on the East Coast."

"What is your next move with Cain and his cargo service?" asked Karen.

"We have agents staking out his terminal in New York. They will be following every crewmember on the plane. Your report says they loaded 1200 pounds of marijuana in Fairbanks. They would need a truck or van to transport that much marijuana. Crew members could be carrying smaller amounts of other drugs in luggage or personal vehicles, and we will be following up on that possibility."

"Do you have any information about how the cocaine and heroin are transported out of Alaska?" Karen inquired.

"We are investigating, but so far we don't know. Indications are that another pilot, perhaps with another cargo company, is taking it south. Where? We have no idea, but we will be watching the next time Amarada Cargo lands in Alaska. We will be following everyone who makes contact with Mosely Cain."

Karen had thumbed through the entire file Goodyear had given her. "And what does the DEA want us to do?" Karen asked.

"You people have accomplished more than DEA in a much shorter period of time," Goodyear began. "I am asking you to keep us informed of anything you might learn concerning the interstate transfer and transport of these drugs. I think it is likely you will find some minion who knows something of how this is done." He concluded, "I feel this is a reasonable request, is it not?"

"I will have to take all this to my captain, but it seems like a reasonable request to me," Karen offered. "I'm sure Captain Davis will agree. Meanwhile, I have a request for you, Agent Goodyear, and that is that you reciprocate. If you learn anything concerning our murder case or the marijuana growing case, you will pass it along to us. Agreed?"

"Fair enough," he said. "On a personal note I want to thank you for what you have done so far. Your information has put us back in the game. I thank you for that. I also want to say that you have a right to be suspicious of my organization and me. Sometimes we don't play fair. We spend so much time with criminals that we sometimes forget we are all on the same side. You and the rest of AST have been fair with me and in return I will be square with you." With that, he held out a hand, Karen took it and they shook vigorously. He did the same with Stanton. "Thanks again," he said as he left the office.

"What do you make of that?" Stanton asked.

"I'm not sure, but I think I will trust him until he gives me a reason not to. Come on. Let's talk to the captain. He needs to know about the meeting." She picked up her coffee cup, "Bring the DEA file, please, Craig."

Once in the captain's office, Karen expressed the highlights of the meeting with Goodyear. It took several minutes to cover the involvement of Amarada Cargo Company and Mosely "Moose" Cain.

The captain sat quietly, assimilating what he had just heard. Finally, he looked up and asked, "Where does this leave our murder case?"

Karen spoke. "I think we can concentrate on the murder case now. Our problem, as I see it, is that we don't have a good motive. Our informant says he was paid to rig the Cessna to crash, but, as yet, we don't know why. That leaves us with the word of our informant against a prominent business man."

"Any educated guesses?" the captain asked.

"I think this all goes back to the marijuana growing business," Stanton offered. "I have seen a lot of rivals done in by partners in the drug trade. It usually boils down to who will get the profits. My instincts tell me Anthony Dunn will be the beneficiary of Jack Boardon's bad luck. It will be tough, but the Sergeant and I have to make that connection."

Captain Davis turned to Karen. "Did I actually give you this guy as a partner? He sounds too bright to be working with you." He gave Karen a broad grin.

"Sometimes he actually makes sense, Captain."

"Take your Chief Investigator and go back to work. There must be a way to get some evidence on Dunn. See what you can do."

CHAPTER 23

Melvin James had been busy accumulating all the items on the list Mr. Dunn had given him. The two new men had been hired and most of the equipment replaced; however, it was too bulky for his van and too heavy for him to handle alone. He called his boss.

James dialed the number given him by Anthony Dunn. Someone answered with, "Hello."

"Is this Mr. Dunn?" James asked.

"Oh! Hello, Melvin. How are you doing with the list I gave you?"

"I've bought almost all the stuff, but I will need another hand with a truck of some kind. The lights and some of the other things are too large to fit into my van. Do you have someone I can use to take a couple of loads to Palmer?" James inquired.

"Just a minute," Dunn said. He put down the phone and looked up the number for Carlton Lieber. Picking up the telephone again, he asked, "Are you there, Melvin?"

"Yes, sir," came the reply.

"Write this number down. You may want to use him again. I don't want him working on the agricultural end, only labor. He has other talents I use. Do you have a pencil?" James said he did and Dunn provided the number.

"Thank you, Mr. Dunn. I'll call him right away. I hired two more men and they will start setting up tomorrow. That last new property you gave me is going to be a challenge. The ground is frozen and we won't be able to get a permanent water supply to the building until spring. I found a 500-gallon water tank on a small trailer to haul water until then. We should be in business at that location in three days. The trays are ready, but we have to hook up the lights and timers."

"It sounds as if you are making progress, Melvin. Keep me posted on how things are going."

"I will, Mr. Dunn. I'll call this Carlton Lieber right away." Dunn was happy, and that pleased Melvin James.

Twenty minutes later, the telephone on Craig Stanton's desk rang. It was Carlton Lieber, sounding excited.

"Trooper Stanton, I just got a call from a new guy, Melvin James. He wants me to meet him and haul a lot of lights and stuff to Palmer. They have a new greenhouse started up there. I said I would meet him down by the dock in a few minutes, but I wanted to call you first. What do you want me to do?"

"They still trust you, Carlton. Go ahead and do the job for them. Let me know where the new greenhouse will be. And, Carlton, don't go asking a lot of questions and get yourself into trouble. Learn what you can, but be careful," advised Stanton.

"Don't worry, Trooper Stanton. I'll be careful. I don't want to end up like Jack or Bettis."

Craig walked down the hall to report the call to Karen. He was worried for Carlton. Once, in Fairbanks, Craig had worked with an informant who wanted to help. The informant had said something that made his boss suspicious and it nearly cost the informant his life. The dealer he was working for had beat him and left him for dead. That was one scenario Craig didn't care to repeat.

"I just got a call from Carlton. He has been asked to move some equipment to a new grow location in Palmer. I warned him to be careful. He said he would find out where the new place is and let us know."

"It sounds like they are gearing up for another crop. I wonder how many locations they are planning. Last time the crop must have totaled somewhere in the neighborhood of a ton of product. Do you think they will try for that amount again?" Karen asked rhetorically.

"It seems likely," Stanton replied. "It would be nice if we could put a time-lapse camera inside the new place and film the entire operation."

"That's a good thought, Craig. Since they are setting up a grow operation as indicated by the equipment they are installing, maybe, just maybe, a judge will give us a warrant to install surveillance equipment inside the warehouse. We will need an address before we go to the judge, but let's ask the captain."

She called the captain and explained the situation. She asked if he could get a search warrant to install a time-lapse camera inside the building to prove a growing operation and to identify participants. The captain agreed and said he would proceed as soon as Lieber provided a location.

Snow was beginning to fall. The forecast was for a total of about eight inches. The days were getting longer by three or four minutes a day. Dusk still came in the early afternoon. Karen looked at Stanton, bored with office duty.

"Why don't we go to Big Lake and check on the welfare of Mr. Ken Whittle?" She wanted an excuse to get out of the office.

"Do you have a reason to suspect he might be in danger?" asked her partner.

"No. But since he was involved in that shooting and the victim of a burglary-turned-robbery, he might feel safer if he knew we were concerned for his safety."

"You are so full of it," Stanton teased. "You just want to get out of the office. You just hate sitting here waiting for Carlton to call. Right?"

"Right. Do you want to go along or would you rather wait here in the office, thinking the skinny blond might call."

"You are never going to let up about her, are you?" He was shaking his head. "I like her."

"I like her, too, but it's my job to see you stick with the SOPs," Karen said, being sympathetic. "But, I'll bet anyone who has a shirt-full like that wears contact lenses," she giggled at him.

"Alright, alright. Let's go to Big Lake. But if we have a flat tire, you will have to change it while I sit inside the nice warm car."

"You're a real wuss." She giggled again.

An hour later, they drove into the yard of the trapper's cabin. The Super Cub was tied down in front. A full set of nylon covers protected nearly every square inch of the airplane. Whittle's pick-up was nowhere to be seen. The two troopers got out of the car. Karen knocked on the cabin door. She waited and knocked again. No answer. They checked the outbuildings. The tool shed was locked, but the fur shed door was open. There was nothing inside. All the furs were gone. It was snowing harder now.

"Our Mr. Ken Whittle hasn't been here for a couple of days," Craig observed. "I'd say he took off shortly after we talked to him the other day."

"I think you're right. I wonder if it was us or the burglar who scared him out."

"Perhaps he just took a vacation," Stanton said.

"He packed up all his furs; maybe he just went to market with them. It does seem strange though. He took his furs, closed his place up, and covered the Cub as if he would be gone for a while. Let's call in and put a locate-only on his license plate number. If he is still in the area, we should spot him soon."

"It sounds like a good idea to me. Can we go home now, mama?" Craig was laughing.

"I was thinking of stopping in Eagle River. The skinny blond never did tell me who did her hair."

Stanton rolled his eyes in frustration. "I'll drive. You call in the plate number."

"I was thinking of stopping in Eagle River. The skinny blond never did tell me who did her hair."

Stanton rolled his eyes in frustration. "I'll drive. You call in the plate number."

CHAPTER 24

On the return trip to the office, the two officers discussed options. Karen called in the license plate number on Whittle's pick-up, ordering a locate-only. Whittle may not be running, only gone to sell his furs. This is always the frustrating part of any investigation, Karen thought, waiting for something to change or something to happen. In either case, it was out of their control and cops hate not being in control.

They were just pulling into the parking area at headquarters when dispatch contacted them to report the license plate they had asked about had been located. The truck was parked in the long-term parking lot at Ted Stevens International Airport in Anchorage.

Instead of parking, they decided to go to the airport and inquire around. They may be able to find out where Ken Whittle was off to. Their first stop was the Alaska Airline ticket counter. They talked to the head ticket agent, knowing it was a long shot. The ticket agent, her name tag read Cynthia, was a slightly overweight black lady with a broad smile and winning persona.

"I remember that guy!" she exclaimed. "He came in yesterday afternoon. He told my agent that he didn't have a reservation but needed to get on a flight right away. All he had with him was a carry-on. The reason I remember was the agent called me to help him. The only flight with a vacancy was going to Denver. He said he would take it. I thought that was strange, most people want a specific destination when they leave. He just wanted to go. Then he pulls out a wad of $100 bills to pay in cash. Nobody pays in cash anymore. But he had ID and cash, so we sold him a ticket to Denver. That flight left yesterday on time at 2:43 p.m. As far as I know, he was on it."

Craig looked at Cynthia in amazement. He wrote her personal information in his notebook along with some notes about Whittle, the flight number, time, and destination.

"Cynthia, you are the most helpful witness I have ever had. Thank you," Craig praised her observations.

In the long-term parking lot, they checked Whittle's pick-up. There was nothing unusual there. "He's running. Bettis scared him," Karen observed. "I think I screwed up, Craig. I think Whittle took something from the wreck before I got there. Whatever it is, someone wants it back. It looks to me like they sent Bettis to retrieve it, he got caught and killed. Whittle knew what they were after, got nervous, and packed his tent. Did you notice all the traps hanging on the side of the tool shed? I'll bet he pulled all his traps before he left. I'll bet he stays missing for a long time."

"What do you think was in the airplane? What did he take?" Craig asked.

"You read the report. There was a metal briefcase in the plane. In fact, it hit Jack in the back of the head and killed him during the crash. When we inventoried the contents of the briefcase there was only $1,500 in it. What if it was full when Whittle found it? What if he took the money out of the case and put $1,500 back inside. The case had blood on it. Whittle knew the case needed a reason to be in the airplane, so he planted enough cash back inside to look legitimate. He hid the rest of the money in his airplane until we came and retrieved the Cessna. He went back to his place, counted his loot, and put it in his big gun safe. Someone sent Bettis to get it. They will probably send someone else. Whittle got scared and ran." Karen looked at Stanton. "What do you think about that little scenario?"

"Your deductive reasoning amazes me," Craig said. "I don't know how you did it. You took all these little pieces and stacked them together to make a case, and a darn good one. I think you have come up with the motive for the burglary at Whittle's cabin."

"We need to find Whittle," Karen said, staring at Craig. "Hey! Do you think Goodyear would be willing to look for Whittle for us? He has the resources to follow him all over the United States. He said he would help. I wonder if we could get good old Sam to find Whittle for us."

Craig was smiling. "We might have the captain ask him, politely."

"Good idea. Let's go back to the office."

The captain laughed when he heard the story. "The two of you have built a really beautiful house of cards with your suppositions. I have to agree that it sounds good, but we are still dealing in fantasy. I'll tell you what I will do," he said. "I will call Goodyear and ask him if it's possible for him to locate a 'witness.' In the meantime, it's a locate-only, and, unless you can get some evidence to support your theory, it will remain a locate-only. Understand?"

"Yes, sir, Captain," Karen said as she rose from her chair. Craig followed her lead.

Craig's shirt pocket began to vibrate as they walked back to Karen's office. He fumbled the cell phone out of the pocket.

"Stanton," he answered.

"Trooper Stanton, this is Carlton Lieber. I have that location for you. I'm on my way back to town now."

"Call me when you are in town. We will meet you at the Lucky Wishbone," Stanton instructed.

"What is that all about?" Karen asked.

"Carlton has the location of the new greenhouse. I told him to meet us at the Lucky Wishbone." He grinned at her. "Feel like chicken for lunch?"

They chose the most remote booth they could find. Craig ordered at the counter for the both of them. He had just returned to the booth when his phone vibrated again. Carlton was coming down 5th Avenue. Craig's order number was called and he placed another order for Carlton when he picked up his own

Carlton was acting nervous again, his eyes darting around the room at the customers. He came to the booth and sat. Just then, a number was called. Craig gave Carlton the ticket and told him it was already paid for.

"When Carlton returned, he immediately started on the lunch. "I don't like this place," he said.

Craig smiled and replied. "Don't you like chicken, Carlton?"

"You know what I mean," Carlton answered, chewing on the crispy chicken. "Too many people in here. Someone may recognize me."

"I can see where having lunch with two uniformed troopers could damage a person's reputation," Stanton said.

"You know what I mean." Carlton continued to chew on the chicken. "They gave me a key to the greenhouse." He slipped the key out of his pocket and placed it on the table. "You can make a copy if you want, but I have to have the key back by tomorrow. No one will be around at night, but the crew will be working on the place all day. They have the trays built and have started filling them with dirt. The heat is on and as soon as the temperature comes up they will start to plant. The lights are installed, but they ain't hooked up to the timers yet. There is a water tank parked inside to stay warm. A new guy took Bettis' place. His name is Melvin James. Nice guy, but he pushes hard. By the way, he mentioned he answers to Dunn."

"Well, thanks, Carlton. You earned your lunch today. I'll have your key back to you by tomorrow." Craig smiled at Carlton. Don't worry about the other people in here, Carlton. You are the only one in the place who is not a trooper."

Lieber's head jerked around, and then he realized he was being played. "Sometimes you ain't very nice, Trooper Stanton."

Karen sat without saying anything, barely able to keep from laughing at the banter around her. She finished her chicken, and wiped her hands and face with a napkin.

She slid out of the booth. "I think we had better go before we damage Carlton's reputation any further," she said with a grin.

She looked back to see Carlton continuing to eat as they left the restaurant.

Back in the office, they went to see the captain. Karen provided him an update on the new greenhouse location. She told him she had a key to the place and that it would be vacant at night.

Captain Davis made a couple of notes on his desk pad. "Good work. I think we will be able to get a surveillance warrant for the place. I'll call the judge right away.

If we get it, I will have the crime lab team get with you to set up the cameras. I'll call you when I have word."

"This has been a very good day," Karen commented.

Craig agreed. "Let's have a 7UP and celebrate."

CHAPTER 25

It was snowing hard when the crime lab team met them in Palmer. The property was another old farm. The house looked good, but there were no tracks of persons entering or leaving the bungalow. The drive and parking area had been plowed earlier in the day, but the new snow was covering it quickly. With the snow coming down this hard they decided to park right at the door. The new snow would cover their tracks soon after they were finished.

The three men from the crime lab held a mini conference to determine where the cameras would be placed. The youngest member of the team did the climbing to place the surveillance cameras in the rafters. The others camouflaged the wiring and microphones. Karen and Craig looked around the building while the others worked. It was plain to see that the new crop was ready for planting. Karen had cautioned the installers that the lights were yet to be hooked up to the timers so there was a danger of the newly installed camera wiring being discovered. They were taking extra precautions to hide the wiring.

Less than a half hour later, after testing the cameras and mikes, the crew exited the barn. The entire crew stopped in Palmer at the Noisy Goose restaurant for dinner. While eating they informed Karen that the signal from the cameras could be accessed from the main road in front of the farm. It would not be necessary to go into the barn for that purpose.

"We will go out there every other day and retrieve the images. We can screen them and bring you copies if you would like." It was the senior sergeant informing them of the process.

"Let me know right away if there is anything suspicious happening out there," Karen said. "We're heading back to the office now. It's been a long day." With that, she and Craig left them to finish their dinner.

On the way back to town, Craig said, "Give me that key and, after I drop you off, I'll get a duplicate made. I'll get the original back to Carlton."

Craig dropped Karen at the front of the headquarters building and drove out of the parking lot. It had been a long day and Karen wanted to finish a couple of notes and leave for the day. It was Friday night and she should be going on a date or something exciting, but she was just too tired. Twenty minutes later, she turned off the light in her office and went to her trooper pick-up. She started the engine and swept the snow off the windshield and mirrors. She climbed into the truck and drove out of the parking area. She had decided to stop at the Dimond area WalMart to pick up a couple of things.

She drove south from Tudor Avenue on the New Seward Highway. The 65 mile per hour traffic was slowed to 45 by heavy snow and low visibility. She turned off the highway onto the Dimond Blvd. exit. There were several inches of snow on the roadway making it difficult to steer her truck. There are three right turn lanes at the Dimond Blvd. traffic light. She chose the farthest left lane, the light turned red and she made an easy stop.

Suddenly, a blue Chevy Suburban struck her from behind, pushing her into the busy intersection. At the same time, a large, white, dual tire pick-up truck with a huge snowplow on the front was coming through the light from Karen's left. The young man driving the plow truck used lightning quick instincts to drop the blade to the ground before the impact. That action slowed the truck somewhat, but the heavy plow struck the trooper vehicle on the driver side with tremendous force.

Karen's truck was slammed sideways and spun halfway around. Inside the vehicle, her head struck the left side window knocking her unconscious. The teenage girl driving the Suburban was also out cold and bleeding. Within ten seconds, eight 911 calls were made from the scene by motorists witnessing the accident. Anchorage Police Department (APD) had three cars on the scene within two minutes.

The first officer on the scene checked the white trooper pick-up and found Karen inside unconscious. His first call summoned an ambulance. Another officer did the same for the young girl inside the Suburban. Two more officers arrived and began to direct traffic. The first officer opened the door of Karen's truck and unbuckled her seatbelt. She was breathing. The impact had deployed the airbag and the entire left side of her face was bruised and bleeding.

While the officer continued to check Karen's pulse, the driver of the snowplow asked from behind him, "Is she OK?"

"Step back," the officer said. "The ambulance is coming." He continued to check her condition.

"Oh, God. I hope she is OK. She just slid out in front of me and I couldn't stop."

"Are you driving the white snowplow?" the APD officer asked.

"Yes. I dropped the blade and tried, but I couldn't stop. No time." His voice was full of emotion.

"Get back in your truck and wait for me. As soon as the ambulance arrives, I'll come to talk with you," the officer instructed the young man.

Road conditions were worsening by the minute. There were twelve to sixteen-inch snow berms between the lanes. Eastbound traffic was allowed to flow, but the westbound lanes were closed. Within minutes, the EMTs arrived, making a U-turn in the closed intersection. The medics quickly examined the unconscious trooper, called the hospital, inserted an IV into her arm, and loaded her onto a stretcher. A medic told the APD officer they were transporting her to Providence Hospital.

Another team of Medics did the same for the young girl in the Suburban. She was beginning to come around but could not remember what had happened.

The APD officer finally walked to the plow truck and asked the driver for his license. "Are you hurt?" he asked.

"No, I'm OK, just a little shaken up," the young man replied.

"Dropping that blade was quick thinking. The little bit of snow in front of it probably cushioned the impact enough to save her life," the officer said. "I'll call in and check your license, and then you can go. You will have to come to APD and make an official statement. Do you know where it is?"

The driver nodded. "I'll be working all night with it snowing like this. I can come in when I get off in the morning." He paused a few seconds. "Can you give me her name? I would like to go to the hospital and check on her in the morning."

The officer finished with the required information and returned the license to the driver. "Her name is Sergeant Karen Holmes, AST. They took her to Providence Hospital. As soon as the wrecker takes the trooper truck away, you can go. We need to get the traffic moving again."

"Thanks, I'll come to APD in the morning," he said as he walked back to his truck, which surprisingly had suffered almost no damage.

A trooper car with red lights running sped to the scene. The driver, a tall slim trooper jumped from the car, approaching the APD officer.

"I'm Stanton. Karen is my partner. Is she OK?"

"I don't know. She was still unconscious when they loaded her in the ambulance. She was T-Boned by this snowplow," he motioned with his thumb, "after being rear-ended by that blue Suburban. She's headed for Providence."

"Thanks," Stanton said, returning to his car. His first call was to Captain Davis.

He caught up with Karen in the emergency room at Providence Hospital. The small treatment room was full of nurses, doctors, and technicians taking blood. Craig was pacing the hallway when Captain Davis arrived.

"How is she?" Davis asked.

"I don't know yet. They are still working on her. Nobody has had time to stop and talk with me." Just then, there was a loud moan from the treatment room.

"What are you doing?" a half-awake Karen asked.

"Take it easy. You have been in an accident," the nurse was saying.

"Get all this junk off me. I have to go." She was still fighting.

Craig and the captain moved to the curtain at the door. "Karen, take it easy. They have to check you over," her captain said.

"I have to get out of here, Captain."

"No, Karen. Just lay there and take it easy. We have you covered."

She seemed to relax somewhat. A nurse was injecting an IV line with a sedative.

"She will be fine. Nothing is broken, but she has massive bruising down her entire left side. She will be stiff and sore for a while, and she will have a beautiful shiner on that left eye. She hit her head pretty hard. The doctor is keeping her to be sure she doesn't have a concussion, which I think she has. She is going to be out of it the rest of the night. Why don't you two come back in the morning to visit?"

Davis gave the nurse a card. "Call me if there is any change at all."

The two men went to the front lobby and found a cup of coffee. They stood around sipping the hot, strong, foul liquid—not talking, just pacing and waiting. Finally, Davis tossed his cup in the trash basket and gave out a huge sigh.

"I guess we aren't doing any good here," he said.

"You know, Captain, I haven't worked with many partners, but there could never be a better one than Karen. I hope she is OK"

"Me, too, Craig. Me, too."

CHAPTER 26

Craig Stanton was in the hospital by 6:30 Saturday morning asking for the room number for his partner. He was carrying a bouquet of roses he had purchased at the Huffman Avenue Safeway store. The woman at the desk gave him the room number and he walked to the elevator. On the fourth floor, he stepped out of the elevator and checked the signs for directions to the room. There was a small commons area halfway down the hall. There, sitting alone was Captain Davis.

"Good morning, Craig," the captain greeted. "Did you get any sleep?"

"Some. Have you seen her?"

"No, the doctor was in her room when I arrived. He should be finished soon," the commander spoke quietly.

Craig was about to sit when a nurse came in and called to the captain. "You can go in now. The doctor has finished."

The two men walked quietly to the room, tapped on the door and entered. Karen was awake, sitting up in bed attempting to drink a container of orange juice. The left side of her face was a brilliant blue-green. Her left eye was swollen shut and her left arm below her shoulder matched her bruised face.

"Are you up to a couple of visitors this morning?" the captain asked.

"Come in, Cap, and bring my partner with you."

"Some girls will do anything to get flowers," Craig teased. He found a plastic container near the sink and filled it with water. The roses fit nicely.

"What did the doctor tell you," asked the captain.

"He wants to keep me a few days. The x-rays didn't show anything broken, but he says I have a concussion. They want to watch me in case of blood clots from the bruising. I hurt all over. I am bruised down my entire left side to my ankle. I remember being hit from the rear, but I don't remember anything about being hit on the left side. Are the other drivers all right?"

"They are both fine. The girl who hit you from behind was wearing a seatbelt and only had a bruised knee. You would have been a lot worse if the plow driver hadn't dropped his blade at the last second. That was quick thinking on his part." There was sadness in the captain's voice.

"I will have to thank him when I get out of here." It was difficult for her to speak through the swollen cheeks and lips. "You may have to work alone for a few days, partner."

Craig smiled at her. "I don't want you to scare the customers, looking like you do. Can I bring you anything: food, books, make-up?"

"Maybe in a few days, but right now I just want to rest and hide my face."

"I think that's a good idea," said the captain. "Craig and I will leave and visit again later. Don't hesitate to call us if you want anything at all. Get well."

"Thanks, Cap. I will. Craig, stay on top of Carlton." She was still giving orders.

Before leaving the hospital, the two men held a short conference. Craig said he would check on Karen a couple of times a day and that on Monday, he would get back on the case. Both men expressed their concern for Karen and her injuries.

Craig visited twice a day throughout the weekend. He was in uniform and on his way to the office when he stopped in to see her on Monday morning. The blue pallor was beginning to turn green and was slightly less distinct today. The swelling had lessened and she was speaking more clearly. The doctors had ordered her out of bed and walking. It was painful, but she complied.

"Keep getting better, Karen. If you need anything just call. I can deliver on state time. See you tonight." It was sad for Stanton to see his partner in this much pain.

When he entered the office, he checked in with his boss. Craig gave him a progress report on Karen and told him he would do some follow-up on their current case. Davis cautioned him about being out there alone. It was essentially the same advice he had given Karen when the case started.

Stanton had called Carlton and arranged to meet him at a Tesoro gas station in Peters Creek. He wanted to see Carlton and give him his key. Craig had made two duplicates, one for himself, and one for Karen.

The trooper was filling his car with gas when Carlton came into the station. The informant sat in his old pick-up with the window down while they conversed. Stanton returned the key and thanked the mechanic. Carlton said nothing had been done over the weekend because of the heavy snow. The crew would be back on the job today, though. Carlton gave a small wave of his hand and drove away. Craig checked the time and thought it possible Laura Toombes could be in her office. He thought he should check in on her, you know, to be polite.

He drove the short distance to Eagle River and the real estate office. The "Open" sign was on and the lights were glowing when he arrived. He wiped his feet before entering the carpeted office. She heard him, looked up, and gave him a big smile.

"Is your boss in?" he asked.

"Not yet," she replied.

"Good, I came to see you anyway." They smiled at each other like a couple of teenagers. "Do you have plans for this evening?" Craig asked.

"Nothing important," she gave him the ultra-white smile again. "Are you going to come over tonight? I'll cook dinner if you will."

"It will be after seven this evening. I have to visit my partner at the hospital first."

"She's in the hospital? What happened?"

"She was involved in a traffic accident Friday evening. She'll be OK, but she's pretty beat up."

"I'm sorry to hear that. I like her. She tries to act tough, but she is really funny. Tell her I will be glad to help out if she needs anything." Laura Toombes was showing genuine compassion. Craig liked that.

"Thank you. I'll tell her. I'll call you tonight when I leave town. Can I bring anything?"

"Just bring yourself."

During the drive back to the office, it was hard for him to keep his mind on his duties. The plows had worked all weekend to clean up the streets, which had received more than a foot of snow. All the main roads and streets were clear now and the crews were working on the side streets. He turned on Muldoon Road and made his way back to the office. His schedule had been easy when Karen was in charge, but now it was up to him to keep the case alive. He spent most of the day organizing his work. He made a list of questions to be asked and answered. The captain had passed on some of Karen's administrative duties that would need his attention.

Late in the day his cell phone rang. It was Carlton who advised him that the crew was planting seeds in cups, which would be transplanted to the growing trays after the seeds sprouted. Craig made a note and began to close up for the day. He wanted to see Karen, but mostly he was anxious to drive to Eagle River and see Laura.

The people in the office had all signed a get-well card Craig was to deliver to Karen. When he arrived in her room, he found her asleep. He added water to her flowers, dropped the card on her table, and left again. He noted the swelling in her face had gone down even more than this morning. That's a good sign, he thought.

In his personal vehicle, he headed for Laura's place. This time of day, it would take at least a half hour. He called to tell her he was on the way, and then stopped at a neighborhood liquor store and bought a bottle of red wine to go with dinner. The porch light was on when he arrived.

He tapped on the door. It opened almost immediately. She looked ravishing. He stepped inside and she closed the door behind him. He turned to say hello and was met with arms around his neck and a wonderful kiss on his lips.

When she backed away, he said, "You do have a nice way of saying hello."

It was late when he drove back to town and his own apartment. It had been a wonderful evening.

Tuesday morning came early. He showered, dressed, and drove to the hospital. Karen was sitting up in bed expecting him.

"I see you came by last night," she commented. "Sorry I missed you."

"You needed the rest more than you needed to see me," he replied. "Are you feeling any better?"

"A lot better," she informed him. "I'm not as sore and stiff as I have been. The swelling is going down and I'm walking better. That was a nice card the office bunch sent. Thank them for me, would you?"

"I will, but they know already." He studied his hands a minute. "How soon before they will let you come back to work?"

"Next Monday," she said. "No flying for a month, though."

"When will they let you out of here?"

"I am hoping for tomorrow. The doctor said he would see how the bruising was responding and, if there is no sign of clotting, I will be able to get out of here. Can I call you for a ride home?"

"I'd be hurt if you didn't." He meant it. "The case has come to a standstill without you."

"What's been happening since I came in here?"

"Oh, no," Craig chided. "You don't go back on the payroll until next week. Next week we will talk about it."

"Are you still seeing the skinny blond?"

"As a matter of fact I had dinner at her place last night. I forgot to get the name of her hairdresser for you."

"How could you have forgotten a thing like that?" she laughed.

"If you are going to start on me about my date, I'm leaving for work. See you tonight. Call me when you need a ride. Glad to see you're feeling better."

They each smiled and waved as Craig made his way to the door. At least her sense of humor is intact and not bruised. I hate to admit how much I miss her teasing, he thought.

CHAPTER 27

The week had been uneventful and unproductive for Trooper Craig Stanton. Carlton had called twice, but added nothing to what they already knew. Karen's administrative duties, handed him by the boss, were keeping his time filled. He had driven Karen home early in the week and had checked on her twice a day since. She was a good partner, a good friend and she used her brain. Stanton admired her intellect and, though he complained, enjoyed her sense of humor.

Friday evening he volunteered to cook dinner for the two of them at her place. The weather had warmed to a plus 20 degrees and had not showed in three days. Stanton heated the gas grill on the back deck and marinated steaks. He had not brought wine, thinking it may react to the medications Karen was taking. Karen constantly asked what was happening at the office and Craig continued to put her off. "Monday," he would say.

Her facial bruising was fading and she covered it well with make-up. She had a slight limp when she walked but did her best to disguise it. After dinner, he offered to drive her to Girdwood to the ski resort just to get her out, but she refused. She said she was tired. Stanton said good night and left her alone.

After Craig, left she put on a set of sweats and began to exercise. She started with sit-ups, push-ups and stretching exercises. She found the pain to be stronger than her endurance, and she was sweating profusely within a few short minutes. She took it as long as she could tolerate before pouring and gulping a large glass of water. After a hot shower, she stood in front of a full-length mirror and surveyed the yellowing bruises that extended from her cheek to her ankle.

"You're a fine mess, aren't you, girl?" she said to herself. "But you will be back on the job on Monday, Good Lord willing."

Through the weekend she exercised even more and for longer periods. She was getting stronger and the stiffness was going away. It had been three days since she had taken any medication for the massive headache she was suffering. The doctor had been right; she needed a week of rest to heal and rebuild her strength.

There was a knock on her front door at seven o'clock Monday morning. She answered, dressed in a new uniform, to see Craig Stanton waiting to take her to the office.

His first words were, "Have you had breakfast yet?"

"I had a glass of juice," she said. "Let me get my jacket and we can go."

Stanton drove south on the Old Seward Highway past O'Malley Road to a little local restaurant with a great breakfast. The place is old, as is the owner, Judy, but the waitresses are friendly and seem to know all the customers by name. They ate breakfast without much conversation, and Karen found she was hungry after all.

On the drive to the office, Craig informed Karen that she was the proud owner of a new work vehicle, a GMC, SUV. He had transferred all her personal gear to the new vehicle.

"The vehicle was previously a K-9 unit and I didn't know if you wanted me to take off the K-9 decals, you old dog." He laughed at his own joke.

"Leave them on, at least until I get a new partner," was her quick reply.

The captain met her in her office when they arrived. "Welcome back, Karen."

"Glad to be back, Captain." She found a huge bouquet of flowers on her desk and a banner on the wall reading "WELCOME HOME." One by one, the dispatchers and receptionists came to her office to repeat the message.

When the crowd cleared and she and Craig were alone, she looked at him with watery eyes. "I don't know how I would have managed without you, Craig, thank you for everything you did. I'll never forget it."

He looked at her, grinned, and scuffed his foot on the floor, looking down at his feet. "Aw shucks, Ma'am. It weren't nothin'."

There was a new coffee cup on her desk. It had the trooper emblem and her name printed in gold. She picked it up and admired it.

"A gift from the gals out front," Craig informed her.

Under the cup was a note for her to call Goodyear. She picked up her new coffee cup and walked down the hall to fill it for the first time. It was nice to be back among her friends.

She checked her watch and decided she had time to sift through the stack of paper on her desk. Craig had organized and filed most of the stack and left her a note with the items listed. By the time she finished it was time to call Sam Goodyear. When he answered, he cut her off and asked to come to her office. She agreed to the meeting, dialed Craig, and asked him to come to her office for the meeting.

Fifteen minutes later Goodyear appeared at her door, a visitor badge hanging from his lapel. "Good morning, Sergeant. I heard about your accident. Are you feeling OK?"

"I once crashed an Apache Helicopter in the Kuwait desert. That was worse."

Goodyear didn't know what to make of her response, but let it pass. "I have some news for you today," he said, smiling. "Your locate-only bulletin on Ken Whittle— we found him. He is living in a cheap hotel room in New Orleans. He's keeping to himself and spending a lot of time and money at the floating gambling hall on the river. We don't have anything to arrest him on, but we think the money he is gambling away may not be his."

"We can't make him a full-time job, but we will try to keep him located," Goodyear said. "Another thing, your mystery pilot, Moose, we found him. Mosely Cain. He is living with a woman in New York City. He has another pilot making the run this week while he lies around with his girlfriend. Local agents were grateful for the information. The name tied together another case for them. He is suspected of being the supplier in a huge pipeline of cocaine and heroin. What may interest you is the fact that he is the main supplier of very high quality marijuana on the streets of New York. Your local growing operation may be the source of that marijuana. I can't believe how many doors you have opened for us with the information you gave me. Congratulations to the two of you. I am grateful."

"Have you found out anything about the pipeline to the West Coast?" Karen asked.

"Not yet, but we're working on it."

"What about the Amarada Cargo plane? Is it scheduled to land in Fairbanks on this trip?"

"The New York office told me he is taking a southern route and will be entering the U.S. at San Francisco. Maybe Moose doesn't trust his pilot with drug deliveries or maybe it's just the regular route, we don't know," Goodyear said with frustration in his voice.

"Sooner or later they all slip up," Karen advised. "We just have to be patient until they make a mistake."

Goodyear lifted himself out of his chair. He was surprisingly agile for a man of his girth. "I have to get back to the office now, but I wanted to give you the update and personally check on your recovery. Glad you're back on the job, Sergeant." With that he left her office.

After he had gone, Craig looked at Karen. "I don't think we can wait for them to make a drug case in their office. I think we need to put some pressure on Dunn." He gave her his best "I've got a secret" grin. "I have been saving a bit of news for you. The other night when I had dinner with Laura she mentioned that Dunn was getting calls on his cell phone from someone she had, at first, thought was two different people. She said whoever it is has two first names. He is either James Melvin or Melvin James. Carlton said Melvin James is the new crew boss at the Palmer grow site. How is that for good news?"

"And all this time I thought you two only talked about her hairdresser," Karen quipped.

"Mostly we do, but now and then we work on something else."

"How are we going to confront him with this without giving up our source or ruining our camera surveillance at Palmer?" It was less a question than just thinking aloud.

"I don't know yet, but the important thing is we have the information. How would it work if we asked him if he knows Melvin James? We can say his name came up in an investigation. It might make him nervous enough to make a mistake."

"I'll have to think about that one for a while." Karen was being cautious. "He has two very lucrative businesses to run, one legitimate and one not. I don't think he will run unless he thinks we will arrest him. But remember, we are still short on evidence. I think we can push him a little, but if we get too accusatory, there is a good chance he will run. He has money and he has a turbine powered airplane to run with."

"I guess I just expected things to be simple." Craig paused a moment and added, "What are we going to do about Whittle? He may stay in New Orleans until his money runs out."

"I haven't thought that one out either." She smiled at him. "It must be the blow on the head. It slowed me down." She got up from her desk and said, "Let's take a look at my new car."

Late in the afternoon Karen was beginning to ache throughout her entire body. She was starting to think she had returned to work too early. She had taken one of the pills her doctor had prescribed and was sitting at her desk with the overhead light off when her desk phone rang.

"Sergeant Holmes," she answered.

The accent on the other end of the phone was so thick she could barely understand him. "Offsuh Holmes, this is DEE-tective Boudreaux of the NO'lins PO-lice. Are you the one who was looking fo' a man name a Whittle? Ken Whittle?"

"Yes, detective. I have a locate-only bulletin out on him. I understand he is in your city."

"Yessum. He's he-a. Only thing is he got hisself killed. Somebody jus walk up behind him and stuck a knife in his back," Detective Boudreaux reported.

"Someone stabbed him?" She sat up and turned on her desk light. "When did this happen?"

"Jes 'bout a hour ago. Looks like he left his hO-tel to go gamblin' and somebody walked up behind him on the street and stuck him. He dead now fo' sure."

"Have you checked out his hotel room?" Karen asked.

"Yessum, we did that, but somebody beat us to it. Somebody tore his room all apart before we got there. They mussa been lookin' fo somethin' by the look of it." Boudreaux then asked, "What was you wantin' us to keep an eye on him fo?"

"He is a witness in a murder case here in Alaska. He is a trapper and one day he just packed up and left town. We just wanted to know where he went."

"Well, somebody found him 'fo you did. Give me yo' mailin' address and I will send ya'll a copy of the report."

She gave him her office address and thanked him for notifying her.

"Some DEA agents were asking around about him. I asked why and they say 'cause you wanted it, tha's hows come I called you. If we find out anything', ah'll give you a call." With that, Boudreaux hung up the phone.

She punched the intercom button for Stanton's desk and asked him to come to her office right away.

When Stanton came in, she related the entire conversation, with graphic accent. When she finished she looked at Craig and asked, "Do you get the feeling we are operating behind the curve? Every time we get a lead, something happens. We hear about Bettis and he winds up dead. We suspect Whittle of stealing money from the wreck and he takes off. When we find him, someone kills him. Something isn't right with this case."

"I don't want to make you feel bad, Karen, but you don't look like you can care much about any of that right now. You need to go home and get some rest."

"That's where I was headed when that phone call came in."

"Do you want me to drive you home?" he asked.

"No, I have a new car. I'll drive myself home, but thanks for the offer. See you in the morning." She turned out the desk light and slowly pulled herself out of her chair.

Stanton watched her walk down the hall, noting that she winced with every step.

When Stanton arrived the next morning, Karen was in her office. She looked rested, but Stanton vowed to himself to get her out of the office early.

"Good morning, Boss. How are you feeling this morning?" he asked.

"Much better, thank you. It was a very long day for me yesterday. I learned I am not as strong as I thought I was. I may quit early today if I start to wear out."

"I think that is a very good idea. Those bruises are healing, but I'm still worried about blood clots." Stanton could see the concern in her eyes also.

"How would you like to take a drive to Eagle River this morning? I think you were right yesterday when you wanted to press Dunn. Let's go up there and pay him a visit. I'll have a conversation with him while you visit with the skinny blond."

"It's tough duty, but I can handle it," Stanton admitted. "How do you intend to approach Mr. Dunn?"

"I'm going to use your suggestion and hit him with the names of Don Bettis and Melvin James to see how he reacts. He will deny knowing them, of course; but I want to try to draw him out, to get him to volunteer something."

"When do you want to leave?"

"He doesn't seem to like getting to work at an early hour, so how about an hour from now?"

The two troopers saw Dunn's SUV in front of the office when they arrived. Karen was walking on the snowy sidewalk and up the stairs with careful steps, consciously trying to avoid a fall. Entering the office, they said "Good morning" to the tall blond secretary and asked to see Mr. Dunn. Craig said he would wait out front for Karen. Laura flashed him a big smile when he said he was waiting with her.

Dunn opened his office door to welcome them. "Come in, Come in," said Dunn.

"I'll just wait here," Craig offered.

"I'll just be a few minutes. I know Mr. Dunn is a busy man." With that, she followed Anthony Dunn into his inner office.

"Have a seat, Sergeant Holmes. What can I do for you?"

"I just want to ask you about a couple of names that have come up during our investigation. You have been so helpful in the past. I hope we don't offend you." She gave him a friendly smile. "We are still investigating the death of Jack Boardon and some of his employees names have come up during the interviews. You have said you knew or knew of, Don Bettis, the man killed in the robbery attempt a Big Lake."

"Yes, I didn't really know him, but he was some sort of crew boss for Jack. But then, I have told you that."

"And I appreciate your help, Mr. Dunn. We have had another name come up. He, too, worked for Jack Boardon. The name is Melvin James. We have no indication he has done anything wrong, but your friend Jack had a large amount of marijuana with him when he crashed. This leads us to believe he may have been involved in the sale of drugs. Have you ever suspected your partner of anything illegal?" Karen was prodding him.

"Heavens, no. Jack was my friend. He was my business partner in a number of properties. I told you we served in Kuwait together. We were close. I may be wrong, but I think if he were involved in something like that I would have heard about it." He had said nothing new.

"I don't know how this name fits in, but there is a man by the name of Mosely Cain somehow affiliated with Jack Boardon. I am told he owns a large cargo plane and flies all over the world. Do you know him?" Karen was testing him again.

Dunn rubbed his chin vigorously before answering. "When Jack and I were in the military, flying A-10s, there was a guy we used to drink with, a transport pilot. I think his name was Mosely Cain. We called him Moose. Boy he was a big man. I haven't seen him in years. I can't speak for Jack." He massaged his chin again. "Was he involved in some illegal business with Jack?"

"I really can't say, Mr. Dunn. I am just following up on a name that came up in the course of the investigation. This whole thing is truly baffling. No one who knew him ever heard of him doing anything illegal or mysterious, yet Jack had all that marijuana in his plane when he died. I just can't figure it out."

"I wish I could help you out, Sergeant, but if Jack was involved in something illegal, I am not aware of it," he said, looking innocent.

While Karen was talking with Dunn, Craig was doing the same with Laura Toombes.

"Do you really like me or are you just using me to get to Mr. Dunn?" she asked.

"I really do like you, and I want to spend a lot more time with you, but as long as you are a principle in our investigation I am not allowed to have personal contact with you. I have already bent the SOP. I promise, though, as soon as this case is resolved I plan to spend a lot more time with you." Craig's excuse was genuine.

"The sergeant doesn't like me, does she?" Laura asked.

"Ah, don't worry about her. She just likes to heckle me about you. She is a wonderful partner and a very smart person. Did you know she is a helicopter pilot?"

"Wow! She must be smart. I have to give her credit for that."

"I think she is just a little resentful of how beautiful you are," Craig added.

"Do you think I'm beautiful, Craig?"

"You know I do. I promise to call you as soon as I can." The door to Dunn's office was opening. He quickly blew her a kiss and stepped away from her desk.

As the troopers walked toward the door, Laura called to Karen. "The Curling Iron," she said. "Mindi Carson."

Karen turned around, puzzled, "What?"

"My hairdresser is Mindi Carson at The Curling Iron," Laura said again.

"Thanks, Miss Toombes. I'll call her."

Karen carefully traversed the steps and walk.

In the car Craig asked, "Well, how did it go?"

"I'm not sure, but I think the needle made it under his skin. It rattled him a little when I asked about Melvin James and Mosely Cain. We will have to wait and see what it brings, but it clearly unsettled him for a few seconds."

"Did we learn anything?"

"Perhaps. He mentioned that he and Jack met Mosely Cain while serving in Kuwait. Cain was a transport pilot. The three of them used to drink together in those days. That tells us that he, Dunn, is acquainted with every name on our list. It isn't good enough to get him into court, but he is sinking in a quicksand of circumstantial evidence.

CHAPTER 29

Dunn watched from his office window as the two officers left the parking area in front of Eagle River Realty. Once he was certain the troopers had left his office, he took his cell phone from his pocket. He dialed a local cell number and waited.

"Hello," a sleepy voice answered.

"Mel, its Tony Dunn. Wake up and listen." He heard shuffling on the other end and suspected Melvin James was still in bed.

"OK, Mr. Dunn. I'm up. What do you want?" James asked.

"I just had a visit from the Alaska State Troopers. Among other things they asked me about you. They wanted to know if I knew who you were. I told them nothing, but what I want to know is what have you done to put them on your trail? Have you been drinking again?"

"No, Mr. Dunn. I'm finished with that life. I don't know why they were asking about me?"

"I want an anonymous operation up there. I'm warning you if you become a liability and bring the law around our operation I'll dump you. You got that?"

"Yes, sir, Mr. Dunn, but I haven't done anything to call attention from the troopers. I hardly ever go to town and I stay around here when I'm not at the greenhouse. There isn't any reason for them to be asking about me." He suddenly had a thought. "Mr. Dunn! Could someone be talking? I mean someone working here. Could someone be talking to the cops?"

"I suppose that's possible, but whatever the reason, find out and fix it. And, do it quick. The new warehouse will have power by tomorrow and I want it planted by the end of the week. We have a business to run. Get out of bed and go run it, or I'll replace you with someone without a public image." Dunn punched the end button cutting the conversation off.

His next call was to a cell phone in New York. It was answered on the second ring.

"Moose," came the short answer.

"Moose, Tony Dunn."

"Hey, Tony, how are things in Alaska?"

"They've been good until this morning. I just had a visit from the troopers. They asked about you. More specifically, they asked if I knew you. I told them we had met in Kuwait, but that I hadn't seen you in years. They didn't pursue it, but I thought it was strange for them to ask at all. They were asking in regard to Jack. They are still investigating his death."

"That is strange, but maybe they are just checking on a list of names they came up with and my name came up along with yours."

"I hope so," Dunn said. "What about that other problem? Are you going to be able to do something about that?"

"Already done," Moose said with a little pride. "I have a man in New Orleans who does that kind of work. I called him and he took care of it yesterday. Your cash, or what's left of it, is on the way to you by Fed Ex."

"That was quick work," Dunn said, sounding relieved. "By the way, we will have the second greenhouse on line by the end of next week and I just closed on a property I will use for the next one. This guy, Melvin James, is a whiz. He says he can speed the grow time and increase the THC level by making some adjustments in the timers and the type of fertilizer we are using. He already changed the humidity settings. If he is correct with his adjustments, we will have a new crop ready by the end of May. In the meantime we are looking at another planting date for some other properties and if all that takes place as it should, we will be able to turn out a crop of roughly a ton every six weeks."

"It all sounds good, but I don't like my name coming up with the troopers. Try to find out where that came from."

"I have to ask this, Moose, but with these new greenhouses being set up I am running short of cash. Is it possible for you to front me a delivery in the meantime? I can pick it up as usual, ship it south and pay for the product within a few days." Dunn hated asking, but Jack had left him short.

"You know this is a cash only business, Tony, but in this case I understand." He was thinking, then said, "I can front you a shipment, but it won't be the usual amount. Half. Half the usual amount up front and only this one time. We have been friends a long time, Tony, and I want to stay friends. You understand. You know how it is."

"Yes, I understand, and I appreciate it. It's just that buying all this property and setting them up has run me dry," Dunn explained. "Thanks."

"I'll call you and let you know when to pick up the stuff," Moose said before hanging up.

———

Karen sat quietly on the trip back to Anchorage. She was thinking about Ken Whittle and his untimely demise. This was all a drug related case, so it didn't surprise her that when Whittle left town someone would be looking for him. Karen had sent out a nationwide locate-only bulletin on him and he had turned up rather quickly. How would someone outside the law enforcement community find him that quickly? Whittle had been running. It wasn't likely he told anyone where he was going or how long he would be gone. The fact that he'd been killed on the street meant the killing could have been random, but after someone killed him they also searched his room. That made it a planned act. What made him so important?

This entire case had been this way, Karen thought. Whittle had obviously stolen something out of the wrecked Cessna. What? Probably cash. Don Bettis had tried to recover the stolen money and had been killed in the attempt. Who had sent him? Whittle had felt enough at risk to run, taking the money with him. Somehow he had been located in New Orleans. They had waited for him on the street, stabbed him, robbed him and then searched his room. Probably found the cash and fled. Something about it just wasn't right in the sergeant's mind.

She was deep in thought about this case. Our Mr. Helpful, Anthony Dunn, is acquainted with almost everyone whose name appears in this case. He knew Bettis; he knew Boardon; he knows Mosely Cain; and he has connections all over the world through his past military career. But so far there is not one shred of evidence to tie him to any of those names with the exception of Jack Boardon, and Jack is in no position to talk about it.

Our only witness is Carton Lieber. Unreliable at best, but he is still feeding information, incomplete probably, to us. The only solid thing we have is the camera surveillance at the new greenhouse in Palmer.

It is important that we find out how the bad guys found Ken Whittle. There has to be a leak somewhere. They didn't figure it out on their own, but who would have given out that information?

"You are being awfully quiet," Stanton commented, interrupting his sergeant's thoughts.

"Sorry, just thinking. I have been going over the facts in this case and nothing adds up. When we think we have one thing, Whittle, figured out, he ups and gets killed. It was damned inconsiderate of him."

"Mind if I ask a question about Whittle?" Stanton asked.

"Go ahead. I have been asking myself a lot of questions I can't answer, one more can't hurt."

"My question is how did Whittle get found in New Orleans? This wasn't just some tourist getting mugged. They found him and killed him. Probably for the money he took from Jack Boardon. We had 50,000 cops looking for him and they found him as fast as we did. Doesn't that strike you as more than a coincidence?"

"Stanton, you amaze me. That is one of the questions I have been sitting here asking myself." She was grinning and shaking her head. "How about this? You told your skinny blond; she told her boss; and he told one of his old war buddies to off Whittle in Louisiana?"

"I know you are joking, but I think it happened just about like that. Not me or Laura, but someone with the information passed it to someone who had him killed."

"You're right, Craig. I think the same thing." She was grinning again. "Think about it. It's always about a profit. Who is making a profit? In this case, you are the only one. You ended up with a cute blond girlfriend and everyone else lost everything."

"So, you really do agree she's cute?"

"She can't be all bad. She gave me the name of her hairdresser."

They pulled into the office just in time to end the jokes.

<h1 style="text-align:center">CHAPTER 30</h1>

Late in the afternoon FedEx delivered the report from New Orleans Police Department. It was short with the medical report attached. Single knife wound to the back near the spine. Long slender blade, like a commando dirk, Karen thought. The wound was clean, in an upward motion, cutting the aorta. Death came quickly for Whittle.

The report stated the contents of Whittle's pockets were scattered on the sidewalk and his wallet was missing. Since the attack came only yards from the entry to the hotel, they checked with the desk clerk and were able to identify the victim. A records check on Whittle turned up the locate bulletin.

By the time local police checked the hotel room, it had been ransacked. The disarray ended at the dresser, so it was assumed that whatever the intruder was looking for was found in the dresser.

The report concluded by saying NOPD had contacted Sergeant Holmes of AST, who had filed the locate-only bulletin, to report the death.

The report also stated there were no known suspects and attributed the death to a mugging, common to New Orleans streets.

Karen put the report on her desk and leaned her head back to think. Her head was aching again. New Orleans police didn't have much to go on and didn't seem to find it unusual that the victim's room was searched before the police arrived. She had to admit to herself that it was possible the killer found the hotel room key in Whittle's pocket and used it to enter the room knowing the resident was dead and just hoping to find something valuable. Karen didn't like that scenario at all. Everything pointed to an assassination. The knife used wasn't a small switchblade. In the words of the medical examiner, it was a commando type dirk and the stab wound indicated a trained professional had used it. No, thought Karen, this wasn't a coincidence or random chance. It was planned and carried out for a purpose. The money!

Karen called Stanton to come to her office where she gave him the report to read. She waited until he had finished to ask what he thought.

"I don't think I can draw the same conclusion they did. This wasn't a mugging," he said.

"You know, Craig, I like having you around because you agree with me a lot," Karen commented. "At first I didn't think much of having a partner to watch out for me, but the deeper this case gets the more I think the captain was right. We are dealing with ruthless people. Not just local drug dealers, but with a nationwide, or even worldwide, syndicate populated with ruthless people. Think about it. Someone from here had to have contacted someone in the Lower 48 to get to Whittle and kill him. Whoever sent the killer had inside information in locating him. That wasn't a coincidence. It had to come from information generated by our locate bulletin. This had to have been done by someone with enough reason and contacts and enough money to carry out an assassination half a continent away. These people are scary."

Stanton was thoughtful for a moment then asked, "Do you have any thoughts about who might have given out the information on Whittle's location?"

Karen was shaking her head. "I have thought about it a lot. Logically, it had to be someone connected with this case. My gut tells me it's someone connected to Dunn. Dunn has friends everywhere. Dunn was partnered with Boardon. Dunn, according to Lieber, met with Moose Cain in Fairbanks. Dunn hired Bettis and now this Melvin James. They are marijuana cultivators working for Dunn. There has been a new greenhouse started in Palmer, owned by Dunn. Everything points to Dunn. Someone in our chain is affiliated with Anthony Dunn. As I see it, that is the only way Whittle could have been found and killed." She shook her head again and smiled. "It has to be you and your girlfriend."

"If you don't quit blaming me and Laura for all your unknowns, we won't name our first-born child after you."

"You know what I mean, Craig. I'm frightened. There are three people dead in this case already. The last one, Whittle, was killed by someone with inside information. That means someone on our side is passing on information. That frightens me. Who can we trust? We have to find out where the leak is and plug it."

"You're right, Karen. I don't mean to take your thoughts lightly. I agree 100%. I do think, however, that we should get the captain on our side," Stanton said, giving Karen a concerned look.

She dialed the intercom and asked to see the boss. He said he would be in her office in one minute.

Captain Davis is a lanky, handsome man with dark wavy hair. His uniforms always have a knife-edge crease in the sleeves and pant legs. The man is a professional police officer, top to toe. When he enters a room, he defines the word authority. That feeling presented itself at Karen's office door less than a minute later.

Karen gave him a summary of the police report on Whittle and listed her concerns. The first concern in her mind was the leak within her own ranks. It had shaken her trust in the people she worked with and with whom she shared information.

"We need more evidence before we can arrest Dunn," Davis said. "I agree the first matter of importance is the leak within our chain. Do you have any feeling for where the leak could be?"

She looked at Stanton and grinned. "No, sir. I wish I did. I don't think it was a random find by someone reading the locate bulletin. I think it was someone from here, Alaska, who called someone in the Lower 48. No one outside of law enforcement would have known about the locate bulletin. I can't think of anyone working with us who even knows Dunn. I have to admit I'm lost."

"Just a thought, Karen, but have you checked to see if Goodyear and Dunn are acquainted? It doesn't seem likely the information came from our department, and he is the only one outside AST who knew we were looking for Whittle." The captain's question hit her hard.

"Oh, my gosh!" she exclaimed. "You don't suppose Dunn and Goodyear are old war buddies, too? His name never crossed my mind." She turned to Stanton. "Run a check on Goodyear's military history. See if he served in Iraq at the same time as Dunn and Boardon."

"I'm on it," he said, nearly sprinting from the room.

"Sorry I missed him on the list of possibilities, Captain."

"No need to apologize, Karen. I'm just a fresh eye looking at an old problem. You and Craig are doing an excellent job. I know how frustrating it can get when you can't seem to make all the pieces fit into place. Keep at it and something will glue it all together for you. They always make a mistake, always."

"Thanks, Captain. I will keep you updated on the progress, if there is any."

The captain stood to leave. "By the way, is Craig still seeing Dunn's secretary?" It caught her by surprise. "How did you find out about that?"

"I'm your commander. They pay me to know these things." He smiled and waved as he left the office.

Moments later Stanton returned with a printout in his hand. "Goodyear was an MP on the same base at the same time as Dunn. It looks like you were right about him having all kinds of connections."

"That links Dunn to all three killings. Now, how are we going to prove it?"

"I don't know, but while I was checking on Goodyear I had a call from Lieber. He wants to meet. He says there is another greenhouse starting up today."

Karen gave it some thought and said, "I think it's time we rocked Carlton's boat a little. Where do we meet him?"

"He wants to go to a burger joint on O'Malley Road, WeBe's."

"I know the place. Good spot. Good burgers. I guess he didn't want to go back to the Lucky Wishbone," she chuckled.

In the restaurant, they all ordered and sat down. Lieber seemed relaxed today. He also seemed hungry, only speaking between bites of burger and gulps of milkshake.

"These guys are really something. They are opening another greenhouse now and they told me the plan was to re-open at least two others they have used before. Mel James is pushing the crew hard." Carlton had another bite. "Another thing, Mr. Dunn called me and said he would be going to Fairbanks in a few days. He wants me to get the King Air ready to fly. Nothing to that, just fuel it up and give it a general inspection."

"What does he intend to do in Fairbanks, Carlton?" Stanton asked.

"He don't tell me that stuff." Carlton finished his milkshake. "I ain't no executive in his outfit, you know. I'm just a gopher. You guys have me doing more for you than I ever did for him, and he pays me."

Karen took the lead. "Anthony Dunn has not confessed to rigging anyone's airplane to crash, either, Carlton. At this point, you are on the hook for the murder of Jack Boardon. If you want to quit, we can always arrest you for murder."

During the drive back to the office, Stanton could not help laughing about the fear he had seen in Carlton's eyes when Karen said she would arrest him for murder.

Karen, too, snickered. "It's not entirely an empty threat."

"I know, but his reasoning powers leave him a couple of sandwiches short of a picnic. I thought he was going to wet his pants when you told him."

"I wish I could think of some way to put that same fear into Dunn. We need a plan," she said. "By the way, your little tryst with the skinny blond has reached the captain's desk. He mentioned it to me this morning. You had better cool it for a while"

Craig had the same fear in his eyes Carlton had shown. "You didn't tell him, did you?"

"You know better than that, Craig. But be careful."

CHAPTER 31

After she finished her shift for the day, Karen went to the gym to exercise. She quickly became aware that her body was not entirely healed. She worked hard at stretching exercises and made an attempt at the weight machine. Her left side ached. The weight machine gave her excruciating pain in her left shoulder. The stationery cycle made her left leg hurt too much and she had to quit. What started out to be a one-hour workout turned out to be ten minutes and a shower. She found she was limping as she walked to her vehicle. By the time she reached home, it was necessary to put an ice pack on her left shoulder.

Karen was sitting in her living room, sipping an iced tea when the phone rang. She tried to reach it with her left hand, but winced in pain. When she finally got the phone to her ear and said hello the party had hung up. She checked the caller ID and found it was Craig. She dialed him back.

He must have had the phone in his hand for he answered in half a ring. "Hello," he said gruffly.

"Hey, Craig, it's me."

"Sorry Karen. I was sitting here thinking about what you said about the captain knowing Laura and I were dating. I have been worrying about it all evening."

"You have nothing to worry about, Craig. If he intended to do anything about it, he would never have mentioned it to me. I think he wanted me to warn you. He wants you to know someone has seen and reported you, maybe an old boyfriend. If you are serious about this girl, then cool it for a while. Let her know you are caught between her and the SOP manual."

"I guess you're right. I would hate to jeopardize my career over this, but I really am crazy about this girl."

"Call her and explain the situation. If she cares about you, she'll understand. See you tomorrow."

"Yeah," he said and hung up.

She was about to go to the kitchen for another ice pack when the phone rang again. Checking the caller ID, she answered, "Hello, Lou."

"Hi Karen, how are you feeling?" Mankawitz asked.

"Not too well tonight, Lou, thanks for asking."

"What's the matter?"

"I went to the gym and quickly learned that my left side isn't healed yet."

"Want me to come over with a bottle of liniment?" Lou offered.

"Thanks, Lou. You are a true friend. I think I'll go to bed with an ice pack and read a while."

"Hope you get to feeling better. I'll call again the end of the week. Bye."

Karen hobbled to her bedroom and readied herself. Finally, she slid under the blankets, welcoming the warmth. She awoke two hours later. The light was still on and her ice pack had melted. She dropped the plastic ice pack to the floor and turned out the light, pulled the blankets around her shoulders and went back to sleep.

The next morning, she found she was able to walk without limping too badly and decided she would go to the office but would stay behind the desk the entire day.

It was mid-morning when Stanton came in. From the doorway, he could see the pain on her face.

"Are you sure you should be here today?" he asked.

"No, I'm not sure at all. I went to the gym last night and I overdid it. I'm paying for it today. Where have you been?"

"Take two hours off my time sheet. I met Laura and explained things to her. You were right, she did understand. I won't be seeing her until this case is resolved."

"You can have the two hours. I'll deduct it from the comp time you have coming. I think I may learn to like her, someday. I thought she was just looking at your uniform, many women does that, you know. The other thought is that she really is a blond and doesn't know any better. I guess I will have to take her to lunch and find out." She turned in her chair and winced with pain. "I won't be going out of the office today, Craig. What are you going to do?"

"I thought I might go up to Palmer and check out the new greenhouse addresses. Without you, I will have to be more cautious. But, I need to see how much activity each location is getting. I've learned there are five men on the crew with Carlton bringing supplies. I would like to know what they are doing at each location, too."

"Call me on the cell phone when you get to Palmer and stay in touch while you are there. Be careful."

"I will, Mom." When he left her office, he stopped to see the captain. He told the captain about his dates with Laura and the conversation they had this morning. The captain smiled and thanked him for his honesty.

"One other thing, Captain. Karen is not doing well this morning. Would you keep an eye on her for me?"

"Yes, Craig. I will."

It was a forty-minute drive from the office to the first farm in Palmer. There were no vehicles at the site, so Trooper Stanton drove to the big barn. There were fresh tire tracks leading up to the doors, and footprints in the snow going into the building. The doors were locked with a huge padlock. Not wanting to be found on the property, he climbed into his patrol car and left the area.

A short trip on the same arterial led him to the side road where the potato warehouse was located. Again, no vehicles were visible. He stepped out of the car to check the tracks. It was the same scenario as the other site. No one was there, but there was a lot of activity at the warehouse. He was climbing into his car when a white van pulled into the drive behind him blocking his exit. Craig waited as a tall, scruffy looking man got out of the van.

"What are you doing here," the man asked angrily. "This is private property."

"Yes, I know it's private property, but there has been a lot of vandalism in the area and I stopped to see if they had been here. It's just a welfare check," Craig said without smiling.

"Well, we haven't had any vandalism here. Now get the hell out."

Craig fished a card from his shirt pocket and handed it to him.

"That has my name and contact number, in case you have any problems on your property. By the way," Craig asked, "what is your name, sir, for my report?"

"It's none of your business, but I'm Melvin James. I'm the caretaker here."

"Thank you for your cooperation, Mr. James. You have a nice day, now, you hear?"

James moved his van and Craig backed his car out of the drive. "Nice to meet you, too, Mr. James. We will be seeing each other again soon," Stanton thought as he backed away.

Once away from the area Stanton pulled to the side of the road and dialed Karen.

"Sergeant Holmes," she answered.

"It's Stanton. I wanted to let you know I just met Mr. Melvin James. He came to the potato warehouse while I was checking it out. He's an unpleasant fellow. He was adamant about not wanting me around," Craig chuckled. "Do you think it was something I said?"

"You do have that effect on some people."

"I told him I was checking vandalism in the area. He seemed satisfied with that. I'm on the way back to the office now."

"Thanks for checking in, Craig. I worry about you."

"You didn't send any lunch money with me, Mom," Craig said facetiously.

"Come to the office and I will fix you a peanut butter and jelly sandwich."

"Bye, Sarge," he said.

Craig had several reports and a lot of activity reports to catch up on. With Karen on the injured list, it seemed a good time to do the office work. He found himself wishing something would happen to break the case. Patience was never his long suit, and while they struggled to find hard evidence, Dunn was still on the street. Three people had died as a direct result of this case and he hoped they could get resolution before anyone else was added to that list.

CHAPTER 32

Thursday morning Craig wandered down the hall to Karen's office. He was sipping a cup of hot coffee and eating a cake donut when he arrived.

"You are pretty selfish this morning, Craig. You didn't bring me a donut." It was a friendly morning greeting.

"You have been in that chair all week and I didn't think you wanted the calories," he replied.

"You are so thoughtful." She picked up her own new cup with her name on the side and took a long drink. "Do you have anything exciting for us to do today? I think I need to get out of the office and stretch my bones."

"I might, if you want to get out." He sat in the chair in front of her desk. "Lieber called a couple of days ago and said Dunn was going to Fairbanks the end of the week. It's getting toward the end of the week. I have been trying to figure out how to keep an eye on him in Fairbanks without notifying Sam Goodyear. If he is our leak, we would be tipping our hand. Do you have any ideas?"

"I've thought about that, too. I was wondering how many friends you still have on the drug team in Fairbanks?"

"I can muster a few," he said. "Do you have a plan in mind?"

"Not really, but we can come up with something."

"How about this? We get some of the Fairbanks drug unit to watch the deal go down, let him load the stuff and fly back to Anchorage. We pick up the surveillance here and follow the drugs. When he ships this package out of the state, we follow it and see where it leads. I know we stand a chance of losing the trail, but we have never had a trail before. The Fairbanks team will document the deal there. We follow the dope and when we pick up it up on the other end we have hard evidence on everyone." Stanton gave her his favorite grin. "And we all live happily ever after. Do you like it?"

"With a few refinements, I like it," she said. "Do you really think we can pull this off without Goodyear getting wise?"

"What have we got to lose?" He finished his coffee. "Think we can sell this to the captain?"

"There is no way he is going to let us follow the drugs down to the Lower 48, but he has friends in high places and I would be willing to bet he can get someone in California, or wherever the drugs go, to tail it to the distributor on the other end." She pushed her chair back and lifted her body out of it without showing pain. "Let's go talk with the captain."

An hour later, the plan was in place and the captain was on the phone to a California Drug Enforcement Bureau Commander. The arrangements were made, and with great anticipation, they waited for the call from Carlton.

Stanton got the call from his informant at 10 a.m. Friday morning.

"Trooper Stanton, this is Carlton Lieber. I just got word to have the King Air ready to fly at 4 o'clock this afternoon. What do you want me to do?"

"Did he ask you to go along today?" Craig asked.

"Not yet, but he don't like to get the plane out and put it away, so I think he will."

"Do what you would normally do. Would you usually go with him?"

"Sure, I like the trip and sometimes he buys me a good dinner when we get back." Carlton was bragging; it had only happened once.

"Have a good trip, Carlton."

"Thanks," Carlton said and hung up.

———

Dunn called his blond secretary into his office to inform her that he would be out of town for the rest of the day. He gave her a list of things to take care of while he was out and said he would see her on Monday. A few minutes later, he climbed into his SUV and drove away.

As soon as she saw him drive away, Laura Toombes took her cell phone from her purse and dialed Craig Stanton.

"I thought you might want to know that Mr. Dunn just left the office and said he would be out of town the rest of the day. He said he would be back on Monday," she reported when Stanton answered. "Does this help?"

"Yes it does, Laura. Thank you." He paused for an instant and said, "I miss you."

"I miss you, too," she replied. "Will I be able to see you soon?"

"Very soon, I hope. I will call you as soon as I can."

Craig rushed to Karen's office with the news. They called the captain to let him know, then notified the Fairbanks drug team.

"Let me call a friend at the NTSB and see if he can tell us when Dunn leaves and when he plans to return."

"Mankawitz," came the voice on the other end.

"Lou, Karen. I need your help."

"Anything for you, Love."

"Our suspect is going to fly his King Air to Fairbanks this afternoon and return later this evening. Is it possible for you to get his flight plans? We need to know when he plans to arrive in Fairbanks and when he plans to arrive back in Anchorage. Can you do that for us?"

"That should be simple enough, I'll call you back as soon as he files."

"Thanks a lot, Lou. You're a sweetheart."

She hung up the phone and looked at Stanton. "Now we wait," she said.

"I didn't know you were so friendly with Mankawitz," Stanton commented.

"Oh, yes, we have been friends for a long time," Karen said casually.

"Are the two of you an item?" Craig asked, with a smirk on his face.

"Not like you and the skinny blond," Karen replied without looking up from her desk.

"I'll tell you what, Sarge," Craig said. "I won't mention Lou if you promise not to mention Laura. Deal?"

"Deal," she replied. "Let's go to lunch and while we're out we can go to Lake Hood and take a look at Dunn's hangar. Try to find a good place to sit and watch."

Pipers Restaurant in the West Coast International Inn has great food and is close to the airport. They ate a big lunch and planned the evening activities. They tried to anticipate every contingency, but as they both knew, it was an impossible task. They talked by phone to the leader of the Fairbanks team, learning the location of Amarada Cargo's hangar. The team leader was familiar with the area. They were ready.

After lunch, they drove the scant mile to the other end of the lake and drove past the hangar. The airplane had not yet been taken from the hangar. The hangar, a huge yellow metal building with a paved parking ramp in front of the door, was across a road/taxiway from the end of the lake. Karen was acquainted with the owner and operator of an engine shop on the lakeshore. The shop's office window offered a perfect view of the front of Dunn's hangar. Karen talked to the owner who gave them permission to use his office. He also said they could park their car inside the shop, since all the mechanical crew would be gone for the day.

The two troopers were leaving the engine shop when Carlton Lieber called.

"Mr. Dunn wants to be ready to fire up the twin at five. It will take me a couple of hours to check everything out and be ready to go. He said he wants oxygen tonight, so I guess he's going at altitude. I'm on the way to the hangar now." Carlton was unusually succinct.

They returned to the office to confer with the captain. Item by item they went over the plan. Every conceivable move must be anticipated. They went over the plan, and then they went over several possible variations. When they thought they had covered everything Karen and Craig returned to the engine shop. They backed their car into the shop and closed the tall electric door. Craig started to bring a night vision scope, but since the area was well lighted, he dismissed the idea. The shop owner had furnished two chairs and a pot of coffee for them. He had also thought to turn off the lights in the office.

They took up their positions and watched as Carlton walked around the plane taking off pilot tube covers, removing gear leg locking pins and propeller covers—all the things a pilot should do himself. Carlton's truck was already inside the hangar, and at 4:36 p.m., Dunn drove his SUV inside and closed the doors.

Dunn had a short conversation with Carlton and the two of them climbed aboard the King Air. A few seconds later, the engine began to spin. The two troopers watched as the big twin taxied toward the North/South runway. It was clear to the north; they should have a beautiful flight.

Karen was watching the plane's lights fading to the north when her cell phone rang. It was Lou.

"Dunn just filed an in-flight flight plan," Lou announced. "Are you ready to copy?"

Karen wrote all the information down as Lou recited. She thanked him and said she owed him one.

Next, they called the Fairbanks team to let them know what time to expect the King Air. They thanked her and said the Amarada Cargo plane was due within the hour and they were set up on the stakeout.

"I guess we're ready." Karen said.

It was 7:26 p.m. when Stanton's phone rang. It was the Fairbanks' drug team reporting.

"Hi, Craig, Fred Williams. The Beechcraft is taxiing to takeoff now. We have the exchange on tape. No audio, but we have great video of Dunn and the big man from Amarada Cargo. We didn't see any money change hands, but they had a long discussion and Dunn waved to his man on the airplane to take the package. His man loaded the package and Dunn climbed aboard. Dunn waved to Moose before closing the door. It all seemed very friendly. At any rate, the King Air is just now taking off. If he flies directly to Anchorage he should be there in less than two hours. Thanks for the tip. We had no idea this exchange was a regular thing here in Fairbanks."

"Thanks for your help. Like I told you before, this is about more than a drug deal. We can't afford to have the DEA find out about what we are doing. We think a man was killed due to a leak and we suspect the leak is at the DEA office. I know you will, but watch that Amarada Cargo plane. We think it is a regular supplier and pipeline to the Far East. I'll let you know what happens on our end. Thanks, Fred. I owe you." Stanton had written several notes while talking and was scanning them after he hung up the phone.

"Dunn just took off from Fairbanks and probably headed here. That gives us time to find a sandwich, if you want one," Craig advised his partner. "Fred told me they got the whole transaction on tape. No audio, but good video."

"I hope this is the turn-around point in this investigation. We have spent a lot of time collecting information, but none of it is evidence. It's pretty frustrating." She paused then turned to Craig. "Let's go to Sea Galley and have a salad."

"I thought you would never ask," he said.

There wasn't much conversation during dinner. Both officers looked at their watches regularly. Forty minutes later they drove back to Lake Hood to park inside the engine shop. They had just settled in to wait when the King Air taxied to a stop in front of Dunn's hangar across the ramp from their vantage point.

They watched as the air stair lowered and Carlton climbed down. He entered through the man-door and moments later the huge bi-fold hangar door began to rise. Carlton backed his truck outside before the door reached the top. Dunn came from the plane carrying a box. With the hangar door open and the lights on, his movements were easy to see.

Dunn took the package to the rear of the hangar and placed it on a desk. Next to the desk, on top of a file cabinet was a long, white box with blue printing. Karen focused her binoculars to read the printing. "ALASKA FROZEN SEAFOOD" read the label. Dunn placed the package inside the seafood box, stuffed the ends with paper from the waste basket, put the foam insulated lid in place and covered it all with the cardboard box lid. He expertly taped, with clear cellophane tape, all the edges and ran tape around each end and the center. He inspected the job, and, appearing satisfied, he took something from the desk. Karen surmised it was a shipping label. He read it carefully and placed it on the top of the fish box. He took a sheet of yellow PERISHABLE labels from the desk and pasted them on every side of the box. He then carried the box to his SUV and placed it on the back seat. He climbed into the truck and backed out of the hangar.

By this time Carlton had attached the small motorized tow bar to the front wheel of the plane. Once Dunn's SUV was out of the way, he maneuvered the plane into place inside the hangar. Leaving the tow bar hooked to the plane, he turned out the lights and closed the door. Karen and Craig saw the two men talking before Dunn drove away. Carlton, in his old truck, followed Dunn down the taxiway/road.

It only took a few seconds to open the back door and drive the patrol car down the road behind them. They followed Dunn and Carlton to the downtown area where the two men went inside O'Sullivan's Restaurant. Craig found a parking place on the street and the two waited for their quarry to return. An hour later Carlton came out of the restaurant alone. He got into his truck and drove away. Five minutes later Dunn did the same. They followed Dunn to his home in Eagle River where he drove into his attached carport and took the box from his car before locking it.

Karen asked Craig to wait until the lights went out in the house before quitting for the day.

Initially both officers were quiet on the drive back to the office. They were nearly back into the city when Karen turned to her partner. "Well, what is your take on what we just witnessed?"

"Dunn is a very thorough man," Craig said. "I think he packaged and labeled that box for the next leg of the trip. We don't know when, but that fish box will be shipped somewhere soon. My guess is tomorrow. We will have to keep an eye on Anthony Dunn until he delivers it for shipping. I wish we could see the shipping label."

"I think you're right. We will have to be here in the morning, early. We can't afford to lose sight of the package. That box is our evidence, not only for the drugs, but it contains the motive for Jack Boardon's murder." She gave a long sigh. "How do you want to split the stakeout? Do you want the morning or afternoon shift?"

"I'll drop you at the office and you go home and get some rest. I want you in good condition and rested. I'll go back and watch his place tonight and follow him tomorrow. I'll call you if he goes anywhere except the office." His signal was on and he was turning into trooper headquarters.

"Thanks, Craig, I need the rest. I'm beginning to ache pretty badly. A soak in a hot tub and some sleep should take care of that." He stopped behind her SUV. "I'll call you in the morning."

Stanton filled a thermos with hot coffee at a quick stop store. He picked up a large bag of popcorn and a deli sandwich. Stakeouts are long and boring and this stuff will keep you awake, usually.

He parked on a street that was high above Dunn's place. It was unlikely the realtor would be checking above his own level for surveillance. Craig sat in the car eating junk food and listening to country music all night long. The sky was light when Dunn appeared in the morning. Stanton followed as Dunn's SUV moved toward the Glenn Highway. Both vehicles were moving toward the city when Craig's phone jingled.

"Where are you Craig?" Karen asked.

"Driving toward town," he replied. "I have no idea where he is going."

"I am at the office. As soon as he stops, let me know where and I will relieve you. You must be pretty tired by now."

"Wired on coffee and junk food, but I will be happy to give him to you. I need a shower."

"Call me as soon as he stops. See you in a little while." Karen was concerned about the physical and mental condition of her partner.

Ten minutes later, Stanton called her. "You aren't going to believe this. He's at Lilly's," he chuckled. "Good thing we aren't meeting Carlton there this morning."

"I'm leaving the office now and should be there in five minutes. Where are you parked?"

"In back of the store next door; I can see both traffic exits from here."

Karen was lucky and hit all the lights green. She made it in four minutes. When she pulled alongside his car, he stepped out and got into her new GMC.

Looking around inside, he commented, "Nice clean car, want to trade? Mine is full of candy wrappers and spilled popcorn."

She was amazed he was still in good humor after all the hours on the job. "Any hint of where he may go from here?"

"None. It's Saturday, I doubt he will go to the office. He's your problem now. I'm going home. Call me if you need me," he added.

A half hour later, Dunn came out of the restaurant. She followed him to a dry cleaning store and a super market. He stopped at his bank and put a card into the ATM machine. She saw him take money from the machine, but had no way of telling how much it was. The rest of the morning and early afternoon followed the same pattern. She continued to follow him at a safe distance, then a few minutes after two he turned toward the airport and his hangar. She stopped near a small building on the lake and watched him get out of his SUV, open the back door and take out the fish box. He carried it into the hangar through the small man-door. A minute later he came out again. When he drove away she was tempted to follow, but opted to stay with the drug package. Parking behind the engine shop and entering with the key from the night before, she sat at the same window she had occupied the night before and watched. There was no one in the shop and it was quiet. She made a pot of coffee and prepared for a long wait.

CHAPTER 34

Marshal Dillon, "Yes that's my real name," awoke in the downtown hotel used by most of the airlines to house their aircrews. Dillon was a product of the 60's. He was never sure about his father. The stories his mother told him kept changing. What he did know was that she had been a flower child in San Francisco protesting the Viet Nam war, burning bras and smoking weed. She had never seen a doctor while she was pregnant, only once did she go to a public health clinic to confirm she was pregnant. When her son was born, three young women from the commune attended as midwives and helped care for the baby in the early days. Television was a hot thing and Gunsmoke was the biggest thing on TV. It just seemed natural to name her son after her hero, Marshal Matthew Dillon.

When Marshal was only six months old, she left the commune and tried to find work. She found it necessary to abandon her flower-child trappings and become more conventional. Initially she waited tables in neighborhood restaurants, finding she had a certain affinity for the work. Marshal spent more time with sitters than with his mother in those days. As her skills improved, she found work in better establishments. As her pay and tips increased, she found better care for Marshal. They lived in a rented apartment on the hill overlooking the wharf. She stayed in that apartment for many years.

Marshal Matthew Dillon attended school nearby. He was a decent student, but a sickly child who missed a lot of school. While growing up he acquired a taste for aviation. He lived and breathed flying. At 19 years old, working for a furniture store delivering goods, he began to take flying lessons. He attended community college when he had the time and money, eventually getting an associate's degree. One of his flight instructors put him in touch with a school in Arizona that taught aviation. He was able to get into the school and worked his way through an Airline Transport Pilot certificate. Marshal flew for any small flying service or commuter airline that would hire him. Three years later he had enough hours in the pilot's seat to apply for a job with a rag-tag cargo airline. A year and a half later they went broke and he was unemployed.

While hanging out with some buddies at the San Francisco airport, he heard about Federal Express hiring pilots. He applied and was hired. He, like most pilots, started in the right seat as second officer. Dillon was a skillful pilot and soon progressed to the left seat. His appearance kept him from being a passenger airline pilot. In uniform he didn't exude the kind of confidence needed to keep the paying riders calm. At five feet five inches tall and 145 pounds, his uniform shirts always gapped at the neck and his hat rested on the top of his ears, making him look more like a misplaced schoolboy than an accomplished airline pilot.

Marshal Matthew Dillon was the first officer on the San Francisco-Seattle-Anchorage freight run. Flying the new Boeing 767, he looked out of place in the cockpit, but when he began flipping switches and starting engines, everyone knew he was an expert. The corporation had rewarded his skill and diligence with more responsibility. He was the check-pilot for the West Coast and was invited to regular staff meetings.

On this particular morning, Marshal Dillon hired a cab to return to the FedEx warehouse, a huge complex on the south side of Anchorage International Airport. Once there he asked for the courtesy car, an old Ford Bronco with FedEx signs on the doors. It wasn't much, but it was free to the air crews for local running around. Dillon started the Bronco and drove to the other side of the airport to a hangar near Lake Hood. He had a key in his pocket and opened the man-door to enter. He found a seafood box on the desk, picked it up and left the hangar, locking the door as he left. He tossed the box on the back seat of the Bronco and drove away, back to the warehouse. He tossed the box in a closet reserved for crew baggage inside the plane and commenced his pre-flight checklist.

Karen was half-asleep when the Bronco arrived at the hangar. She was surprised when the man driving an old FedEx Bronco had a key to open the hangar. Her binoculars in hand she read the license number on the Bronco. She wrote it in her notebook along with a description of the man driving it. Then she called Craig, who answered his phone immediately.

"The pick-up guy is here," she reported.

"I'm on my way. Stay with him."

When Dillon came out carrying the seafood box, Karen abandoned her seat in the shop and ran to her car. When the Bronco drove away, down the taxiway/road, she followed. When Dillon returned to the warehouse and parked the Bronco, Karen parked her SUV across the ramp near the old National Guard Headquarters. She watched Dillon carry the box to the big cargo plane, climb the stair and disappear inside.

She had her notebook out again, writing the aircraft number and times in it. Next she pulled her cell phone from her pocket and dialed her captain.

Captain Davis was at home when the call came.

"Captain, a FedEx employee picked up the package at Dunn's hangar and took it to an airplane parked at the FedEx warehouse. He is inside the plane now. I think he's a pilot."

"That's good news. Give me the aircraft number and I will notify my man in California. Good job, Karen. This may be the turning point in this case. Pass that on to Craig when you see him."

"I will, Captain. He's on his way down here now. Do you want me to check with the office over here and find out where this plane is headed?"

"That won't be necessary. The aircraft number will give them all they need to follow the flight," the captain said.

Ground crews had finished loading the plane and were closing the big cargo door by the time Craig arrived. He parked alongside Karen's SUV and slipped into the passenger seat.

"Anything new?" he asked.

"Nothing here, but I talked with the captain. The authorities in California are being contacted. Once the plane leaves here it will be up to them." She was apprehensive about losing sight of the evidence.

***

Twenty-five miles east of Anchorage, Anthony Dunn waited for a phone call. Marshal Dillon was to have picked up the package this morning. Once it was safely on the airplane, he was to have called Dunn. It was getting late and Dunn was becoming impatient. Dillon was scheduled to take off in twenty minutes. Trying to calm himself, Dunn went to the kitchen and heated water for a cup of raspberry tea. He was pouring the water in the cup when the phone rang.

"Yeah," he answered curtly.

"Tony, it's Marshal. I'm loaded and ready to take off. I'll call you when I deliver the package."

"Good. Try not to keep me waiting on the other end. You know what to do about the payment."

"Yes, sir, Mr. Dunn. Gotta go, my crew is coming aboard. Be talking to you later."

Relaxed now, Dunn took his tea into the living room and turned on the TV. The Bears and Packers were in the second quarter, tied. He kicked off his slippers and put his feet on the couch. He placed his cup on the floor and leaned back to watch the game.

Both Karen and Craig returned to the office as soon as the big Boeing 767 lifted off from the runway. The landing gear went up and a climb rate was established. It didn't take long for the FedEx cargo plane to disappear.

Back in the office, each officer transcribed their notes, copied them for the files, and met in Karen's office. It was not yet noon.

"You must be very tired, Sarge. Are you going home now?"

"Yes. It's been a long night and I need some sleep. What are you going to do?"

"Nothing. I am doing nothing. I think I will take a short nap and watch some football," Craig said in a weary voice.

"See you tomorrow," she said.

At home, she took a hot shower and piled into bed. She slept four hours and awakened refreshed. In the kitchen she fixed some toast and milk and ate while planning the rest of the day. She decided on the gym. She had overdone it the last time and she planned to be more careful today. She slipped into some sweats and headed to the gym.

She stretched for a while before stepping on the treadmill. She made it thirty minutes without ill effects. She drank some water and found an open weight machine. Five minutes on it made her shoulder ache, so, wisely, she stopped. She tried other machines, but ended her program on a stationary bicycle. It was a short session, but she made up for the extra time in the big blue hot tub, Soaking longer than her normal time turned out to be a wise thing to do. She showered and dressed and, during the short walk to her car, found she had few aches. Her body was beginning to heal.

Monday morning found her sorting through a mountain of memos and paperwork that had made its way to her desk during the weekend. Among the memos was one from Captain Davis, who wanted to see her when she came into the office. She called his office to see if now was convenient; it was. He had said to bring Stanton.

Minutes later, they were seated in front of his desk. "You two did a fantastic job over the weekend. I think we may have a motive for Boardon's murder. Let me back up a bit. That box the two of you tailed from Fairbanks to Anchorage and sat on all night, then tailed to the FedEx offices, was picked up again. The plane stopped in Seattle, but nothing happened. My friends on the King County Sheriff's

Department kept an eye on the pilot and the plane while it was on the ramp there. It took off again for San Francisco."

"I had drug units in both San Francisco and L.A. waiting. It was my friend in L.A. who learned where the plane was headed and set up the stakeouts. The name of your pilot is, now get this, Marshal Matthew Dillon. A scrawny little runt of a guy S.F.P.D. has had on the radar for a long time but could never catch him. They saw him take a frozen fish box from the plane and load it into his personal vehicle parked at the FedEx warehouse. He checked out and drove out the gate. His pilot's credentials have kept him safe for years. The pilot drove into town and met with a man in a suit on Fisherman's Wharf. Dillon lives near there and he went home. There must have been cash exchanged at that time, but the officers couldn't see it."

Captain Davis continued, "Another pair of S.F.P.D. officers followed the fish box. The suit went to a bar on the west side of town and took it inside with the officers in tow. They said it was beautiful. They followed the box right into the bar owner's office. These guys were so intent on looking inside the box that they never saw those two officers coming until all of them were in the office. The bar owner and the leman were both so shocked by the officers that they never said a thing. When my friend called this morning, the bar owner and the leman were in custody. The drugs had been tested and found to be one-kilo bricks of both heroin and cocaine. The two of you are responsible for putting a cork in a major drug import pipeline. Any questions so far?"

"Lots," said Karen. "First of all, how does this tie us to a motive for Jack Boardon's murder?"

"Try this," offered the captain. "Jack Boardon was meeting Moose Cain to make an exchange with four hundred pounds of marijuana and some cash. Jack was going into business for himself. He was trying to cut Anthony Dunn out of the loop and out of the profits. He called Dillon to set it up. Moose called Dunn to let him know what was happening. Dunn had Carlton Lieber rig the plane to run out of gas. It hasn't been confirmed, but Dillon has said there was $100,000 on the Cessna when it went down. The money belonged to Dunn. It's also the reason Don Bettis was sent to Whittle's cabin and probably why Whittle ran. We are still in the dark as to how Dunn found Whittle."

"They learned all this from that puny little pilot?" Karen asked.

"Yup! Moose Cain and Marshal Dillon have been friends for many years. Dillon says they met during a drug deal in Arizona. Since they are both pilots, they hit it off, remained friends and have since done a lot of business together."

"We still have nothing on Dunn except one more unreliable witness to testify against a respectable real estate agent. We can't arrest him yet," Karen said wearily.

"You are right, Karen, but we have enough to make him very nervous. I think we need to update Dunn on our progress. We have enough to arrest him on drug charges." Stanton wanted to put cuffs on the realtor in the worst way.

"I'm not sure that is a wise move." Karen was pessimistic. "We could arrest him and he would be out on bail before the day is out. He has a lot of money stashed someplace and a very fast turbine engine plane with which to retrieve it. He has the means to skip town and be gone forever."

Suddenly, Stanton sat up straight. "Carlton Lieber," he said. "When Dunn hears about the FedEx pilot being arrested, he's going to go ballistic. He may figure out Carlton is the leak in his kingdom and try to stop it up. Carlton may be in danger."

"I would have to agree with that," said the captain. "We had better take some steps to protect him. In the meantime copies of all these reports are on the way and when they arrive I will see you have copies, Karen."

"Thanks, Captain. Stanton and I will take care of Lieber." The two officers left the office, mulling over these latest revelations.

"How do you want to handle it from here?" Craig asked his partner.

They were in Karen's office, forming a plan. "We have enough evidence to call in the drug unit and take down the three greenhouses at Palmer. If we arrest the five workers and get Carlton at the scene, it may take some suspicion off him. That would put a crimp in Dunn's operation, and cost him a crop and a lot of equipment to say nothing of the properties themselves."

"Do you think he might get scared and run?" Stanton asked.

"He didn't run the last time his crew was busted. He just started a new greenhouse in another location. I'm not sure how long he can afford to keep on losing like this, but that's what he did last time." Karen stared at the ceiling a minute, then asked her partner, "Do you agree?"

"You have been right so far. I think I have to go along with you. How do you want to handle it?"

"That's what I was thinking about. Why don't we call the lieutenant from the drug unit and have him meet us here in my office?"

Stanton was nodding approval.

Lieutenant Bill Tolliver wasted no time getting there. "What's up?" he asked upon entering.

Karen and Craig gave him a rundown on the events of the last few days. Tolliver was busy scribbling notes in his notebook while they talked. Karen gave him an outline of her plan to catch all five of the greenhouse crew plus the foreman and Carlton Lieber. She wanted all seven at the scene when they made the raid.

Tolliver made a couple of adjustments to the plan and called his office to send a car to watch for the men. He warned the men he sent that all seven had to be present when it went down.

"I have a lot to do. I'll call you as soon as we have confirmation they are all on site."

"Here we go," Stanton said with a gleam of anticipation in his eyes.

"Indeed," replied Karen. "Here we go!"

CHAPTER 36

Craig Stanton was antsy. Waiting was never his long suit. He wanted to make something happen, but the plan was in place and waiting was all there was left to do. Karen, too, was uneasy.

"This is where things always go wrong," she thought. It was easy to see Craig was having trouble just sitting and waiting.

"Craig, what happens if, during the raid, one of the hired hands phones Dunn? What will he do?" It was an idle thought, but a valid point.

"He may decide to run. There is really no way to know. We can't just sit outside his office waiting for the raid to go down." Stanton was showing his frustration.

"We could call Carlton and have him find out when the crew is going to be at work. We could ask him to be there to tip us to a time and have the drug team there when they arrive." Karen was trying to get an advantage, but this was a risky one.

"Talking to Carlton makes me nervous. Let's get something to eat and talk about it," Craig suggested.

"That beats sitting here biting my nails."

The two officers left the office, making their way downtown and out C Street to the Outback Steakhouse. Craig ordered coffee and a burger with everything; Karen ordered a plate of hot wings and iced tea with lemon.

They both dug into their food as if they were starved, neither of them talking about the case. Craig quickly finished his sandwich and fries, wiping his lips and hands. He took a long drink of coffee and looked Karen in the eye.

"I must have been hungry," Craig commented.

Karen's hot wings were almost gone, too. "What do you think about my idea, calling Carlton, I mean?"

"I don't like it, but I can't think of anything better to do. It's difficult for me to trust Carlton," Stanton confessed.

"I know the feeling, but you are right. We can't just sit in front of Dunn's office and wait. We can wait until Tolliver's boys call, but maybe we can hurry the process by calling Carlton. If he knows we are trying to keep him alive and well, he may become more dependable." Karen knew she was rationalizing, but what was the gamble? "You realize the only thing we gain is time, our time?"

"One other thing bothers me, Karen. If Goodyear is our leak, he will soon know about the bust in San Francisco. He will surely call Dunn right away and, if the raid hasn't happened yet, Dunn may decide to clear out before the raid. Remember, we aren't after Dunn just for a drug deal; we want him for murder. That makes him a greater flight risk and much more dangerous."

"OK, Craig, you convinced me. When we get to the car, call Carlton. Find out when he expects the growers to be working and tell him he has to be there. We can pass that on to Tolliver and make a date with Dunn."

They split the bill and went to the car. The temperature was falling again. The slush in the parking lot was turning to ice that crunched under their feet. Karen started the SUV right away and started the heater to defrost the windows and make it comfortable to sit inside while they made the phone calls.

Stanton had Carlton on speed dial. He punched the buttons and waited. When Carlton answered, Stanton asked, "Where are you, Carlton?"

"I'm on my way to Palmer. What do you want?"

"I need to know when the whole grow crew will be working, all six of them."

"Right now, why?" Carlton asked.

"Which greenhouse?"

"The old potato shed, why?"

"Listen very carefully, Carlton. I'm trying to save your butt. This is the only way to keep you alive. Go to the potato shed and keep the crew there until my men arrive. Whatever you do, don't let on they are coming. You could be a victim before they get there. Understand?" Stanton hoped he had frightened Carlton.

He hung up and dialed Tolliver. "Bill, Craig Stanton. Get your men on the road. My guy is headed to the old potato warehouse now. He says the entire crew is there, working. Karen and I will head to Eagle River to keep an eye on Anthony Dunn. Call me on my cell phone if you need me, and let me know when we can go inside to pick up Dunn."

"Got it, Craig, good work. We are on the way now."

Karen called Captain Davis and brought him up to speed. Things were falling into place quickly.

Craig called Laura Toombes and, with what he hoped was an innocent voice, asked, "Hi, Laura, Craig. Is your boss in?"

"Yes, he has been in his office all afternoon. Would you like to speak with him?"

"No, thank you, Laura, and please don't mention I called."

"Sure, Craig, anything you want." She couldn't help but ask, "Will I be seeing you soon?"

"Very soon, babe. Gotta go now, but I will call you soon." With that, he hung up.

"He is in the office now." Excitement crept into Craig's voice. "We had better call for back-up. When they raid the Palmer greenhouse, we will need to have someone outside when we go into the office." He looked at his partner with another of his wicked grins. "This is going to be fun."

Two AST units responded to the call for back-up. Karen and Craig met them a few blocks from the real estate office. They instructed both men to follow to the office when they moved in. They were to stay in their cars unless summoned by Craig or Karen. They knew the drill. Now they all waited for word from Palmer and Tolliver. It seemed to take forever, but in reality, it was less than an hour. Tolliver contacted Craig on his cell phone.

"Great intel, Craig. Everyone was here and didn't know a thing until we came into the greenhouse. All seven are in custody and being transported as we speak. I have a crew here to inventory and seize everything," Tolliver chuckled. "Do you have any idea how big a growing operation this is? There must have been bigger busts, but it's the largest one I have ever seen. Nobody seems to know who the big boss is, but the crew boss isn't saying anything. He wants a lawyer. We are taking them to Post Street Correctional Facility for booking."

"Thanks for the report, Bill. We are going to the real estate office now to pick up Dunn. We'll let you know when that takes place."

Karen was looking at Craig. "Did they get all of them?"

"Yes, all seven. They are heading to jail now."

"Good, then let's make our move." She motioned out the side window for the other two cars to follow; she put her own SUV in gear and drove to Dunn's office. Karen and Craig marched, shoulder to shoulder, up the steps to the office door. Craig opened the door. Laura Toombes smiled broadly when she saw him.

"Is your boss in?" he asked.

"Yes, wait a moment and I will announce you."

"Please don't do that. We will announce ourselves." He then said quietly to Laura, "Please stay behind your desk in case there is trouble."

She nodded and sat back down.

Karen took the lead. She walked across the office, and without knocking, opened the door to a surprised Anthony Dunn.

"What do you want?" he said, irritated.

"Anthony Dunn, you are under arrest for the distribution and sale of dangerous drugs. Please step out from behind your desk."

He was reaching for the telephone when Karen clamped her hand on his wrist, stepped past the end of his desk and quickly pulled the wrist up behind Dunn's back. She had handcuffs on him before he could protest. She led him out of the office and pointed him toward her SUV. He was escorted to the car without a coat and placed in the back seat. Craig went back inside to talk to the secretary.

"Laura, Mr. Dunn is under arrest and we are taking him to the Post Street Correctional Facility for booking. He will be afforded a phone call when the booking is complete. I know this office is a busy place and you should continue to take care of business as usual until you are notified by Mr. Dunn or his attorney."

"Oh, Craig, I didn't know he was doing anything illegal. I don't want to be involved in anything like that. Do I have to worry about being involved?" Laura was nearly in tears.

"No, Laura, this doesn't involve you, and I hope it won't affect our relationship. This is why I wasn't able to see you. Do you understand?"

"Yes, I think so. Call me as soon as you can," she said.

He winked at her and nodded.

Dunn was silent as they drove him to jail.

CHAPTER 37

At the jail troopers requested all the prisoners be separated. They didn't want them having a conference to organize their story. Dunn was held in an attorney visiting room until the others had been booked and searched. One by one they were taken back to holding cells to wait for their chance to make their phone calls.

Dunn was cooperative during the booking process, taking it all in stride. After he was fingerprinted, and while cleaning the ink from his fingers, he asked to call his lawyer. Officers working the booking desk knew her well, a shapely brunette with the mouth of a sailor. Her name was Gweneth Hall. She was often called to the jail to represent people accused of dealing drugs. She was good at her job and managed to get most of her clients off without jail time.

Karen and Craig waited in an office, drinking coffee and chatting with jail personnel. Dunn had told them he would talk to them when his lawyer arrived. They waited an hour for her to show. All the while Dunn seemed calm and relaxed. Karen had seen this woman in action on prior occasions and learned it was her strategy to keep the officers waiting for a very long time before showing up and even longer while she met with her client before letting him talk with the troopers. She would likely tell Dunn to say nothing to the troopers. She would demand to know all the charges before she even saw her client. That's just how she operates, Karen had told Craig.

Finally, Hall was admitted to the attorney visiting room to confer with her new client. She seemed to know Dunn on sight. She entered the small room and closed the door behind her. Hall's briefcase had been searched and, once inside, she put it on the floor and opened it, taking out a yellow legal pad and ball point pen. The narrow window in the door allowed the officers to see inside, but they could not hear what was being said. The two troopers waited, drank more coffee and waited some more. Stanton was becoming impatient, but Karen calmed him down, telling him to sit down and wait.

Forty-five minutes later, Hall opened the door and motioned for Craig and Karen to come in.

"My client wants to know what he is charged with," she stated flatly.

"Transporting dangerous drugs for sale. The quantity is large and he will be considered a major drug dealer," Karen announced.

"You say 'dangerous drugs.' What kind of dangerous drugs?"

"Mr. Dunn is accused of transporting a large quantity of cocaine and heroin from an unnamed person in Fairbanks, Alaska, to Anchorage, Alaska, where he prepared a package disguised as frozen seafood which was picked up and shipped out of the state. All of which has been documented. Copies of the reports will be made available to you by the court." It was all Karen could manage to keep a straight face while reciting the charges.

"Thank you, Sergeant Holmes. I have instructed my client to remain silent except to identify himself when asked. My client is a businessman and will have a need to make several business calls, if you can arrange that for him."

"I will see what I can do for your client, Ms. Hall. You must understand that these will not be considered attorney calls and are subject to being monitored by the jail facility. Please make sure he understands the rules," Karen advised.

"He understands." She turned to face Dunn. "I'll have you out of here when they take your butt to court in the morning." With that she closed her briefcase, stood up and motioned for Karen and Craig to move away from the door so she could exit.

Karen called the correctional officer on duty to take Dunn to a cell and asked that she and Craig be let out to their patrol car. Once outside the fence, she pulled to the side of the road and called the captain to ask an Assistant District Attorney to meet them at the trooper office.

"This is one meeting I am going to enjoy," Stanton remarked.

"Don't set the wedding date yet, Craig. This is still an open case and the SOP manual is going to keep you from getting frisky with the skinny blond. Be very careful, partner." It was a friendly warning, but it carried teeth. If he ran back to Laura too quickly, he could jeopardize their case and his career. They rode back to the office in silence.

The meeting with Assistant District Attorney Joe Malone convened in the office of Captain Davis. Malone was introduced to Craig Stanton before they began to discuss Dunn and the points of the case.

"My first question is what are we going to do about Carlton Lieber?" Craig asked. "He is our only real witness in the murder of Jack Boardon. We requested he be at the warehouse when the others were arrested in order to keep suspicion off him. He was only there because we asked him to be."

"Your captain told me about that and I think I have it worked out. Tomorrow, at arraignment I will ask the judge to dismiss all charges against him. I will state that he had only been at the warehouse to deliver some sacks of fertilizer and got caught up in the raid. I think the judge will go along with that and Mr. Dunn should be satisfied with him being released. You must remember, though, that drug dealers are a paranoid class of people and Dunn may be suspicious anyway," Malone explained.

Karen sat up straight and said, "We have three dead bodies right now and I would hate to come up with any more. Like Craig said, Carlton is our only link between Dunn and Boardon in connection with the murder. Carlton is going to jail for helping Dunn rig the Cessna, and he knows it; but if he thinks he will be going up on a murder one charge, he may change sides again."

"I understand your concern, Sergeant, and I promise I will try my best to keep him safe. I don't want him thrown under the bus any more than you." Malone seemed to understand.

"Good, now where are we with regard to Mosely Cain?" asked Davis.

"It has been very difficult to follow through on him without alerting anyone in the DEA office. Department of Justice personnel have been monitoring telephones listed to Moose Cain and to Sam Goodyear. Goodyear has made several calls to Cain, so your suspicions were correct. DOJ officers are monitoring all calls made between Cain and Goodyear. Those calls, with a search warrant, are being recorded," Malone said.

Karen had another thought. "I just remembered something that New Orleans detective, Boudreaux, said when he called. He said some DEA agents had been asking about Whittle. You don't suppose they are the ones who killed him, do you?"

"The locate-only bulletin went out through the federal network from Goodyear's office. They may have been looking for him for that reason only," Captain Davis said. "You are right to be cautious, though. We can't tell the good guys from the bad at this point."

Malone spoke. "Let me just caution all of you. Most of this case is outside of Alaska jurisdiction and is, therefore, out of our hands. It is further complicated by the very thing you just discussed. I think it will be necessary for us to focus on the things within our jurisdiction and not worry about the rest, at least for now. We have what looks like an airtight case on those arrested today. We will prosecute Dunn and his men for growing marijuana to sell. The arrest and confiscation of their new crop and their grow equipment, as well as seizing three more properties in the Palmer area, has taken a sizable bite out of their ability to continue. Karen, you and Craig have put an end to one of the largest drug networks the State of Alaska has ever seen. You are to be congratulated." Malone reached out to shake both their hands.

"I think Craig will agree," Karen said, "this is a very hollow victory for us. We didn't start out to catch a drug dealer. That was secondary. We started out to catch a killer, and we are still looking for evidence in that murder case. In the process of following up on the case, we helped get two more men killed. I don't feel very good about that."

"Don't chastise yourselves. Those men died while performing illegal acts. You are not responsible for what happened to either of them. Malone is correct; the two of you have accomplished more by accident than anyone else has done with a full investigation." Davis then turned to Malone. "What time are these men being arraigned? Karen and Craig will need to be there."

"I'll let you know as soon as I find out," Malone said as he stood and stretched. "I am going back to my office now. I will probably be there most of the night. My clerk will most likely throw a rock at me when I break the news to her. I'll call you in the morning."

Karen asked her boss, "Where do we go from here, Captain?"

"The two of you had a big day. Go home. Get some rest. We will worry about it all tomorrow," said Captain Davis, knowing he, too, would be working most of the night.

The seven men arrested at the greenhouse had been isolated from each other since being brought to the jail. Now, late morning the next day, a Department of Corrections van was waiting in the sally port to transport all of them to court for arraignment.

Mel James whispered to the man next to him in the van.

"Pass it on, plead not guilty, and don't say anything else. The court will get us lawyers." The message was passed from one man to the next until all of them were looking at James and nodding agreement.

The van was full of prisoners, so the Judicial Services Officer, a state trooper, loaded Dunn into the back seat of his patrol car for transport to the court. The crew in the van was taken to a holding cell in the courthouse. Dunn, at his lawyer's request, was taken directly to the courtroom where he was seated at the defense table alongside Gweneth Hall.

"Keep your yap shut. I'll handle this," she whispered to him.

Preliminary court procedures were obeyed after the judge had taken his seat. He had carried with him a tall stack of legal folders, presumably one for each of the morning arraignments. He was looking thoughtfully at the open folder on his bench. "Are you ready to proceed, Ms. Hall?" he asked.

"Yes, Your Honor," she acknowledged.

The court clerk read the charges filed against Anthony R. Dunn, along with a description of the circumstances precipitating his arrest. When she had finished, the judge asked, "Anthony Dunn, do you understand the charges as they have been read to you?"

Gweneth elbowed her client. "Yes, I do, Your Honor," Dunn answered.

"How do you plead to these charges?" asked the judge.

Gweneth Hall stood to answer. "My client wishes to plead not guilty, Your Honor. I ask that bail be set and my client be released in order that he may return to his real estate business."

The judge looked at the prosecution's table. "Any objections, Mr. Malone?"

"Yes, Your Honor. The State of Alaska considers Anthony Dunn a flight risk. He appears to be a wealthy man and he owns a twin turbine engine aircraft capable of taking him anywhere in the world. He is known to have worldwide connections within the drug trade."

"That has yet to be argued in court, Mr. Malone." The looked at and spoke to the court clerk. "I am setting bail at $100,000, cash only. Next case."

"Can you come up with a hundred grand cash?" Gweneth asked Dunn.

"Yes, but it will take until late today to get it here."

"Bank transfer?" she asked.

"Yes, foreign," he replied.

"Can you assure me it will be here today?"

"Of course, I have the money, but the bank will have to have some time to transfer it to my local account."

"I'll front you the bail money, but it will cost you. You will have to wait in the holding cell here in the courthouse until I can get a cashier's check over here. Wait here while I make arrangements with the clerk of the court."

Dunn watched her operate. She talked with the clerk, got a copy of the release forms and made a call on her cell phone. She spoke to the clerk again and came back to the defense table.

"The check will be here in five minutes. We can wait here until it arrives. I will take you back to the jail to get your personal property." As she was talking, the judge gathered his files and left the courtroom via a door behind the bench.

It took eight minutes for the check to arrive, another five to get a signed release and one to get out of the courtroom. Gweneth drove Dunn to the Post Street jail to retrieve his personal items taken from him at his booking. Once outside, he used his own cell phone to call his office.

"Laura, I am going home to shower and change clothes. Is everything all right at the office?"

"Yes, Mr. Dunn. What happened? They just came and took you away." She sounded very concerned and confused.

"It will all be OK, Laura. Now, what is immediate this morning?"

She gave him a list of things he had scheduled and another list of transactions to be filed with the recorder's office.

Gweneth Hall was driving Dunn to his home. He turned to her. "You need to get back to the court. Drop me here and I will take a cab home. I want you to represent those other men they arrested, not you personally, but your office. I want all of them bailed out today. Have Mel James meet with me at that little Italian restaurant in Wasilla at one o'clock. Let me know what is happening in court with all of them."

She stopped her car to let him out. "I'm on my way. Don't forget my check. I want it today."

"You will get it. Now, just go and do what I told you." Dunn had not yet decided what his next move would be, but he knew he had to call Moose and let him know what was happening. Also, he was awaiting word from Dillon. It wasn't like him to be late on reporting his delivery. Things had suddenly become very complicated.

The cab dropped him at his house where he showered, changed into a clean suit and called Cain. Moose listened intently as Dunn gave him a play by play account of the previous day.

"It is going to take some time to regroup. I can't afford to lose any more property and I can't afford to set up any more greenhouses until I recoup some of the money I have lost this week. I need the cash from the delivery Dillon is making to start things moving again. My problem there is that I haven't heard from him. The reason I called you is to ask if, with all the grief the law is giving me here, you are getting any hints they are tracking you."

"No. I thought the thing in New Orleans might backfire, but everything seems to be normal. What is your next move, in court, I mean?"

"I don't know yet." Dunn's voice revealed tension. "My lawyer is at court right now bailing out the crew they arrested yesterday. She is a crafty little thing. I guess I have to trust her to pull something off. Usually she attacks the troopers or the DA and gets cases thrown out on technical points. Maybe she will do that this time. I have to wait and see. I'm meeting with my foreman in an hour to see where we stand at the greenhouses. I just wanted to touch base with you and keep you in the loop on the legal situation here. I'll call you again when something changes."

"I know you are having cash flow problems right now, but I am going to need payment for the delivery I fronted you. You had better contact Dillon and see if everything is on schedule," Cain reminded his business associate.

"That is my next call. See ya."

Dunn could feel a stress headache beginning to form as he dialed the number for Marshal Matthew Dillon. There was no answer.

With a huge sigh, Dunn closed his phone and prepared to go to his office. Once there he quizzed Laura about anything the troopers had said the day before. She said she didn't know anything and had been frightened by his arrest.

"I don't want to be involved in anything illegal, Mr. Dunn. I like working here, but if there is a chance I will get arrested, I'm afraid I will have to quit." She was looking at him with those big, blue, sad eyes.

"You have nothing to worry about, Miss Toombes. This is all a big misunderstanding. My lawyer will have it all worked out soon. I assure you there is nothing improper happening in this office. You are safe here, Laura. I appreciate your loyalty. It means a lot to me. In fact, I think I can put a little something on your check this month to reward that loyalty." Dunn meant what he said, for Laura had become more of an office manager than a secretary or receptionist.

"Thank you, Mr. Dunn," she said.

"I have a lot to do here, but I have a meeting in Wasilla at one. I will be on the phone if you need me. It should be a short meeting and I will be back by two-thirty,

I hope." With that he turned and left the office. She relaxed once again and wished Craig Stanton would call her.

Mel James met Dunn at the front door of the restaurant. The two men were shown a seat in the dining room. It was mostly empty of customers at this late lunch hour. Dunn ordered coffee while James ordered iced tea. When the waiter left to get the drinks, Dunn asked, "What happened? How did they get wise to our new operation?"

"I don't know. We were working in the potato warehouse, transplanting all the seedlings to the trays and adjusting the lights. Bad luck for Carlton, he came to deliver some fertilizer just before they raided us. The judge thought he was just a delivery boy and dropped all charges against him and released him. The judge started to appoint a public defender for all of the rest of us when some young lawyer showed up and said he represented the six of us. Later he said you had sent him. We all plead not guilty and we all have the same court date in three weeks. The new lawyer told us he would get with us later this week to plan a defense." The waiter came back to take their order. When he left again James continued. "Mr. Dunn, I don't want to seem like a wimp, but I don't want any trouble with the law. I had that once and I don't want to go through it again."

"I understand your feelings, Mel, I don't know what happened. I am trying to find that out right now. My greenhouses have been taken down twice recently. I can't afford that. Something put us on their list of things to do. I don't know what, but I will find out. In the meantime, I need you to keep the crew together for now. I will pay them at least until after things are settled in court. I'm short on cash right now, so it won't be a lot, but they can all stay in that old farmhouse over on the Old Glenn Highway, you know the one." The waiter came again to bring their food and refill their drinks. "Call me every day and keep me informed about the morale of the crew. I have to be getting back to the office now, but I need your help."

James nodded agreement and remained seated as Dunn left the restaurant. "What have I gotten myself into," he wondered.

<h1 style="text-align:center">CHAPTER 39</h1>

About the same time Dunn was meeting his foreman in Wasilla, Carlton Lieber was getting his truck from the impound yard where it had been taken the day before when the raid took place in Palmer. The fees took nearly all the cash Dunn had given him. He was broke and his employer had been arrested. All this was leaving Carlton with a feeling of doubt about his future. He was beginning to think it wise to quit Dunn and find other places to ply his mechanical trade.

He had only driven to the first stoplight when his shirt pocked jingled. "Carlton Lieber," he answered.

"Hello, Carlton. Craig Stanton. Are you OK?"

"Oh, yeah! I'm just great. I was arrested, spent the night in jail and had my truck impounded. Yes, sir, things are working out real good for me since I met you. I ain't sure I can afford to talk to you anymore. I wish you guys would leave me alone."

"Carlton, Carlton, is that any way to talk to the one friend you have? Who got you out of jail? Who got your charges dropped? Who said he would take care of you and keep Dunn from suspecting? I would think you could show some gratitude."

"Let's see, how is this working out for me? The guy I worked for was thrown in jail. The men I worked with were all thrown in jail. My business as a mechanic is down to one customer and he was thrown in jail. Yeah, things are working out real well."

"Count your blessings, Carlton. Remember who it was that helped to murder one of your customers. Now, if you want to quit, I can come over and arrest you on a murder one charge. Would you feel better about that?"

"I never wanted to be a part of any of this, none of it, right from the start. I didn't want to fix the Cessna to crash, but Mr. Dunn forced me. I didn't want to turn in the men I worked with, but you forced me. I'm not in charge of my life anymore and I can't stand it. I ain't no narc. I ain't no snitch. I guess I ain't much of anything else either, but there ain't no way I can keep doing this." There was a frantic tone in Carlton's voice. "You have to get me out of this."

"Patience, Carlton. We are working on it. You have to remember that we can't allow anyone, not even you, to help someone murder his partner. Murder is a bad thing, Carlton, and you knew that before you did the job for Dunn. Like I said, Karen and I are the only real friends you have. The others are going to go down for growing marijuana and Dunn is going down for distribution of drugs, but that is not what we want him for. We want to get him for the murder of Jack Boardon. A murder that you participated in. You have already admitted to your part. You could be in jail awaiting trial for murder right now. Instead, you are out here helping us. Is that such a bad trade?"

Carlton was driving toward Lake Hood and the hangar owned by Anthony Dunn. "I ain't got no real job. I ain't got no money and I ain't got no place to call a home. You ain't exactly turned my life into a success story."

"How about this, Carlton? I'll stop and get you some Chinese take-out and drop it off at the hangar. At least you won't be hungry. Besides, we need to have you on the inside a while longer."

"Do I have a choice?"

"About the Chinese food? Yes. About staying on the job? No."

———

Moose Cain was entertaining a lady friend when the call came from Marshal Matthew Dillon.

"Dammit all, Moose. I thought you had someone on the inside who would keep me safe from arrest," Dillon said, showing his anger.

Cain sat up on the bed, surprised. "Arrested? What happened, Marshal?"

"Someone was watching me when I picked up the package in Anchorage, and they had someone waiting when I got to San Francisco. They let the package go when my contact picked it up and followed it to the other end. They busted everyone, including me. What happened to your fool-proof-plan? I am probably going to lose my pilot's license over this. What happened?" Dillon was venting again.

"This is the first I have heard about this. I do know they busted Dunn in Anchorage, along with his entire growing crew. They seized all his property and equipment, as well as taking the current crop. They hit him hard. I'm sorry they got you, too. I didn't know about that. Give me some time and I will call to find out how this happened. I'll call you back later." Cain was trying to understand how his network had failed. Someone had dropped the ball. Looking at his phone index, he found the number for Sam Goodyear and punched SEND.

"Goodyear," answered a voice on the other end.

"Sam, Moose. What happened up there? I got a call, just now, from Dillon. He was busted in San Francisco. Why didn't we get a warning? Are you sleeping up there?"

"You are the second call I've had in the last thirty minutes. I just learned the troopers busted Dunn and hit his warehouses. I never got word about any of this. Protocol dictates they notify me when there is going to be a major bust. That is to prevent one agency from stepping on the action of another. They never notified me or my office." Sam was as puzzled as Cain.

"What about Dillon?" Cain asked. "He thinks someone followed him when he picked up our package in Anchorage and tailed the package all the way to the final delivery in San Francisco. He says the local police got everyone: Dillon, his contact, and our San Francisco distributor. I want to know, Sam. How did our entire system fail so miserably without any warning?"

"I can't answer that, but I will make some personal calls now and contact other offices in the morning. Don't worry, Moose. I'll get to the bottom of this by tomorrow," Goodyear promised.

"It's my job to worry, Sam. It looks like you dropped the ball and it got a lot of people busted, to say nothing of the loss in product, both imported and domestic. We cannot afford failure. Fix it or I will have to fix you." With that warning, Mosely "Moose" Cain ended the call.

The more he considered the problem, the more he was sure the failure in his network could only have come through Sam Goodyear. Every failed connection hinged on him. Cain now had to determine if Sam's failure was deliberate or if someone had found him out. In either case, Goodyear was becoming a liability. He had become a liability that was destroying an extremely profitable business venture as well as jeopardizing many old and dear friends, friends dating back to the first Gulf War in 1991. Goodyear had been effective for a very long time and would be difficult to replace, but he must be replaced now.

Karen was in the office early the next morning. She was finishing her administrative tasks when Stanton stepped in.

"Good morning," she said.

"Mornin'. I've been thinking," he said without preamble. "We have Anthony Dunn staggering a little. I think we should go up and see him. Give him a left hook, so-to-speak. What do you think about telling him we are still investigating Jack's death? We say we could never come up with a motive for the killing, but since he had drugs in his airplane, we suspected that was the connection. We now know Dunn is also in the drug business. This would seem a logical step toward a motive for Dunn to kill Boardon."

"Oh, I like that," she said, smiling. "Do you think he will rise to the bait?"

"I doubt it, but he may be off balance enough from our previous visit to make a mistake or get careless. I just think it might push him a little."

"I don't suppose you considered that you will be seeing the skinny blond while you are there?" Karen was teasing her partner.

"It never crossed my mind" was his instant reply.

It was just about ten miles from the trooper office to Anthony Dunn's real estate office. The weather was overcast with a temperature of seventeen above zero. A nice day.

They were nearly there when Karen broke the silence.

"I suppose you want me to kick him in the pants this morning. You always want me to be the bad cop, while you shine your pearly whites at the secretary."

"As a matter of fact, I want to be there to see the look on his face when you let him know we consider him a suspect." They both had a chuckle over that.

When they entered the office, Laura gave Stanton her best smile. Stanton smiled back. "We need to see your boss. Is he in?"

"Yes, I'll let him know you are here." She picked up the phone, and then looked at Craig. "Are you going to arrest him again today?"

He smiled again, "No, not today."

She told Dunn the troopers asked to see him and he said let them in. It was obvious he wasn't happy with the intrusion by the stern look on his face.

"What do the two of you want of me today?" he asked sharply.

"We are still investigating the death of Jack Boardon, Mr. Dunn. Until now, we could never come up with a motive, but after the activity of this week, we must ask you about your association with Jack. Were you in the drug trade with him? I mean, since we now have you connected to the marijuana growing business and since Jack died with 400 pounds of marijuana in his possession, we wondered if you two were partners in the marijuana business. If so, we thought it would make a great motive to kill him." Karen was twisting things a bit, and smiling at the result.

Dunn was instantly angry. "Get out of my office. And call before coming here again so I can have my lawyer here when you arrive. I will instruct my secretary not to allow you in the office without a prior appointment. Now get out."

Stanton smiled and waved to Laura as he passed her desk. In the car, he broke into a fit of laughter. "We wanted a reaction and boy did we get it. I think we accomplished our mission and unnerved him enough that he may begin to make mistakes." He slapped Karen on the shoulder and laughed again. "You were great, partner! You were great!

CHAPTER 40

Stanton and Karen Holmes were both removing their coats in Karen's office when the receptionist buzzed to say there was a visitor to see them. Karen walked to the front to see who it was.

Sam Goodyear was waiting at the front desk. He smiled at her and asked if he could come into her office to "chat" a few minutes. Karen assigned him a visitor pass and escorted him to her office where Stanton was waiting.

"Hello, Agent Goodyear," Craig greeted as he walked into the office.

"Hello, Trooper Stanton. How are you?" Goodyear replied.

"I'm doing great, how about you?"

Karen interrupted the pleasantries. "What is it you came to see us about, Sam?" Goodyear turned back to face the sergeant. "I just came over to see how your investigation is coming along. I hadn't heard from you for a few days. There is a rumor in our office that you, I say you meaning the troopers, made a big drug raid in the Palmer area this week."

"Yes, that's true. The drug unit did that. I'm sure if you talked with Lieutenant Tolliver he would be happy to give you the details," Karen informed him.

"I heard it went well for you and that you arrested several men at the Palmer site and also took Anthony Dunn into custody. I'm happy it all went well for you."

"Again, Sam, Trooper Stanton, and I had nothing to do with the Palmer raid. We were assigned the task of arresting Anthony Dunn. Everyone has been arraigned and released on bail. All this is public record. Why are you here asking us about it?" Karen knew what Goodyear was getting to, but wanted to taunt him a little bit.

"Oh, yes, I checked it out with the court. You did a good job and are to be congratulated. However, I do have a question about the whole affair. In the past our agencies have had a policy of informing the other when a large bust is taking place. I can't find where that happened in this case. I'm sure it was just an oversight on your part, but it was a departure from normal procedures. Can you tell me how it happened?"

"I can't speak for the Lieutenant, but I'm sure if you walk over to his office he will be glad to bring you up to speed on the entire raid. It must have been an oversight if you weren't notified beforehand. Would you like me to call the Lieutenant and ask him to come to my office and brief you on the raid?" Karen was baiting him again.

"That won't be necessary. I'm sure he will send me a copy of the file. Strangely, though, the rumor at my office is that you and Stanton were in charge of the raid."

"That's the trouble with rumors, they are seldom accurate." She paused a moment, then added, "Is there something specific you would like to know about the raid, Sam? Perhaps I can help you."

"No, I am just curious about why our office didn't receive prior notification," Goodyear commented. "There is another thing that made me curious. What made you connect Anthony Dunn to the greenhouse operation in Palmer? I've always heard he was an honest and successful real estate agent. I can't imagine him involved in a marijuana growing business."

That was her opening. "Are you acquainted with Anthony Dunn? You speak as though you know him," Karen nudged.

"I don't really know him, but I have met him a few times at public functions." Sam Goodyear was admitting nothing, but he knew his connection to Dunn was under suspicion. He stood to leave. "Well, I have to go, but I hope this lapse in protocol can be corrected and not happen again. Thank you, Sergeant." He turned to leave.

"Don't forget to leave your visitor pass at the front desk," Karen called after him.

Craig Stanton watched the door for a few seconds to be sure Goodyear was gone, and then turned to Karen, smirking. She was smiling and shaking her head.

"Well, Sarge. We set out to shake the tree and look at the nuts that are falling out. Goodyear has the same as admitted knowing Dunn. He was here to see what we knew. I love the way you handled him," Craig complimented his boss.

"I think we need to talk to the captain about what just happened. Come on, Craig, let's go fill him in," Karen said.

"Do you think we should tell Tolliver?" he asked.

"Yes, but we had better talk to Captain Davis first."

Stanton nodded agreement and the two walked to the chief's office at the end of the hall. They tapped on the door and Davis waved them in.

"What's up?" he asked.

Karen grinned. "Craig and I just had a visit from Sam Goodyear. He was very curious about the raid in Palmer and the arrest of Anthony Dunn. He was also a little upset that his office had not been notified about the raid prior to it taking place."

"How did you handle it, Sergeant?" Davis asked.

"I referred him to Tolliver. I said he was in charge of the whole Palmer raid and that Tolliver would be happy to fill him in on what took place. I don't think I gave him any information, but he certainly wanted to know about Dunn's arrest."

"Did he ask anything about the California seizure and the arrests there?"

"No, he didn't," Karen answered.

"I think he saw he was getting nowhere with you and gave up. I expect he will contact Tolliver and see if he has better luck there. I would also bet he asks Bill about the FedEx pilot and the seizure in California." Davis drummed his fingers on his desk and added. "I had better call Bill Tolliver and bring him up to speed in case he gets a visit from Goodyear today."

"We will be in my office, Captain. There is a lot of report writing to do. Let us know if Goodyear contacts Tolliver." With that, Karen and her partner returned to her office.

———

Sam Goodyear was thinking hard as he drove toward his office. As he turned onto 5th Avenue, he pulled into a parking meter spot and stopped. He took his cell phone from his pocket and dialed the New York number for Moose Cain.

"Yeah, Sam, what did you find out?" Cain asked after seeing the number of the caller on his phone.

"They are playing it close to the vest. They didn't tell me anything. They referred me to the head of the drug unit, a guy named Tolliver. I have dealt with him before. I might be able to get something from him, but not today."

"Did they say anything about Tony Dunn?" Moose asked.

"Not much. They told me he had been arrested in connection with the marijuana growing business in Palmer, but they didn't volunteer anything. The troopers are keeping this investigation quiet, I mean really quiet," Goodyear said.

"Did they mention Marshal Dillon?" Cain inquired.

"No, and the way the conversation was going I was afraid to ask. They seemed awfully suspicious."

"Use your agency connections and see if you can find out what happened to Marshal. Things are getting out of hand up there. We're losing a lot of money and product. It appears to me that Tony is becoming a liability and I'll have to decide what to do about that. Tony Dunn has been a friend a long time, but when he decided to end his partnership with Jack, he put all of us on the trooper radar. I may have to do something about him soon. In the meantime, find out what happened. We can't route any more product through Alaska until we have some answers. I don't want to have my airplane taken in a surprise raid. Get on it, Sam, and do it quickly." Moose didn't wait for a reply; he just pressed the END button on his phone.

Sam Goodyear sat at the curb thinking. Tolliver probably knew the answers and Sam needed to get them from him. He checked his mirrors, crossed four lanes of one-way traffic, and made a left turn on C Street, heading back toward the Trooper Headquarters.

He parked in front of the building occupied by the drug unit. Inside was another receptionist who called Bill Tolliver to come to the front desk.

Lt. Tolliver met the squatty federal agent at the front desk to escort him to his own office. Once there, he offered Sam a cup of coffee, which was politely refused.

"What can I do for you, Sam?" Bill Tolliver asked.

"Have you talked to Sergeant Holmes or Trooper Stanton?" Goodyear asked.

"Not since this morning. Why?"

"I went by her office earlier and talked to them about the raid in Palmer and the arrest of Anthony Dunn. They referred me to you and said you had been in charge of the raid and would fill me in on what took place. I think I made them uneasy when I asked why my office wasn't advised before the raid. I told them I thought it must have been an oversight, but they wouldn't tell me anything."

"Don't blame them, Sam. The DA is still working on the files and they are forbidden from giving out information," Tolliver explained. "I am bound by the same regulation, but if you have a specific question I can answer, I will be happy to do it for you."

"I knew there was a good reason, Bill. And I do have a couple of questions, if you don't mind."

"Ask away, I'll answer anything I am allowed to, Sam."

"Well, first, I was curious about how you found the new greenhouses in the first place," Goodyear said.

"Oh, nothing magical, Sam. We were checking out some properties with high power bills and came across this group. We even had surveillance cameras and sound recorders in one of the buildings. We had been watching them for a while," Tolliver revealed.

"Nice work, Bill," Goodyear gave him a verbal pat on the back. "I still can't see how you tied Anthony Dunn to the greenhouses."

"Oh, we didn't tie him to the greenhouses except by ownership. That wasn't why he was arrested," Tolliver admitted.

"Then, why was he arrested?" Sam looked puzzled.

"We learned he had brought a large quantity of cocaine and heroin into Anchorage on his airplane and hidden it in his hangar. We staked it out and tailed the man who picked it up. This was another case of unrelated circumstances leading to finding drugs." Tolliver had Goodyear listening carefully.

"Wonderful police work, wonderful, Bill. You are to be congratulated. How soon will it be before I can get a copy of the reports?" Sam asked.

"I can't say for sure. It depends on what the DA says. I expect he will release them to you within a few days. In the meantime, if you have any more specific questions I can answer for you, just give me a call. Always happy to cooperate with the feds." Tolliver stood and reached out to shake hands with his guest.

Goodyear drove away trying to digest what he had just learned. A mile down Tudor Avenue, he pulled into a Tesoro Station and called Cain.

CHAPTER 41

Tolliver walked into Karen's office with a Cheshire cat grin on his face. "You hit that nail on the head," he said. "Goodyear just left my office. He was definitely looking for information. I camouflaged the truth some, but gave him what he wanted. I'd be willing to bet he is on the phone, right now, reporting to whoever his boss is. Thanks for the heads-up, Karen. I can't remember the last time I had that much fun." He ended his speech with a giggle, "Hee hee hee."

Karen was joining his mirth now and she, too, was chuckling. "I'm glad I was able to give you a bright spot in your day. What, specifically, did he ask?"

Lieutenant Bill Tolliver could barely control his glee as he gave her an account of his conversation with Goodyear. "The part I liked the best was that you had read him right. He went too far with you and knew it. When he came to see me, he was more careful and totally patronizing. I will be typing up my report later today and I will see you get a copy of it." He turned to leave the office, then turned back to say, "Man that was fun."

Karen could hear him chuckling as he walked down the hall. She went to fill her coffee cup and stopped by Craig's desk to update him on Tolliver's visit. She knew he would get a kick out of it just like she had. When she finished her story, the two of them had a laugh about it and about Tolliver's reaction.

"I had a call from Laura Toombes this morning. She said she thought she was about to be fired because of a FedEx package that came to the office," Stanton told Karen.

"Wow! What happened?"

Stanton continued, "It seems that sometime after we arrested Dunn a package was delivered to his office. When Dunn came back, Laura had been so busy she forgot about it until this morning. She got it out and gave it to him and he hit the roof. He cussed her out for not getting it to him right away. She tried to explain that he had been in jail and then out of the office and it had slipped her mind. She said he screamed at her that he had been waiting for this package and that her actions were inexcusable. He took the box into his office and closed the door. A few minutes later he left the office with the box under his arm, loaded it in his SUV and drove away without saying when he would be back.

She was crying when she called me. I asked her if there had been a return address on the shipping label and she said there wasn't. While we were on the phone, she went to Dunn's office and found the wrapping papers in his wastebasket. She has cut the shipping label from it and is faxing it to me. Perhaps we can trace its origin with FedEx."

"I may have misjudged the skinny blond. Maybe her roots are dark after all."

"Be careful, Sarge. You may start to like her."

"I hate to admit this to you, Craig, but I already do."

Just then, the receptionist came to his desk with a fax printout. It was the shipping label.

"See if you can trace it and let me know what you find out."

"The routing numbers are on the label, it should be an easy task. I'll get back to you as soon as I hear." Craig was grinning as he left Karen's office.

Sam Goodyear had been trying to reach Mosely Cain by telephone for nearly an hour. He had left messages on Cain's voice mail without success. Finally, there was a call from Cain.

His opening words were, "What did you find out?" Cain snapped.

It instantly irritated Goodyear. He wasn't used to being talked to that way. "I'm not your whipping boy, Moose. I'm having a bad day of my own."

"Yeah, you're right, Sam. So, what have you learned?" Cain said in an apologetic tone.

"First of all they said they had been watching the greenhouses for a while because of abnormally high power use. That is logical and probably true. They also said Dunn was not arrested in connection with the greenhouses. He was arrested because he had forwarded a package of drugs from Anchorage to San Francisco via a FedEx pilot. They didn't give me any names. They didn't mention where Dunn got the package, only that he repackaged it at his hangar and left it to be picked up by the pilot. They said they had staked out the hangar on a tip, but they wouldn't say where the tip came from. It doesn't appear they are aware of your connection with Dunn. It also means they will keep looking for the source of the drugs." Goodyear paused.

"Why haven't you been kept in the loop?" Cain asked.

"They aren't saying, but they have stayed within jurisdictional lines and, possibly, thought it wasn't necessary. I'm beginning to think you were correct in your thinking about Dunn. He may now be a liability," said Goodyear.

"Are you thinking he should be eliminated?"

"It certainly is an option that would end a great deal of public probing," Sam commented.

"Do you want the job, Sam?"

"It isn't my usual line of work."

"You are the only asset I have in Alaska capable of doing the job," Cain said.

Sam Goodyear gave a long sigh. "Look, Moose, if I'm the last option, I'll take it on—but it's not a job I want."

"I understand, Sam. You and I have done a lot of things together, some of which included this kind of work. I think, for our mutual benefit, this needs to be done before the DA starts making deals and Dunn starts trading. Tony and I have been friends a long time, but he has become used to the good life and I think it likely he will trade you and me for a lesser sentence, or even immunity. I don't think it wise to take the chance."

"I won't do it for free, Moose. This may be the undoing of my career and I really can't afford that yet," Sam demanded.

There was a short silence, then, "One hundred fifty thousand, cash, and a position running a new port of entry when we change out of Alaska. Things are getting too hot up there. You can help me select a new entry point."

"OK, Cain. How soon?"

"Whatever is best for you and your plan, but it has to be soon in order to keep him away from the District Attorney," Mosely Cain said.

"I'll get back to you when I have a plan." Sam was not looking forward to his new task.

Karen was working on time sheets when Craig came into her office.

"Want to guess where the FedEx package was shipped from?" he asked.

"New Orleans," she said.

"How did you know?"

"It had to be the money Whittle had left when he was murdered. You know, Craig, this means Dunn is tied to Whittle's murder as well as Jack Boardon's." She was thinking, and asked her partner, "What do we do with this information? Arrest Dunn? Talk with the DA? Or should we just shoot him?"

"My choice would be the latter, but it's probably not a good option," Craig said, grinning. "I think we should talk to the DA about what we need to arrest him."

"I agree," said Karen. "Let me finish here while you call him and make an appointment to see him this afternoon."

Minutes later Craig called her to say they were to be at his office at noon. Joe Malone had to be in court for an arraignment at 1:30. At noon, the two troopers were standing in Malone's office. Karen carried a file she had constructed on Dunn.

The next hour was spent reviewing the case history, Jack Boardon's death, Leon Bettis' shooting, and Whittle's stabbing. They outlined the burglary, the ransacking of Whittle's room in New Orleans, and that the package had been delivered to Dunn's office. For an hour, they exchanged views.

"Too bad we didn't get the money when it came to the office. As it stands, I don't see enough evidence to indict Anthony Dunn for murder. We have a good case on the drug charges, but we need more solid, tangible evidence on the murder charge. Sorry, I wish there was more I could do. You have a good circumstantial case, but a jury is going to want more." Malone looked at his wristwatch. "I have to be in court in ten minutes. I'll call you later today and we'll try to come up with some options. I'm sorry, I have to go." Malone walked out of the office ahead of the troopers.

Karen and Craig were on the way to lunch when Carlton Lieber called. "Meet us at the Lucky Wishbone," said Craig.

"Aw, man, I hate that place," Carlton whined.

Craig ordered three lunches and was picking them up from the counter when Carlton arrived. "Why do you always want to come here?" asked Carlton.

"Because the food is good, Carlton. Eat your chicken." By then, Craig was wiping his fingers and sipping his iced tea.

Carlton kept his voice low and his eyes darting around the cafe. "I haven't been paid in a while and I came to ask if you can come up with some cash. Mel James hasn't seen Dunn and can't pay me. Dunn hasn't paid me for the last work I did for him and I can't even afford to buy a meal. I have to have some money."

"I'm buying lunch, Carlton," Craig teased.

"That ain't funny, Trooper Stanton. I'm desperate," Carlton said, eating a chicken leg.

"How much do you need, Carlton?" asked Karen.

"A hunnert would do me 'til my other money comes in," said a relieved Carlton.

"Follow me to my car when we leave. Take the cash as you walk by, don't stop to talk."

"OK, Sergeant. Whatever you say. I ain't a wantin' to cause no trouble."

Karen and Craig left first with Carlton following a few seconds behind. Karen stood beside her SUV holding her hand low as Carlton walked by. He snatched the hundred dollar bill from her hand and whispered "Thanks" as he walked by.

Inside the car, Craig was grinning at his hard-nosed partner. "You're just an old softy," he muttered.

CHAPTER 42

Sam Goodyear had been a DEA agent for a long time and had many contacts in the criminal world. There were some things he would need if he were to eliminate Anthony Dunn and not get caught himself. In Wasilla, there was a criminal by the name of Eddy Luton. Eddie had been an informant for Goodyear on many occasions. Luton had connections everywhere. He could supply anything for any job. Luton was a mousy little man with a high pitched voice, earning him the nickname "Squeaky." Goodyear called his snitch and asked to meet him in Wasilla that same afternoon. Luton was at the rendezvous, a Parks Highway turnout on the north side of town, on time.

The two vehicles parked driver to driver, neither driver getting out of their vehicles. Goodyear rolled down his window. "Hi, Squeaky. How have you been, I haven't seen you for a while."

"Just fine, Sam, and yourself?"

"I'm doing fine, pal. But I need some things in a hurry. Can you help me?" Sam asked.

"Depends on what you need," Luton replied.

Goodyear handed him a list written on a page from his notebook. Luton studied it a minute.

"How soon?" he asked.

"I need the stuff by this evening," Sam replied.

Luton looked at the list again. "The fairgrounds in Palmer at 7:30. Five hundred dollars, cash."

"I'll be there," Sam said, rolling up his window and driving away.

Goodyear knew Dunn was not a heavy drinker but that he did occasionally like to sip a good scotch whisky. He stopped at a liquor store in Wasilla to purchase a bottle of Johnnie Walker Blue Label. Not wanting to drink on an empty stomach, he found a steakhouse near Lake Wasilla for an early dinner. He ordered a Porterhouse, baked potato, salad with Russian dressing and coffee. He ate at a leisurely pace, as he had a lot of time to kill and plans to make. Dunn had an elaborate alarm system in his house making it necessary to get inside while he was at home. Recent developments in the transportation business gave him an excuse. The Johnnie Walker gave him a means of rendering Dunn incapable of struggle. The plan would work and it would look like he got drunk and fell asleep. After three cups of coffee, Goodyear saw the time getting close to 7 p.m. It was time to go. He paid his bill, stepped into the cold breezy evening air, and took a deep breath.

Goodyear waited for Luton near the back gate of the fairgrounds. It was a short wait. Again, they parked window to window. Luton handed Sam a paper box containing several items. Goodyear checked them off and handed an envelope to his snitch. "We never met," he said to Luton, who nodded and drove away.

He checked the contents of the box again to be sure he had what he needed, then called Anthony Dunn.

"Tony Dunn," Dunn answered the phone.

"Tony, Sam. We need to talk. I'm in Palmer and can be at your place in a few minutes. I'll bring a new bottle of scotch."

"I could use a drink tonight. Come on over."

Traffic was light and he was at Dunn's house in twenty minutes. Goodyear walked up to the front door carrying a velvet coffin containing the bottle. He rang the bell and waited.

Tony Dunn answered the door wearing lounging sweats and a tee shirt with leather slippers on his feet. "Come on in, Sam. Good to see you. Have you heard from Moose?"

"That's why I'm here. He wanted me to talk to you about what happened to Dillon. He's worried." They walked to the kitchen where Sam placed the blue box on the table. "Got a couple of glasses?" he asked.

"Sure." Dunn opened a cabinet and brought two crystal glasses to the table.

Sam used his thumbnail to break the seal on the bottle. In his palm was a small packet of white powder. In the old days, this powder was called a Mickey Finn. Sam wrapped his palm around the glass and held the bottle over it, obstructing the view of the powder drifting down into the glass. He poured a generous portion of scotch into the glass and handed it to Anthony Dunn, and then he poured another stiff drink into his own glass. He held his glass high as to toast. "To better times," he said.

"To better times," Dunn replied before taking a large drink.

Sam took a tall drink from his own glass before asking, "What in the world happened. How did the troopers get wind of the shipment in your hangar?" He took another sip of the expensive scotch. "The drug team commander for the troopers told me they had your hangar staked out and followed the drugs all the way down the West Coast to the delivery point in San Francisco."

Dunn took another long pull on his drink. "I don't know. I wish I did. My mechanic was the only one who knew, but he was with me the whole time. There was no way he could have told them. I even took him to Fairbanks with me. I have been over it in my mind a hundred times and I can't figure it out." He was feeling the warmth and took another drink, pushing the empty glass toward Sam to be filled again.

"Whatever happened, we lost a lot of product along with the means to carry it safely to the West Coast. This was a bad hit." Sam pretended to sip his whisky.

Dunn was now enjoying the way he felt. "Yes it was, and Dillon will probably lose his commercial ticket over this." He laughed loudly. "Wow, this is hitting me hard. No more for me. I'll finish this and call it good."

Sam talked and kept an eye on his victim. Moose says we will have to move the port of entry from Fairbanks to the Lower 48 somewhere. It will be inconvenient, but the transportation link has been broken." Sam was watching Dunn begin to sway while sitting in his chair.

The Mickey Finn was taking effect. "You don't look so good, pal. Come on and I will help you into the living room. You can lie on the couch."

"Yeah, sure, you can help me," Dunn slurred.

Dunn was nearly unconscious and Goodyear nearly carried him into the living room. He stretched Dunn out on the couch and covered him with an afghan from the back of the couch. He watched the sleeping man for a minute then walked to his car to fetch the paper box he had bought from Luton.

Sam opened a jar of Vaseline Petroleum Jelly and smeared it generously around the edge of the couch. There were also two brown bottles in the box. He opened one bottle and poured the contents on the carpet behind and on the couch. The other one he opened and dumped in a puddle near the smeared petroleum jelly. He placed both bottles back in the box along with the Vaseline jar. Having never done this before and not knowing exactly what to expect, he wanted to leave as soon as possible. One hundred percent strength hydrogen peroxide is very volatile.

Goodyear took the box back to his car and climbed inside. He wanted to wait and see the results of his work, but he also needed to be seen somewhere else when the fire started. In Anchorage, he drove down an alley behind the Mush Inn Motel. He stopped at a dumpster, threw the box into it, and drove away. Then he hurried to a sports bar on Fireweed Avenue and bought a round for the house when he entered, feigning drunkenness. Sam didn't understand hockey, but screamed and yelled along with the rest of the crowd. He bought two more rounds before staggering to his car where he sat, cold sober, and waited. A couple of minutes later, he pulled out and drove home. All he could do now was wait for the results.

The next morning Sam was drinking orange juice and watching the morning news. One of the featured stories this morning was about a terrible fire at the home of Eagle River realtor Anthony Dunn. "The fire destroyed the home and, when investigators went inside the charred house, they found the remains of a person. The remains have been sent to the crime lab for identification. It is presumed that the remains are those of the owner of the home, Anthony Dunn," reported the commentator, using a sad tone.

Sam Goodyear smiled and drank another glass of juice before calling Moose Cain.

"It's done," Sam reported.

"Are you sure? No slip-ups?" Cain asked.

"I just heard the report on the morning news."

"I'm going to miss Tony, but it had to be done. Why don't you take a few days off and meet me in the Bahamas for a couple days of rest? You probably need it right now," Cain chuckled.

"I think I had better stay here and keep my ear to the ground. This is bound to cause some reaction at both the troopers' and the DA's office. I should stay here and see if they call it suspicious. I don't think they will, but you never know." Sam was nervous about an investigation into the fire. He was sure they could not determine the cause, but fire investigators are clever, he thought.

It was 5:45 a.m. when Craig Stanton was awakened by the ringing of his cell phone. He turned on the bedside lamp and picked up the little handset.

"Stanton," he said, groggy and half asleep.

"Craig. It's Laura. Have you seen the news this morning?"

"No, I haven't, you woke me when you called. Why? What's happening?"

"Mr. Dunn, he died in a house fire last night," she said, half in panic.

"What! You can't be serious. When?" Stanton asked.

"Sometime during the night, I guess. The fire department is still over there."

"I have to get dressed and go up there to check on it myself. Thank you for the call."

"I don't know what to do, Craig. Should I open the office today?" Laura asked.

"I suspect that, if it was on the news, there will be a lot of phone calls asking about Dunn. The fire marshal will undoubtedly come to see you sometime today. Yes, I think you should open the office. I'll stop there later, after I talk to the fire department."

"OK, I'll open the office. Thank you, Craig. Please call me later."

He ended the call and dialed Karen. She, too, was awakened by the phone.

"Karen, listen closely. Dunn is dead. He died in a house fire during the night. I think we need to get to the scene and find out if it was accidental."

She was immediately awake. "Pick me up on the way. I'll be at the office."

Stanton had a quick shower and shave before putting on a clean uniform. As he drove to the office, he considered the possibility that this was a coincidence. The more he considered it, the less likely it seemed. Karen was waiting in front of the office.

"I watched the news while I dressed," she said. "We have to find the fire marshal. This can't be an accident. Someone eliminated Dunn to keep him from talking to us or the DA. This makes body number four, Craig. The score is four to nothing with the bad guys leading. We have to do something, and soon. Carlton or Laura could be on the list for all we know."

"I know, Karen. We have to get ahead of them somehow. We have to figure out who is pulling the strings in all this."

Craig was driving as fast as the roads and traffic would let him. He had his over-head lights on and the siren yelping as he weaved in and out of traffic. He had to slow down to make the Eagle River exit. They went directly to Dunn's house. The scene was surreal: four fire trucks, an ambulance, two fire company pick-ups, and the fire marshal's red station wagon, all with red lights flashing. They had blocked the street. The trooper markings on their car let them get past the onlookers in the street.

Karen and Craig stepped out of their patrol car and asked the fireman at the first truck where to find the fire marshal.

"He's inside. If it's important I can get him on the radio," the young fireman told him.

"Thanks, I'll talk to him later. Who is in charge of the response?" asked Stanton.

"Captain Murdock." The firefighter pointed to the next pumper. "That's him up there. He's not too busy now, 'cause we're pulling hoses and sending three engines back to the station."

"Thanks," Craig said, as he walked to the next truck to speak with Captain Murdock. The fire captain saw them coming and waved to them as they approached.

His face was blackened from the smoke and he looked weary. As they approached, Karen recognized him from another case when they had contact.

"Morning, Murdock," she said as they came closer.

"Hey, Sergeant. I didn't recognize you in all the lights. How are you?"

"I'm doing fine. What's the story here?"

"The fire marshal is still I inside, but there is a victim, dead. He had been asleep on the couch. Maybe drinking, there was a bottle of whisky beside him. Between you and me, the origin of the fire is suspicious. It appears to have started right at the couch where he was sleeping. We didn't see any sign he had been smoking or any other sign of ignition. Like I said, suspicious origin. Remember, that's just my opinion."

"Your opinion has always been good enough for me, "Karen said. "We'll let you get back to work and wait for the fire marshal. Let him know when he comes out, will you?"

"Sure thing, Sergeant," said Murdock, waving as they walked back to their car.

"What do you think, Sarge?" Stanton asked.

"I think your initial assessment was correct. Dunn had become a threat to someone powerful, someone with a lot to lose," Karen opined.

"I wish I had some coffee," said Craig.

They sat in the warm car, listening to music on the radio, for nearly an hour before the fire marshal came out of the burned house. Only fifty years old, he looked much older and walked with a distinct limp. As he approached Murdock, he shed the air pack from his back. Murdock said something to the fire marshal and pointed toward the trooper car. He laid his helmet on the air pack and walked toward them.

Both troopers stepped out of the car and said, "Hello."

"Hello, I'm the fire marshal, Wayne Lassiter. Captain Murdock said you wanted to see me."

"Yes, we do. I'm Sergeant Holmes, call me Karen, and this is Trooper Stanton."

Stanton held out his hand to shake, "Call me Craig."

"Pleased to meet you both," said Lassiter. "What's your interest in this fire?"

Karen explained. "The owner of the house, and probably the victim, was a suspect in a case we are working. We arrested him a few days ago on a drug charge. I'm curious about the origin of the fire. Was it an accident?"

"Funny you should ask. I'll have to wait for the lab results to be sure, but it looks to me like arson. Which means your suspect was probably murdered."

Karen gave him a card. "I want to know the results of the fire investigation. Can I get you to send me a copy of the final report? I need it as soon as possible."

"No problem. If this is arson, I will be grateful for the help."

"Do you have an educated guess as to the cause of the fire?" Stanton asked.

"My best guess, judging by what I saw on the carpet near the body, it looks like an old firebug trick. They put Vaseline on the floor, pour hydrogen peroxide nearby, and run. One hundred percent peroxide is flammable on its own, but the Vaseline guarantees ignition. We don't see much of that here. It's what the firebugs use in the big cities to burn old buildings."

"Do you have a time?" Karen asked.

"Nothing exact, but it had to be sometime before ten last night."

"Well, thanks for the help, Wayne."

"Any time, Sergeant," he said as he turned to walk back to the fire engine.

Stanton drove back the direction he had come, driving slowly through the crowded street. "I'm hungry," he said. An hour later, they were back in the office and headed for the captain's office.

Karen briefed the captain on the fire and Dunn. "What I can't figure out is who could have done it?"

Captain Davis leaned back in his leather office chair. "It appears all your suspects are dead. Who is left on the list with enough at stake to have him killed?"

"I only have one name on my list that fits that picture—Moose Cain of Amarada Cargo. The last I heard he was in New York. I guess he could have flown up here, done the job, and flown back, but it seems more likely he hired it done."

"And who on your list has the means, motive and opportunity to do the job?" asked the captain.

"I don't think Carlton Lieber or Mel James has it in them to do a murder, and certainly none of the laborers are likely suspects."

"Right, Karen, but there is one more name you haven't considered."

"I can't think of anyone else," she said.

Stanton nearly jumped out of his seat. "Sam Goodyear!" He was almost shouting. "He was nosing around Karen's office and over at Tolliver's. That's what he wanted the information for, to see if Dunn was making a deal."

Captain Davis smiled. "Now, I think you have a suspect."

Karen was in deep thought, then looked up and asked the captain, "Would you call him and ask if he would stop by my office to talk? We have to find out where he was last night."

"When do you want him here, Karen?"

"Just let me know what time and I will be here." She was anxious to question Goodyear, but tried not to show it.

Karen and Craig were drinking coffee in her office when Goodyear arrived. "What's up," he asked when he came in.

"Have you heard about Anthony Dunn?" she asked without looking at him.

"I heard on the news that they think he died in a house fire this morning. Is it true? Is he dead?"

"That's what the fire marshal is saying." Karen waited for a few seconds to see if he would volunteer anything further. He didn't. "I was just wondering, where were you last night around ten?"

A shocked look crept into his eyes, but only for an instant. "About ten? Let's see. Oh, yeah. There was a hockey game last night and I stopped at a sports bar on Fireweed to watch it. I almost got drunk while I was in there. Hockey fans are nuts, you know. Great game, Toronto pulled it out in the last ten seconds."

"Which bar was that, Sam?"

He gave her the name and elaborated again on the game.

"This fire sure wrecks our case," Karen started. "We still have the grow crew, but we think Dunn was the brains behind it all. He was behind the scheme of forwarding other drugs to the Lower 48, but all that is outside our jurisdiction and is someone else's headache. You will probably be hearing from the San Francisco police about that case, since the drugs came through your bailiwick." Karen was baiting him again.

"I suppose you're right. They usually keep me informed. And, I want to thank you for the heads-up on Dunn. I appreciate the information. Is that all you needed from me?" Goodyear asked.

"Yes, Sam. You seemed upset we hadn't kept you in the loop and I don't want that to happen again. Thanks for coming in."

He gave a wave of his hand and marched from the office.

"Find out what time the bartender that served him during the hockey game comes on duty. Ask him about Sam and what time he came in and what time he left. And see if he can remember ask how much Sam had to drink during the game."

"I know that place. It's a neighborhood bar. I think they open at noon. I'll check it out at noon. See you later, partner." Stanton wanted to get the federal agent in the worst way. Before he went to the bar, he had time to call Laura and see how she was doing.

CHAPTER 44

Karen sat in her office trying to decide her next move. She suddenly had a thought. She spun her Rolodex, found the number, and dialed the fire marshal's office. The receptionist asked how to direct her call. Karen asked to speak with Fire Marshal Lassiter. "Please hold while I connect you," she said.

"Wayne Lassiter," said a tired voice.

"Hello, Wayne. Karen Holmes. We spoke earlier at the fire scene in Eagle River."

"Oh, yes, Sergeant. What can I do for you?"

"I don't want this to leak out to anyone, but we are looking for evidence in a murder case and I am wondering if there is a large safe in that house."

"As a matter of fact, there is. It is a fireproof safe, too, so if there is evidence inside it, it should be intact. Anchorage PD has stationed an officer there to safeguard the scene. After all we may have a murder scene and I want to keep it secure until we determine the true cause of the fire."

"I think that is a wise decision, sir," Karen commented. "I have a request for when you open the safe. I'm looking for a large sum of cash. I don't know how much, but it came to him in a large paper box by way of FedEx. There should be more than fifty thousand and less than one hundred thousand dollars. It's evidence in a murder committed in New Orleans."

"I'll tell you what I will do, Sergeant. We intend to open the safe today. If there is a large sum of cash in there, I will call you. We can only impound the contents until ownership is established and you will need a search warrant to seize it."

"One more thing, Wayne. If you find any items related to the cash, items that could have come in the box with the money, let me know and I will add those items to the search warrant." Karen requested the additional items not knowing what was in the box when it was delivered.

"I'll get back to you when the safe is opened," Wayne said.

Trooper Stanton was entering the sports bar on Fireweed Avenue behind the bartender when he opened the door. The bartender recognized Craig from a previous visit, but couldn't remember the name.

"Sorry, I can't remember your name. You were in here about six months ago looking for some doper, as I recall." He made his comments while walking around turning on beer signs and lights. Finally, he went to some kind of master panel and turned on all the television sets at one time. "What can I do for you?" he asked when he finally stepped behind the bar.

"Last night, around ten, a short, stocky man about fifty-five years old came in here. He said he watched the hockey game, had a few drinks and left. Do you remember him?"

The bartender chuckled out loud. "Yeah, I remember him. What a putz. He came in alright; it was after ten, maybe ten thirty, sat at the bar, and was looking at the hockey game. He had a drink and tried to take up a conversation with one of the customers, Duke Mason. Duke is a die-hard hockey fan. Your guy wanted to know who was winning. He bought a round for the house to make friends. Duke got friendly with a free drink and told him who was ahead. This guy didn't know anything about hockey. In fact, the game was a re-run from yesterday afternoon. Your guy was screaming, yelling, and buying drinks for the house. I thought he was drunk and was thinking about cutting him off, but he hadn't had that much. It looked to me like he was faking."

"You say it was after ten, maybe ten thirty when he came in?" Stanton asked.

"Yeah, I know the time because of the hockey game."

Stanton now had his notebook in his hand. "Your name is Ted, as I recall."

"Yeah, Ted Williams, like the baseball player."

"It is really important that I get accurate times, Ted. I want you to be sure about the times."

"Like I said, I know what time it was because of the hockey game."

"And what time did he leave?" Stanton asked.

"I don't remember exactly, but he was only here about an hour. He staggered out to his car. I didn't want him to drive and was watching him through that window. It was funny. When he got outside, he walked straight as an arrow; and that's when I decided he was faking. Oh, God. He didn't leave here and get into an accident, did he?"

"No, Ted, nothing like that. We think he is involved in something else and we just need to establish time." Stanton tried to ease Ted's mind. "Would you be willing to come by the trooper office and make an official statement?"

"Sure, when?" he asked.

"When you come into work tomorrow? Would that be convenient for you?"

"Yeah, I'll stop on the way to work," Williams said sounding relieved.

"If I'm not in the office, the receptionist can help you. Just write a statement about what happened, being as accurate about the details and times as you can remember. It's very important, Ted. Thanks." With that, Stanton put his notebook in his jacket pocket and walked out.

Back at headquarters, he walked directly to Karen's office. He gave her a report on what he had learned, grinning the entire time. "Good, huh?"

She laughed. "Yes. Good. And I have some news for you." She pulled a sheet of notes in front of her. "While you were out, the captain called me. His contact in New York has been checking the phone numbers Mosely Cain is communicating with. He has called and received calls from a cell phone in Alaska. The number is listed to, none other than, Sam Goodyear. I'm waiting for a call from the fire marshal to tell me if there is a large amount of cash in the safe in Dunn's house. If we can locate the cash, I think we can go to the DA and either get an arrest warrant, or go to the grand jury. Good, huh?"

"This case has been a brick wall at every turn since the start and now everything seems to be falling into place. I don't know why I have this uneasy feeling, though," Stanton said to his partner.

Karen answered her ringing desk phone, "Sergeant Holmes."

"This is Captain Ballantine with the U.S. Coast Guard in Kodiak. I was told you are the helicopter pilot for the troopers in your area, is that correct?"

"Yes, Captain. What is it you need?" she asked.

"The Rescue Coordination Center referred me to you. We have a call concerning a small plane crash on a beach near the Chickaloon River at Refuge Bay on the Kenai Peninsula. RCC helicopters are at another crash site with multiple victims near Denali Park. Our helicopters are on an at-sea rescue, a sinking fishing vessel west of Kodiak. Is it possible for you to pick up that downed pilot? No injuries are reported, but the weather is dropping and this pilot lost his survival gear in the crash. He is on the beach and has a fire, but no shelter and no insulated clothing."

"I was put back on flying status this week, Captain. Give me the GPS coordinates and I will see what I can do." She wrote the numbers on the pad in front of her, called Captain Davis to advise him of her departure and asked to take Stanton. She also asked the captain to call the hangar and advise them she was on her way.

Stanton was in the left seat while Karen piloted from the right. The Robertson 44 is a four place helicopter with a rotor blade on a tall stand above the fuselage. It is not an exceptionally powerful helicopter, but it will haul four people without difficulty. She spoke to him through the headset. Karen headed south, across Turnagain Arm.

"That's Chickaloon River straight ahead. Look for a small campfire. We will probably see it before we spot the wrecked plane. It's not fun flying in this low ceiling. I'd like to have some altitude going across this cold water."

"I think I just saw a flicker to the right of the river. Yeah, there it is. Do you see it?"

"Oh, yes." She turned the aircraft slightly to the right. As they approached the fire, a man became visible. She circled and noted there were no obstacles between the fire and the water's edge. She eased the small blue and white craft to the ground, causing a huge cloud of snow to be blown into the air. She stayed in the pilot seat while Stanton got out to help the downed pilot.

The man was shivering and near hypothermia. "I'm OK," he said hoarsely.

"Come on, I'll get you inside the helicopter where it's warm. Do you have any gear?" Stanton asked.

"No, just what is in my pockets." He pointed toward the beach and the water. "That is where my plane is, upside down in the water. I called to get someone to come and lift it out of here, but I think the tide will get it first."

"We can call an ambulance while we fly back to the hangar. I think you should go to the hospital and be checked out. Cold as you are, you may have injuries you can't feel."

The pilot nodded his assent as he settled into one of the rear seats of the helicopter. He was truly grateful for the rescue. Stanton crawled into the copilot seat again and they took off toward Anchorage and Lake Hood. An ambulance was waiting at the state hangar when they arrived. Stanton took the man's driver's license and copied the needed information to his notebook along with the tail number of the wrecked plane. He was being loaded into the ambulance when Stanton reached him to return his license.

"Good luck, sir," Stanton said.

Karen had noted the flight in her log book and spoken to the mechanic from the hangar who said he would put the bird away after fueling it. Karen thanked him and the two troopers walked to her SUV.

"Let's swing by Dunn's hangar as long as we are in the neighborhood," she said.

"Good idea, partner," replied her partner.

It was only about three blocks to Dunn's hangar and they were surprised to see Lieber's old truck parked by the entry door. Karen stopped the SUV and asked, "Shall we visit Mr. Lieber?"

"We should ask what he is doing here, anyway," Stanton added in a joking tone.

Cautiously they walked to the door, opened it quietly, and peeked inside. There was a light burning on the desk. Carlton was sitting in the desk chair reading. Being as stealthy as possible, they stepped inside, moving toward the light. They were only about fifteen feet away when Karen spoke.

"Good evening, Carlton."

The man jumped completely out of his chair and dropped the book he had been reading. He looked at them wide-eyed.

"What are you two doing here?" Carlton asked.

"We came to check the hangar, Carlton. Nobody is supposed to be here since Anthony Dunn died." Karen informed the mechanic.

"What do you mean he died? I didn't know Mr. Dunn died." Leiber seemed surprised.

"Yup. He died in a house fire last night. It was on the news; I'm surprised you hadn't heard," Stanton delivered the news.

"Oh man! First he gets arrested and then he dies in a house fire. That's bad, man. What happened? What caused the fire, I mean?"

"The fire marshal says it's a suspicious fire. Did you set the fire, Carlton?" Stanton asked.

"Are you crazy? I ain't into that stuff, you know that," Carlton declared defensively.

"What are you doing here, then?" Karen asked him.

"Mr. Dunn asked me to stay here until he could get something going again. He wanted me to do a couple of things on the King Air and he said to watch the hangar because he hid a box here he didn't want anyone to find. He asked me to guard it."

Karen looked at Stanton with anticipation in her eyes. "Where is the box now, Carlton?" she asked.

"Right here." He pointed to a cardboard box between the desk and a file cabinet.

"Have you looked inside the box?" she inquired.

"No. He said to leave it alone and he would come back for it."

"I can get a search warrant to take the box, Carlton, but since you are in charge of it you could give me permission to look inside," Karen said cautiously, not knowing if it were true.

Stanton lifted the box to the top of the desk. Carlton produced a small pocket knife with which he cut the cellophane tape holding the top closed. Inside was a black plastic bag, twisted at the top and secured with a wire tie. Stanton untwisted the wire and opened the bag. Inside, in neat bank bands, was a large amount of cash. Atop the cash was a handwritten note. Stanton put on a rubber glove before picking up the note.

"This is everything. I kept the loose change of about $2,000. Keep the room key for a souvenir," read the note.

Stanton picked up the green plastic key tag. It was the key to Whittle's room in New Orleans. They closed the bag and the box. It needed to go to the crime lab before it was inventoried.

"You did well, Carlton. Tomorrow, I want you to come to my office and we will help you write a statement about all the things you did for Mr. Dunn. I will personally call the DA to ask for a deal for you. You have been a big help, Carlton. Thank you." Karen meant what she said. He would probably go to jail anyway, but he had been instrumental in finding the person who murdered Jack Boardon.

CHAPTER 45

During the drive back to headquarters, Stanton seemed unusually happy. "This calls for a celebration. Why don't you drop me at my car, go home, and get out of that uniform. I'll do the same and take you to dinner?"

"I can't, Craig. I have a date," she replied.

He spun his head around in surprise. "You have a date? I didn't think you ever dated."

"I'm surprised you thought about it at all. You have been so taken by the skinny blond."

"Who are you dating?"

"That's none of your business," she told him with a wry smile.

"I still don't believe it," Stanton said, shaking his head in disbelief. "Well, congratulations to both of you."

"Thanks. By the way, how did you like the little mission this afternoon? It makes you feel good to save someone, doesn't it?" she asked out of curiosity.

"I have never ridden in a helicopter before. It was fun. Landing and seeing the relief on that pilot's face was worth a lot. Yeah, I loved it. Not enough to want to learn to fly a helicopter, but I'd go again if I got the chance."

Karen dropped Stanton at his car and shouted after him as he walked to his vehicle. "See you tomorrow. We will have a lot of work to do. Be here early."

"Yes, Mom," he said as he waved goodbye.

He started his car and while it warmed up, he dialed Laura Toombes. It was the first time he had been able to call her since the fire. When she answered, her voice was sad.

"Hi, Laura, are you OK?"

"Oh, Craig," she sobbed, "this has been so horrible."

"I know, Laura, I know." He tried to console the sobbing woman. "Have you had dinner?"

"No, but I haven't felt like eating since Mr. Dunn died. It's so horrible." She was crying hard now.

"Take it easy, Laura. Do you want me to come by and be with you a while?"

"Not tonight, Craig. I love you, but I have to be alone tonight. I just have to."

Stanton was surprised to hear she loved him but knew there were times a person had to be alone. "Call me if you change your mind. And for what it's worth, I love you, too."

Two offers and two rejections in ten minutes, he thought dejectedly. He was now unsure what to do. He decided to stop and pick up a pizza to take home.

He was eating his pizza, drinking a Coke, and thinking about Karen. He couldn't help wondering who she was dating. What about Laura? She had said she loved him but wanted to be alone. He decided he must not understand people very well.

He thought about Carlton Lieber and about what was going to happen to him. He, after all, was an accessory to a murder. The DA couldn't just excuse that. Carlton was going to go to jail, possibly for a long, long time. He finished his pizza and Coke, turned out the lights, and headed to the shower and bed.

He awoke at five to stagger out of bed and to the bathroom. He shaved and dressed in a clean uniform. He stopped at Judy's cafe for a quick breakfast and coffee before going in to the office to begin a boring day of paperwork.

Karen was at her desk when he arrived.

"How was your date?" he asked.

"I'm not telling." She looked up at him and smiled. "You once asked if I thought you looked 'like someone who would kiss and tell' I might ask you the same question. I don't discuss my personal life at the office. What part of this report do you want to work on?"

"I admire your ethics," he said, grinning at her. "Give me the stuff on Carlton and the box in the hangar. You have to do the one on the rescue." He took the stack of papers and returned to his office. The rest of the morning was spent with his head buried in notes and forms. Just before noon, his cell phone rang.

"Stanton," he answered.

"Craig, its Laura. I'm in trouble."

He sat up and listened more carefully. "What's the problem, Laura?"

"Some U.S. Drug Enforcement Agency agents came to the office this morning, handed me a search warrant and searched my car. They said they found a large amount of cocaine under the seat. I don't do drugs, Craig. You know that. I don't know how the drugs got there. I don't know what to do."

"Where are you now?"

"They arrested me and brought me to the federal building. They said they had a lot of questions to ask. Please, Craig, I'm frightened. Please help me." She was sobbing into the telephone

"OK, Laura, calm down. Just tell them you want a lawyer before you answer any questions. That should slow them down a while until I can find out what is going on. I'll be there as soon as I can."

"Thank you, Craig. I'll do what you say. Hurry, please."

Craig Stanton quickly walked to Karen's office. He gave her a short synopsis of his conversation with Laura. "What in the world is going on? She was never implicated in Dunn's drug business."

Karen sat silent for a moment then announced, "Craig, this is about you and me. Goodyear! Goodyear is trying to confuse the issues and muddy our case. He is going to try to connect you and Laura to discredit you and to taint our case."

"We have to tell the captain about this," Stanton said.

"I agree," she said, picking up the intercom.

In the captain's office, the two rapidly went over the situation. Captain Davis listened intently, searching for options. While the discussion was taking place, the intercom rang. It was the front desk. A DEA agent wanted to see Captain Davis.

"I'll have someone come get him and bring him to my office." He looked at Karen. "Go get him, will you Karen? Craig and I will wait here."

Three minutes later Karen reappeared with a well-dressed man at her side. He was about thirty-five years of age, wavy black hair, and stern expression. He looked like a poster child for a DEA recruiting poster.

"Good morning," he said, presenting his credentials. "I am Stanley La Crosse. I would prefer to speak with you alone, Captain."

"I'll bet you would, Stan." The captain was not impressed with the agent's attitude. "Before we go any further, I want to know the nature of your business here."

La Crosse glanced at Holmes and Stanton but decided to plunge ahead. "I wanted to clear the way with you before confronting one of your officers."

"Get on with it La Crosse. Why are you here?" Davis asked again.

"We arrested Laura Toombes this morning, with a warrant. She is the current girlfriend of one of your officers. We had an anonymous tip that this woman was transporting cocaine for sale. The tip also indicated her boyfriend was supplying her with the drugs. Her boyfriend is your officer, Craig Stanton. I have an arrest warrant o serve on him. I would appreciate your cooperation in this matter."

"Sure thing, Stan." Davis was doing his best to irritate the DEA agent. He turned to Craig. "I am required to ask for your weapon and badge, Craig, department policy."

Stanton nodded and unbuckled his duty belt and placed it on the captain's desk. The captain took it and placed it on the credenza behind him while Craig unfastened his badge.

"Thank you," said La Cross as he reached inside his suit-coat pocket for a copy of the warrant.

"Hold on a minute, Stan. Before you try to serve this warrant, I have a couple of questions." Davis looked the agent in the eyes.

"Certainly, Captain, anything I can do," he said.

"First of all, you said these warrants were issued on an anonymous tip. Just how did you verify the validity of the information?"

"We searched the vehicle owned by Laura Toombes and found a package containing cocaine under the front seat. We arrested her at that time for possession with intent to sell, due to the amount of drugs in her possession," La Cross recited.

"So, your verification came as a result of evidence you found during a search in which the search warrant was made on an anonymous tip. Is that correct?"

"Basically, yes," La Cross admitted.

"I'm not a lawyer, but it sounds like the search warrant was not valid. That means the drugs you seized are tainted evidence and you have no substantiating evidence to prove Stanton is involved; therefore, this arrest warrant is invalid." Davis was enjoying this.

"No one has said the search warrant was not valid," La Cross defended.

"What judge issued each of these warrants?" asked Davis.

"Judge Zukor signed them both."

"Hold on a minute while I call him and ask him a couple of questions." Davis picked up the telephone and began to dial a number he knew by heart. While it was being answered, he said, "Have a seat, Stan."

"No, thank you, I'll stand," La Cross replied.

"Harry, Davis at AST. How was your trip to Australia? Did you win the billfish tournament?"

"I didn't win, but I placed fourth. Not bad considering there were something like 230 entrants," the judge bragged.

"How big was your fish?"

"It was a dandy—1,483 pounds," said Judge Zukor.

"Wow! How big was the winner?" Davis asked.

"1,856 pounds. Listen I'm due in court in a few minutes. Can we talk about this later?"

"You bet, Harry, but before you go I need to ask you something. You signed a couple of warrants for the DEA. I am told the information came on an anonymous tip. I need to know what DEA agent validated the facts for you," Davis told his friend.

"Let me think. Oh, yes, I remember. It was Sam Goodyear. He's some kind of head dog over there."

"Hold on a second, Judge. I am going to put you on the speaker phone. I have DEA Agent La Cross in my office. He is here to serve one of those warrants on an officer in my command." Davis switched the phone to speaker. "Go ahead, Judge."

"Agent La Cross, what is it you want to know? This is Judge Harry Zukor, I signed those warrants."

"Captain Davis thinks the warrants were obtained with false information given to you by Agent Goodyear," Agent La Cross said without conviction.

"Is that correct, Davis?" Zukor asked.

"Yes it is, Judge."

"I am headed to court right now, but I want both of you in my office in twenty minutes and bring the warrants. What you are telling me, if true, would constitute a serious offense. Twenty minutes," Zukor repeated before hanging up the phone.

"You heard the Judge, Stan. We have to be in his office in twenty minutes. That means you have twenty minutes to begin to think for yourself. I'll fill you in on Goodyear later. I am warning you not to notify your office about any of this until after we meet with Judge Zukor. For now let me say that Goodyear is suspected of being an accomplice, or even of committing, the arson that killed Anthony Dunn. Now let's go. You can ride with me."

Captain Davis turned to Sergeant Holmes as he walked toward the door. "Karen, Craig is in your custody until we return. Keep him here," he ordered.

Karen stopped the captain. "If the Judge revokes the warrants, would you see to it that Laura Toombes is released and brought here?"

"Yes, Karen, I will." With that, he and Stanley La Crosse headed for the courthouse.

Davis and La Cross started out the door. Davis told La Crosse he could ride with him and that they could talk about Goodyear while on the way to the Nesbitt Courthouse. La Crosse was uneasy. He wondered if he would be able to trust Judge Zukor given the personal relationship that seemed to exist between him and Captain Davis.

In the car, before Davis had a chance to start the engine, La Crosse asked Davis a very pointed question, irritated with the attitude the captain had displayed.

"Agent Goodyear is a highly decorated officer. What would make you say he is a suspect in murder and arson? That, to me, is absurd."

Davis was grinning. "I don't imagine he was bragging about it while he was in the office. Let's wait until we talk with Judge Zukor; then, if you still have doubts, we will go back to the office and I will show you the evidence we have. Fair enough?"

"Fair enough," agreed La Crosse.

Davis found an official parking area close to the door. The two men went inside the courthouse and found Judge Harry Zukor's office. His clerk asked them to have a seat until the Judge returned. Only moments later she said, "You can go in now. He's back and waiting for you. I would like to remind you he has another hearing in less than an hour, so please keep it short."

Davis told her he would comply and thanked her. It appeared this was the first time La Crosse had been in a federal judge's office and he was awed. Inside, Harry invited them to sit in the high backed, red leather chairs in front of his huge desk.

"I am informing you both that, because of the nature of this meeting, I am recording this hearing. Understand?" Zukor began.

Both men nodded and said yes for the recorder.

"Alright, what makes you think Sam Goodyear falsified information to obtain these warrants? He has been in my office many times to ask for warrants and never have I found him to be less than truthful."

"In the hurry to get to your office, I failed to bring the file we have on Agent Sam Goodyear, but I will furnish you a copy today. Agent La Crosse hasn't seen the file either," Davis explained. "The summary of the investigation goes like this. We have a case which started with a plane crash. It turned out that the pilot had 400 pounds of high grade marijuana in his Cessna when he crashed. The pilot was killed in the crash. We learned that a mechanic had rigged the fuel gauges to read full when, in fact, they had been drained and the plane contained only about a half hour of fuel. We later learned the pilot was carrying a large sum of cash with him. The money was taken by a trapper who discovered the crash. Someone burglarized the trapper's cabin attempting to find the cash. The trapper came home and found the burglar. The burglar pulled a gun, but the trapper had a rifle in his hands and shot him dead. Later the trapper became worried and left the state, taking the money with him. Whoever was looking for the money followed him to New Orleans, killed him, ransacked his room, and took the money, which he then sent back to Alaska. The recipient of the cash was Anthony Dunn. He was found dead in a house fire this week, the same day he received the package of cash. At the time of the plane crash, the pilot was on his way to Fairbanks to meet with a drug importer by the name of Mosely Cain. We suspect Cain ordered the death of the trapper in New Orleans. Are you with me so far?" Davis asked the others.

Both Zukor and La Crosse said yes and he continued.

"We have one common denominator in this case. Everyone is connected. Dunn and the pilot of the Cessna, a man named Jack Boardon, and the drug importer, Cain, as well as Sam Goodyear, were all old buddies from the first Gulf War. They all served there at the same time. Dunn and Boardon and Cain were all pilots. Goodyear was a military policeman. They were all drinking buddies back then. The man shot burglarizing the trapper cabin worked for Dunn. We think Boardon was trying to cut Dunn out of the drug smuggling business. Dunn had him killed. We followed Dunn to Fairbanks where he picked up a large package of cocaine and heroin. He brought them to Anchorage and re-packaged them. He left the package in his hangar at Lake Hood to be picked up by a FedEx pilot, Marshal Dillon."

Zukor held up his hand to stop the conversation. "Marshal Dillon? Is that a real person?" the Judge asked.

"Yes, sir. That's his real name. He is now in custody in California." Davis continued, "Dillon took the drugs through security and passed them to a distributor in San Francisco. The point to all this is that the pivot point, the common factor, is Sam Goodyear. The warrants you signed have the same common denominator. I trust my man, Stanton. Goodyear is trying to impugn Stanton and taint the drug case as well as the murder case."

Judge Zukor was tapping his fingers on his desk. He turned to La Crosse, "What do you have to say about all this."

"I'm sorry, Judge. This is the first I have heard of any of this. I have to say that, if there is proof of any of this, Captain Davis is right to challenge the warrants. I have not seen the reports or the documentation, but I have to assume the captain has it." He turned to Captain Davis. "If you can document any of what you have said, I owe you and Trooper Stanton an apology."

"Now you understand why we never sent copies of this to your office. And, until we can arrest Goodyear, I don't want you to repeat any of what you have heard."

"You have my word," the agent said.

"OK, Captain, send me copies of those reports and I will check them out. If what you have told us is confirmed in the reports, I will rescind the warrants and have Miss Toombes and Trooper Stanton released, and I will have any record of their arrests expunged."

"I will have a trooper bring you a copy as soon as I get back to the office," the captain told him. "Thank you, Judge."

Back in the car, Stanley La Crosse faced Davis. "I meant what I said about an apology. I didn't know about all this. I'd like to help with this case, if you would let me."

"I may take you up on that offer, Stan. We aren't quite ready to arrest Sam, but this will put a rush on it."

Back at trooper headquarters, the two men went directly to the captain's office. Davis ordered copies of the file to be made and one sent to Judge Zukor and one given to DEA Agent La Crosse. He also called Karen and Craig to his office.

When Karen arrived in the office, she seemed excited. Stanton came in behind her. As he entered, the captain handed him his duty belt and shield. "They just didn't have all the facts, Craig."

Agent La Crosse held out his hand for Craig to shake. "It looks as if I owe you an apology. The only excuse I can offer is that I was just following orders. I'm sorry."

"Apology accepted. Now, is it possible for us to work together?" Craig asked.

"The captain convinced me. I will do anything I can to help out," La Crosse said.

Karen interrupted, "Does Stan have access to the file, Captain?"

"Yes, I gave it to him. If you have any additional information about the case, you can share it with Stan"

"In that case, hang on to your hat. While you were out, I had two calls. One from the crime lab; they examined the box of cash. They lifted a print from the note and got a match right away. The print belongs to one Lonnie Beason of New Orleans, Louisiana. He has a criminal record as long as your leg. Lately he has been into drug distribution, extortion and assault."

"It sounds like he could be our Whittle assailant," Davis commented.

"It gets better, Captain." Karen continued, "Beason has been confirmed as one of the names of phone contacts made by Mosely "Moose" Cain. Cain called Beanon's number the day before Whittle was killed. In my book, he ordered the hit on Whittle."

"You see, Stan? Every time we try to connect the dots it comes around to Sam Goodyear." The captain was glad La Crosse was here to hear it first-hand.

"How do you want me to go about dealing with Beason, Captain?" Karen asked.

Davis thought a moment then asked, "What was that detective's name, the one in New Orleans?"

"Ah, you mean DEE-tective Boudreaux, of the NO-lins PO-lice Department," she mimicked.

"That's the one. Give him a call and pass this on to him. Let Boudreaux get first shot at Beason, if he is still in NO-lins." Captain Davis was pleased. This had come to light at an opportune time.

"Craig, I've had a copy of the file made to be sent to Judge Zukor. Go up front and get that file and take it to him. If you can see him personally, fill him in on Beason. When he sees the file, the judge will have Laura Toombes released. You can stop at the DEA office and pick her up and deliver her here. She will not be safe at home until we arrest Goodyear."

"Thank you, Captain. I'm on my way." He smiled at Karen and turned to La Crosse. "And, thank you Agent La Crosse. I hope we can work together in the future." Craig shook his hand again before leaving the office.

Karen watched as her partner walked away. "He's a good man, Captain. He has a good head on his shoulders, as well as a good sense of humor. He's fun to work with. I like him."

"Coming from you, Karen, that is a four-star recommendation. For what it's worth, I like him, too."

"If there is nothing further, Captain, I will go back to the office and regroup. I'll be there when Stanton comes to pick up Miss Toombes," Agent La Crosse said in a solemn tone. "How do you want me to handle Goodyear? If he is in the office when I return, he will be asking questions about Stanton. I may not be able to answer all his questions without raising his suspicions."

"I wanted to go to the grand jury for an indictment, but this will put a rush on his arrest. As soon as you get back call me. I want Laura Toombes and Craig Stanton out of the building when this goes down. I will send four troopers to arrest Goodyear at his office, but I will need you to help in keeping things orderly. I don't think he will resist in his own office, but you never can tell."

"You can count on me, Captain. I'll call you as soon as Stanton and Toombes are out of the office. I had better be getting back now. Thank you for tolerating me and my attitude, Captain Davis. I will try to stay on your good side from this day on." He shook hands with the captain and left.

When he was gone, Karen smiled and looked at Davis. "I think I could learn to like him," she said.

Captain Davis was giving orders to Sergeant Holmes. "Pick three officers to go to the federal building with you. You may as well have coffee and brief your raiding party. It will be up to me to contact security in the federal building about your arrival. We don't want any sort of scene in the lobby. When Stanton and Laura are out of the building, you need to be ready to move in." He was reaching for the telephone.

Karen went to her office, called the front desk, and asked for a list of officers on duty. She wrote the names on a legal pad while the receptionist read them off. Karen quickly scanned the list and told the dispatcher to have Troopers Sloan, Mitchum, and Gomez come to her office right away. She then followed the captain's advice and got a cup of coffee. Within minutes, all three officers were in her office.

"You guys all know each other, right?" The three men nodded, looking at one another. "I have a special assignment and I want you three to accompany me," she began. "As you may or may not know, Stanton and I have been working a murder case. This case has gone from weird to bazaar."

She gave them a short version of the case. "We—you three—and I will be going to the federal building to arrest Agent Sam Goodyear. We think he is responsible for the death of Anthony Dunn. He has had a hand in other crimes, but the arrest will be for murder and arson. Gomez, I want you to handle the actual arrest and handcuffing of Goodyear. You others will back him up in case Goodyear gets physical. I don't anticipate anything like that, but we have to be ready. I will read the charges for which he is being taken into state custody. You all know how this works, just be ready." Holmes paused and looked around at the men.

"Any questions?" They were shaking their heads; they understood. "Get some coffee. We are waiting for Stanton to call and say he is going to get the girl out of the building before we make our play. When he heads for the federal building, we will head out. The marshals are expecting us, so we won't be stopped in the lobby."

Ten minutes later Stanton called to say he was on his way to the federal building. Karen and the three troopers headed out of the headquarters building. They parked both cars in official parking slots at the front door of the building. Stanton had parked near the sally port at the rear of the complex.

Trooper Stanton had his ID checked and was waved into the huge office building. He rode the elevator to the proper floor where the receptionist was sitting at a desk in a small cubical near the entry to the section marked Drug Enforcement Agency. He stopped at the desk and asked for La Crosse. He met Stanton almost immediately.

"Come with me," he said. "She is in an interview room. Bad news, though. Goodyear heard about the warrants being quashed and left the building. I don't know where he went."

"Thanks, Stanley. I had better notify Karen and her party." They continued their march to the back of the offices to a glass interview room. The blinds had been pulled so outside eyes could not see inside the little room. Laura sat in one of the two chairs in the room. There was not a thing on the lone table. Stanton had his phone out of his pocket as they entered. Holding up his hand to Laura, he spoke into the phone to Karen. "Sam split. La Crosse said he heard about the warrants being vacated and left the building. We don't know where he is or where he is going."

"I'll put out a locate-only bulletin on him and his car. I'll call you back as soon as he is spotted," Karen said.

"I'm taking Laura out of here now." Stanton ended his call and turned to Laura, pulled her into his arms and squeezed her tightly. "Let's go," he said.

Stanley La Crosse led the way to the elevator and down to his car. "I might be wrong, but I heard him talking on the phone just before he left. He was talking to someone he knew very well. He ordered the person on the other end to come and get him right away. He listened for a minute and then said Fairbanks, and hung up. I think he may be driving to Fairbanks because he knows we will be watching the Anchorage airport."

"Thanks for the help, Stan. I'm going to stash Laura, then go after Sam." He backed out of the parking space and spun the car into traffic with the red lights flashing. He sped across town to a neighborhood on the south side of town.

"I'm taking you to my place. You will be safe there. You can stay there until I get back. Help yourself to anything in the place. I'd like you to get used to it anyway."

"Oh, Craig, I've been so scared. They came in and handcuffed me, and took me away. They wouldn't tell me anything." She was holding his hand very tightly.

"I know, Laura. I plan to make it up to Sam Goodyear when I catch up with him. But for now, you have to stay put. Don't go out for anything and don't call anyone except me or Karen. I don't want anyone to know where you are. I have to go look for Goodyear."

"I understand, Craig. I'll wait at your place."

He pulled into the drive and hustled her into the house. He gave her a key, kissed her, and said, "I'll be back as soon as I can."

Back in his car, he called Karen again. "La Crosse told me he thought Sam was headed for Fairbanks to be picked up. My guess is that Moose is flying up there to pick him up. It will take a while for him to get here, but we have to find Sam before he can disappear."

"I agree," Karen said. "I'll call the trooper in Talkeetna and have him watch for the car. It will be getting dark soon and it will be a lot tougher to spot him."

"I am headed that way now. I'll start up the Parks Highway and drive all the way to Fairbanks if need be," Stanton said.

"Don't let it get personal, Craig. Do it right."

"You're right, Karen. Don't worry, I'll do it right," he told her.

Stanton was moving quickly. Using his red lights and occasionally the siren in traffic, he passed the Talkeetna exit. The roads were mostly bare, with some snow-pack here and there, as well as a few stretches of black ice. These were becoming more frequent as the temperature dropped. A few miles north of Talkeetna, the local trooper called on the radio.

"I just spotted your subject. He is heading north on the Parks Highway. He is doing the speed limit and driving steady. I don't want to get too close and spook him."

"I'm about 40 miles north of Talkeetna. Do you think I can catch him before Hurricane Gulch?"

"I'd say you should catch up with him about there. Can I help?"

"Can you cruise past him and stay ahead for a while? Until I catch up?"

"I think so. I'll try and call you back."

"Call me on my cell. He may be listening," Stanton informed the trooper.

"I heard that," came Karen's voice. "I have your reds in sight."

Stanton checked his rearview mirror and saw no one. "Where are you?" he asked. "A mile behind and 1000 feet above you."

Stanton stole a quick look back and spotted the helicopter's rotating beacon. "I see you, partner. Let's get him," he urged.

The roads were slippery as he entered the winding road through the Gulch. On the north end of the canyon was a narrow bridge and a sharp right turn. Stanton could see the lights of the agent's car ahead of him. Goodyear must have seen the red lights because he increased his speed.

Stanton was closer now and could see Goodyear's car begin to fishtail as he crossed Hurricane Bridge. This canyon had been given its name for the tremendous winds generated as the air passed through the narrow canyon. Legend has it that men had been blown from the trestle while they were building for the railroad.

Goodyear managed to recover from the skid on the bridge in time to enter the hard right turn at the other end. He skidded again and slammed into the snow bank on the left side of the turn. His car bounced enough to keep him from being stuck in the snow and he continued up the hill.

Karen had now passed them and was circling near the top of the grade. The Talkeetna trooper was parked on the side of the road at the top of the hill. Goodyear saw the trooper car and began to slow. Then, he must have seen the helicopter. He shoved the throttle to the floor and fishtailed again but gained speed as he approached the other trooper's car.

The trooper at the top of the hill pulled his car across the road, not completely blocking it, but with the aid of the tall snow banks, enough to prevent a car from going around him. He sat on the road with his red lights flashing. As he approached, Goodyear could see it was impossible for him to pass and began to slow. He suddenly swung crossways of the road and attempted to make a U-turn. His car wasn't able to make the turn in one motion and he had to stop and back up. By doing this, he lost enough time for Stanton to come close and block the road behind him. Goodyear was stopped now, sitting in his car.

Stanton was out of his car, keeping the vehicle between him and Goodyear. Sam just sat there. Craig reached for his microphone and switched to PA mode.

"You are under arrest, Goodyear. This is Trooper Stanton. Throw out your weapon and step out of the car with your hands in the air." The loudspeaker was very loud in the silence of the frigid night.

Goodyear did not move. He was just sitting in his car, waiting.

"Get out of the car, Sam. Make this easy on yourself."

Then, Sam did something strange. He exited the car on the passenger side without throwing out his weapon and began to walk toward the other trooper car. Slowly, but directly he walked.

Again, Stanton spoke through the loudspeaker. "Give it up, Sam, throw down your weapon. We have no desire to do you harm. Drop the gun, Sam."

Goodyear kept walking ever closer to the trooper car. Karen watched from the top of the little hill. She had landed, but did not get out of her helicopter.

The Talkeetna trooper was behind his car with his own weapon drawn. Goodyear was about twenty-five feet away when he made his move. He reached inside his suit coat to pull out his .40 Caliber Smith and Wesson. He flipped off the safety.

Stanton could see what was coming and shouted on the speaker. "Don't do it, Sam," but the warning was too late. Sam had fired at the trooper who fell behind his car. Sam then spun around to take a shot at Stanton, but he was blinded by the spotlight Craig had turned on and focused on the agent. Sam shot in the direction of the light, but Stanton had moved to the rear of his car.

Craig fired two shots at Goodyear. One struck his gun arm while the other struck him low in the abdomen. Sam's gun went clattering across the icy pavement as he fell to the ground, screaming in pain.

When the shooting started, Karen had leaped from her pilot's seat to help. She saw the first trooper take a hit in the shoulder and fall to the pavement. Behind the car, he struggled to regain his feet, but Karen shouted for him to stay down. She ran to his side, crouching low to prevent being shot at. Then more shots rang out and when she looked, Goodyear was on the ground writhing in pain.

"Are you all right, Craig?" she called.

"Yes, I'm OK. How is the other trooper?"

"He's hit, but I don't think he's too bad. Cover me while I pick up Sam's weapon."

Stanton did just that. The entire event had taken less than a minute, but it had seemed an eternity.

Karen picked up the Smith and Wesson and slipped it into her jacket pocket. "Craig, call for an ambulance from Cantwell. Goodyear is bleeding badly. When you finish, come help me stop the bleeding."

When Craig walked to her side, he found Goodyear barely conscious. The two troopers did their best to stem the bleeding on both men as they waited for the ambulance to arrive. The Cantwell trooper arrived before the ambulance. After checking on Karen and Craig, he found another blanket in his car with which to cover his friend from Talkeetna.

Minutes later the ambulance came and the medics spent some time stabilizing Goodyear before loading him. Karen asked them to help load the wounded trooper into her helicopter. She would transport him to the hospital in Anchorage. More troopers came to the scene and took pictures and video. They picked up all the empty cartridge cases as evidence. The road was closed for over three hours while the process was completed.

Stanton was glad to be back inside his car, getting warm, and driving toward Anchorage. The outside temperature had dropped to minus 41 degrees and the Northern Lights were exhibiting a colorful display. Stanton was too consumed by the events of the day to notice.

CHAPTER 48

It was past midnight when Stanton reached Anchorage. As he neared town, he asked dispatch if Sergeant Holmes had checked out yet. They told him she was in the office. He dialed her phone and waited. A tired voice came on the other end.

"Sergeant Holmes."

"Karen, it's me. Are you OK?"

"Yes, thank you. How about you?"

"I feel as if I had been shot at, other than that I'm alright. At least nothing a good night's sleep won't fix. How is Trooper Evans?"

"The ambulance was waiting when I landed at Lake Hood. He had lost a lot of blood, but he was conscious and talking. That .40 caliber left a big hole, but it didn't appear he had any bone damage and the bleeding had stopped by the time we got to town. I'll go to Providence Hospital later today and see him. Do you want to go along?"

"You bet. He saved my bacon. I need to thank him for the job he did. Have you talked with the Captain?"

"Yes, but only for a minute to let him know we're both OK. The Talkeetna post is responsible to Palmer, Captain Davis was to call his commander and tell him what happened. You sound pretty tired, Craig. If I know you, you are headed in to do the reports. Go home. Someone is waiting for you there. You can come in a little late in the morning and finish the reports. No one is going to court in the morning, so it can wait a few hours."

"Thanks, Karen. I could use some sleep. You know how it is when the adrenalin wears off. I'm going home," a weary Stanton replied.

Sergeant Karen Holmes had been waiting for his call and as soon as she had finished talking to him, she began to put things away and ready for her own departure. It had been a long and eventful day, one she would remember for many years to come.

Craig Stanton reached his home a half hour later. As he pulled into the drive, he saw the lights were on in the living room. He backed his car into the carport and slowly climbed the steps to the front door. He let himself inside as quietly as possible in case Laura was asleep. He needn't have worried. She was sitting on the couch waiting. Her eyes were red from crying and lack of sleep, but she stood when he opened the door.

At five feet ten inches tall and with her blond hair piled high on her head, Laura could have looked imposing. But she was beautiful to Craig. The curls at the side of her face were perfect, and, still in her stocking feet, she ran to meet him at the door. Without a word, she threw her arms around his neck and held him tight.

"I have been so worried, Craig. You have blood on your shirt. Are you all right? Are you hurt?" she asked, not turning loose of his neck.

"I'm fine, but it has turned into a long day. The good news is that you can forget about Sam Goodyear ever bothering you again. We arrested him, near Cantwell, on murder and arson charges. He tried to shoot it out and got himself shot in the process. I think he'll live, but he may wish he hadn't."

"Oh, Craig, you were involved in a shooting? Does this happen often?" she asked.

"Almost never," he replied. "Do you want me to take you home tonight, or would you prefer to stay?"

"I'm staying. You go get cleaned up. I'll have fresh coffee by the time you get done." She kissed him and looked into his eyes with a peaceful expression on her beautiful face.

A few minutes later, he returned wearing pajamas and a robe. She heard him coming, his slippers scuffing on the carpet. She was pouring his coffee when he returned to the kitchen.

"I had to take time for a shower," he said.

She handed him his coffee. He took it and took a small sip. "Good," he said.

"I have something to say, Craig. Please listen and don't stop me before I'm finished. It took me all day to get up the courage to make this speech."

Craig took a longer drink of his coffee and nodded his agreement.

She stared into his eyes. "You and I have only known each other for a short time, but I have grown very fond of you. In fact, I have never felt this way about anyone. I don't know how you feel about me, but if you have any feelings for me at all, I would like you to consider making this a more permanent arrangement. You know, see if we could stand to be with each other on a daily basis."

Stanton put down his coffee cup. He was dumbfounded. "Do you know what you're saying, Laura?"

"Oh, Craig, I was afraid you wouldn't want to try living with me. I'm sorry I brought it up."

"Hold on, Laura. You have it all wrong. I have been trying for days to figure out how to ask you the same thing. I thought if I asked you it would just make you mad and you'd never want to see me again. I'm falling in love with you. I can't help it; I just am." He reached for her and pulled her close. He kissed her long and deeply. When he pulled back, he added, "How about we live together long enough to make proper wedding plans?"

"Really? Craig, do you mean it?" she said almost crying with happiness.

"I saw the limit of my mortality today and I don't want to waste what time I have left in life. Yes, I mean it."

"Oh, Craig, I love you. I love you." She was holding his arm with her head against his shoulder.

"I hate to break up this wonderful moment, but I have to work tomorrow. Can we get some sleep now and take this up again tomorrow?"

"Yes. Yes. Yes," she giggled. "I'll have to go home sometime in the morning and get some clothes and a shower."

From a drawer in the kitchen, he took a set of keys. "This is the key to my car. It's in the garage. Take it tomorrow and get what you need. Keep your cell phone with you."

It was a very short night for Stanton. He was in the office by 7:30. Karen was already working. Captain Davis came in as Craig was pouring his first cup of coffee.

Davis poured his own coffee and said to Stanton, "Great job yesterday, Craig. Get Karen and come to my office with your coffee. We have to talk."

Once in the captain's office with the door closed, Davis asked for a verbal report on the chase and the shooting.

Stanton did most of the talking at first. He detailed the events of the chase and catching up with Goodyear at Hurricane Gulch. He told about the Talkeetna trooper, Dean Evans, blocking the road and Karen landing at the top of the hill. "I tried to talk him into dropping his weapon and giving himself up, but he pulled his gun and shot Evans. He then turned and shot at me. I managed to get off two shots and hit him twice. He went down and Karen moved in to help the other trooper. In what seemed like no time at all there were a lot of troopers on the scene."

"I just spoke with Providence Hospital. They said Goodyear will survive, but it was close. He lost a lot of blood during the ride to Anchorage. He was on the operating table all night and has just now gone to recovery. I have a guard on him." Davis sat back in a relaxed position.

"The two of you have taken this case from an aircraft accident to an international drug business. You have left bodies everywhere, but you successfully followed the case. You were able to uncover Dunn's Blue Sky Real Estate for what it really was, a money laundering business. You were able to follow the results of the marijuana growing business to the heroin and cocaine importing business. Blue sky and green grass, you made it work and got to the root if it all even though there was never any real evidence to follow. In my book that makes you two a pair of the best investigators I have ever had. I'll see there are letters of commendation in your files. You won't get a raise, though," he joked.

"Thanks, Captain, you were part of the team, too. It isn't over yet. We have to get the case to court and we have to find Moose Cain," Karen said in a grateful tone.

"As long as we are here, Captain, I guess I should tell you that Laura Toombes and I are going to be living together for a while until we can work out a wedding plan."

"Thank you for telling me, Craig," acknowledged Captain Davis. "Now get those reports finished and on my desk."

When they left the office, Karen turned to Stanton. "Dapper Craig Stanton and the skinny blond—I never would have guessed," she said, laughing.

It was going to take a long time to bring all the facets of this case into focus and to have the DA get indictments. The Feds were making the case on Moose Cain for importing drugs. Marshall Dillon had been indicted in San Francisco for charges ranging from breaching security to delivery of dangerous drugs for sale.

De-tective Boudreaux was pleased with the information supplied by Karen. Lonnie Beason had been located in Georgia and arrested. Boudreaux and the State of Louisiana were working on extradition warrants.

The night they arrested Sam Goodyear, Mosely "Moose" Cain had rented a Gulfstream IV to fly to Fairbanks. Airport security had notified the Fairbanks Trooper Office there was activity at Amarada Cargo's hangar. When the troopers entered the hangar, Cain ran for the Gulfstream. Without preamble, preflight or clearance, he took off. He had fuelled the plane while waiting for Sam Goodyear. He had no destination in the United States he could call safe. He tried to think of options, and then he decided to fly west. He made a refueling stop in western Russia before flying southwest toward Thailand. He had friends there with the power to keep him safe for a while, at least until he could figure out his next move.

Federal arrest warrants were issued for Mosely Cain. When he landed in Bangkok, he was met by his old friend and business associate, General Li Po. The general helped him re-register the Gulfstream in Thailand, changing the identification numbers.

Several weeks passed with Cain living high, though quietly, in the Thai countryside. The General visited often and the two discussed ways to, once again, export heroin to the Unites State. One evening the two were having a friendly drink and discussing the problem, when there was a knock at the door. Cain answered it to find a squad of Thai police at his door with an international police warrant for his arrest. The arresting Thai officer also had a local warrant for the General. It seems his association with Cain and the drug business had come to light. With the help of the General, Cain was confident he could stop the arrest and extradition to the United States. It didn't work out that way, however, and Cain found himself on a military transport plane being flown to a jail in America.

News of the arrest reached, now Lieutenant, Karen Holmes. When she heard, she summoned, now Sergeant, Craig Stanton to her office. It was a joyous meeting that brought closure to a long and frustrating case.

"When is the wedding, Craig?" Karen asked her old partner.

"Soon, but no date yet. She wants a June wedding. Of course, you are invited."

"Do you mind if I invite myself into the occasion?"

"What do you mean, Karen?"

"I have decided to give my man a 'yes.' Do you think Laura would object to having a double wedding?"

Craig was stunned, "You are kidding, right?"

"No, I'm not. Lou asked me and I told him I would think about it. At first I thought I was too old to start a new life with a new partner, but the more I think about it the better it sounds. Since we have been to shootouts together, I thought it might be nice to have a double wedding."

"Whoa, back up! Who is Lou?"

"Lou Mankawitz, from the NTSB. You've met him. He and I have dated for several years. He has asked before, but until I saw how happy you were about your up-coming nuptials, I never considered it. What about it, will you and Laura consider it?"

Stanton pulled the phone from his shirt pocket. When Laura answered, he explained the surprising news to her. "Karen wants to know if you would consider having a double wedding."

He listened a moment and handed the phone to Karen.

"Hello, Laura."

Laura was excited. "You're getting married, too? That's wonderful. I want to know all the details. You have to come over and we will make plans. We will plan a beautiful wedding and the boys will have to go along with it."

"Yes, it is wonderful. I'll get with you this week and we can make plans. See you soon."

She handed the phone back to Craig. "Did you hear they are extraditing Mosely Cain back to the U.S.?"

"That is good news, Karen. Now we really can get on with our lives."

To contact Ron Walden for book signings or to arrange for him
to be a guest speaker for your group, call or email:
Phone: (907) 252-4471 ••• rwalden99669@gmail.com